THE SORCERER'S APPENDIX

A BROTHERS GRIMM MYSTERY

P. J. BRACKSTON

PEGASUS CRIME

NEW YORK LONDON

THE SORCERER'S APPENDIX

Pegasus Crime is an Imprint of
Pegasus Books Ltd.
148 W 37th Street, 13th Floor
New York, NY 10018

First Pegasus Books cloth edition November 2017

Interior design by Maria Fernandez

Library of Congress Cataloging-in-Publication Data is available.

ISBN: 978-1-68177-530-2

10 9 8 7 6 5 4 3 2 1

Printed in the United States of America
Distributed by W. W. Norton & Company

For my sister-in-law, Chris: a woman of many talents, not the least of which has been managing my brother all these years.

THE
SORCERER'S
APPENDIX

ONE

Gretel raised her hand to lift the heavy iron door knocker but a niggling sense of foreboding caused her to hesitate. It was not apprehension of the variety that might make her pivot upon her kitten heel and hasten away, nor a cold dread that could freeze her, statue-like and statuesque, to the spot. It was merely a niggle, a twinge, a small but annoying twitch of anxiety that made her pause. Both knocker and house gave every appearance of being commonplace and workaday. Nevertheless, this was the home of a sorcerer, and that was sufficient to put Gretel on edge.

Or at least, it was the home of a late sorcerer, which was the reason for her visit, for she was calling upon the magician's widow in answer to a request for her services as a private detective in order to discover the truth behind the man's untimely demise. The fact that there was no longer a sorcerer in residence, however, did not mean that his presence in the house did not, in one way or another, linger. In Gretel's experience, sorcerers never passed up the opportunity to wrong-foot a person. It was not, in truth, a profession that she viewed with much admiration. Sorcerers, to her mind, were little more than tricksters, pranksters, men of scant talent and even less magic, who made their living by sleight of hand, clumsy illusions, and conjuring tricks. They parted the gullible from their money—a fact that at least earned them Gretel's grudging respect—and delighted in nothing better than showing off. But she could forgive their lack of any real ability with magic. She could even tolerate their questionable money-making practices. What she could not forgive, what had actually been known to make her wince, was their appalling fashion sense. They were always to be found indulging an ill-advised fondness for excessive facial hair, swathed in purple satin, splattered with stars and moons, hems trailing dangerously, their every outfit droopy of sleeve and pointy of hat. Such sartorial crimes made Gretel break out in a rash.

But business was business. Her services were requested, there was work to be done, and therefore money to be made. She must put aside her petty dislikes and personal opinions, at least until the job was secured. She comforted herself with the fact that the man was dead, and therefore unlikely to be wearing anything so offensive ever again.

Taking a deep breath, she lifted the lion's paw knocker and rapped hard on the door. No irritating trickery ensued. Instead, there came the sound of locks being undone, and the door was opened by a wafer-thin woman of indeterminate age and a faded loveliness, whose tearstained face and morose countenance suggested she was the widow of the deceased.

"Frau Arnold? I am Fraulein Gretel, come at your own behest. My condolences and good morning to you."

"Oh! You received the . . . the parcel, then?" The woman's voice was as insubstantial as her frame. She wept silently as she spoke, tears not so much brimming and spilling as just plain leaking from her. Gretel felt a fleeting moment of pity for the flimsy creature, which was quickly replaced by impatience. That the woman was shaken by her loss was understandable, but did she have to be so off-puttingly lachrymose about it?

"Indeed I did. Its contents were both disturbing and interesting."

At this Widow Arnold cried a little harder. She gestured for Gretel to step into the house.

The interior was every bit as ghastly as Gretel had feared. They passed through a short hallway strewn with mirrors and crystals and faux magic artifacts, and entered a modest reception room. This was decorated as though it were the great hall of some gothic castle. Sadly, it did not have the proportions to carry off such an ambitious look, and the scruffiness of the furnishings gave the whole place a down-at-heel feel. The midnight-blue ceiling seemed to press down upon anyone standing beneath it, despite the proliferation of spangly stars it boasted. The bulky, carved wooden chairs and tatty, oversized velvet sofa filled the space so that Gretel was forced to sit, there not being sufficient width of clear Persian carpet to accommodate her fashionably full skirts were she to stand. She took out her pocket notebook and pencil, promising herself that a small portion of the fees she was about to begin earning would purchase a new silver case for what were, after all, some of the tools of her trade.

"If I am to take on the case, Frau Arnold . . ."

"Oh! Say you will, for I am quite desperate!"

". . . merely a few questions first. All perfectly normal in such cases."

"Oh! Such cases?"

Gretel began to suspect that her new client might start all her sentences with an exclamation. "Such cases as this, in as much as although there is a suspected murder, there is no body."

The widow gave a little wail.

Gretel pressed on. "At least, not much of one."

The widow gave a louder wail.

Gretel drew back. "Let us first bring our attention to bear on the more . . . on the plainer facts. For it is facts that will solve this case, as they have solved many others."

If Widow Arnold had any thoughts on this comment she kept them to herself.

Gretel proceeded, cautiously. "Your husband . . . Ernst Arnold?" When the widow nodded she continued. "He went into his workshop . . ."

"Oh! He didn't like the word 'workshop.' He called it his *magicarium*."

"His . . . ? Very well, he went into his magicarium at what time?"

"Oh, it was right after breakfast. He said he was going to be working on some new spells, and that he was not to be disturbed. I recall that very clearly because I asked him if that meant I couldn't take him his luncheon, and he told me that I could not, so I said well, then I'd better pack a meal for him to take with him, because nobody works well without luncheon . . ."

Gretel allowed her client to gabble on, having lost interest in what she was saying beyond the second mention of luncheon. Widow Arnold's wits may very well have fled along with the greater part of her late husband's body, but she was right about the importance of feeding the mind if it was to perform well.

And at that precise moment, Gretel felt a dip in her own levels of performance. The clock in the square struck twelve, which meant that somebody somewhere would be eating something, and alas it was not her. At last the widow came to a full stop. Gretel hauled her attention back to the case.

"So he remained working alone for the day. At what time did you notice that anything was amiss?"

"Oh, tea time. Ernst was very particular about his tea. We always took it together at half past four, and though he was determined to work though his midday meal, he said nothing at all about foregoing our tea." She made no attempt to staunch the flow of her tears as she spoke. Gretel decided then and there that whatever facts remained as yet obscured, one thing shone with dazzling clarity: Frau Arnold was besotted with her husband and could be crossed off the list of possible suspects. In fact, Gretel had serious doubts about the woman's ability to cope without her husband. Which led her to her next set of questions.

"Tell me, was your husband a successful sorcerer?"

"Oh yes," she nodded, pride shining through her tears. "Extremely." Gretel glanced around at the contents of the room but could see no evidence of wealth that might bear out her client's assertion.

"And now that he is no longer able to work," Gretel trod as gently as she was able, "has he left you well provided for?"

For once, Frau Arnold did not utter her habitual exclamation, but sat up a little straighter and clutched her pocket handkerchief a little tighter. Her expression could not have been said to actually harden, but it did seem to firm up a smidgen around the edges.

"Ernst was both careful and clever. He told me many times not to worry about money, and that he would always see to it that our needs were met. He even said that . . . should anything terrible happen to him," here she took a wobbly breath, "I was not to fret over my income for he had taken out an insurance policy that would keep me more than comfortable. Only now the insurance company don't want to give me my money."

"Ah."

"They don't think he was murdered at all! They are saying they will not give me my money without a . . . without poor Ernst's body." She fell to weeping again with such emotion that she was quite unable to speak.

Gretel was not surprised to hear of the insurer's stance. When she had received the letter from Frau Arnold along with the only remnant of her husband—the sorcerer's appendix—her first thought had been *eew!* and her second had been *show me the insurer who will pay out on that!* She attempted to console the widow.

"It is customary for insurers to prevaricate and set obstacles in the path of those who have a perfect right to demand payment. Rest assured, Frau Arnold, I am here to sweep away their protestations and overcome those obstacles."

"Oh, you are? You can? Only, they are saying his death was the result of a magic trick gone wrong, and he's not covered for that."

"You are certain they are incorrect?"

"Ernst was such a good sorcerer! And he would never do anything dangerous, he would not risk his own life, for he knew how dear he was to me, and that to lose him would mean a lifetime of heartbreak for me," she insisted, her words rising to a squeak.

"Quite so. In which case, murder would appear the only logical assumption. But who would want to murder your husband? Had he enemies?"

"Oh, there was so much jealousy in the Sorcerers' Circle! It is a highly competitive profession, you know. Anyone as successful as Ernst, well, he was bound to make others feel inferior."

Gretel made some notes. Happy clients. Unhappy colleagues. Insurance company behaving as one might expect. It wasn't a great deal to go on. She decided it best to address the prickly topic of fees then and there. "There is one further matter we must discuss before I proceed . . ."

"Oh, then you will definitely take the case?"

". . . the question of my remuneration. I think you will find my fees competitive," she said, beginning her usual defense, safe in the knowledge that there was no competition to be found within thirty leagues of Gesternstadt, "and that it is standard practice to request an up-front payment, to cover expenditures incurred, you understand, followed by further payments culminating in the final installment when the case is solved to your satisfaction."

"Oh, but I have nothing to give you now."

"What, nothing?"

"Ernst and I recently enjoyed a vacation away, you see, such a lovely time. He knew he would make more money upon our return, only . . . he never had the chance . . ."

Gretel narrowed her eyes. Either Widow Arnold was a simpleton, or else a highly skilled actress, manipulative and calculating.

"Ernst said if I was happy he was happy, and he knew how much I delighted in pretty clothes and treats."

Manipulative?

"And he always agreed that if he was happy he did his best work, so spending money on my happiness was an investment!"

Calculating?

"And look," Frau Arnold brightened for a moment as she turned to pick up a figurine from the table beside her. "He bought me this. We found it in a little shop in a tiny village while we were on our vacation. I had thought to have a ring to celebrate our time together, something with a sparkle to it. A diamond, perhaps. But Ernst saw this and said to me that it was so darling and sweet it reminded him of me and of how much he loved me and there could be no more perfect gift. See? Is it not so very much better than a silly old diamond?"

Gretel lifted her silver lorgnettes from their resting place upon her bosom the better to inspect the roughly made, poorly painted, lumpen china ornament that appeared to be a knock-kneed ballerina who had at some time in her life suffered both rickets and smallpox. It was an object of such singular hideousness that it hurt Gretel's eyes to look at it.

Simpleton.

She got to her feet. She knew she had a choice; she could refuse the case, go home, and forget about the sorcerer, or she could agree to take the case and work without pay for weeks in the hope of solving it and getting the insurance company to pay out so that she, in turn, would be paid. It irked her to realize that in fact this was no choice at all. The money from her most recent case would not last forever. They were nearing the end of summer. Brutal winter winds would soon blow down from the Zugspitze, and she had no wish to face them without funds for sufficient food and fuel to see herself and Hans through to spring. She took a breath.

"Very well, Frau Arnold, I accept the case and we shall agree special terms, given the unusual circumstances, which I will outline later. Now, if you would be so kind as to show me your late husband's magicarium?"

The sorcerer's place of work was a small building at the far end of the garden behind the house. As Gretel approached it she found she had to keep fending off the word "shed." It was, at least, built of stone rather than wood, and its owner's penchant for medieval-revival architecture had endowed it with an arched doorway, an arch above its single, pointy window, and even a rather lonely turret. Despite Ernst Arnold's best efforts, however, the proportions, the lowness of the roof, the ill-fitting door, and lack of space within all pretty much shouted "shed!" Gretel persuaded the widow to leave her alone to look for clues. She had grown weary of the woman's weeping, and besides, there was precious little space in which an unnecessary person might hover.

The walls were lined with shelves that were in turn lined with either books of spells, or jars of heaven-knew-what. There were wands and crystal balls and astrological charts and all manner of sorcerous paraphernalia. At the center was a long, narrow table. It was set out to resemble some sort of laboratory bench for grand and dangerous spells, but Gretel was fairly certain she had seen Hans use one just like it when he had decorated the hallway at home. All in all, the feeling was of corners cut and pennies pinched. Every item looked adequate at first glance, but closer inspection revealed everything to be cheap and of poor quality. She saw no evidence to support Frau Arnold's assertion that her husband had been a successful man.

Gretel voiced her thoughts aloud in the shabby space. "It would appear that the great sorcerer's greatest illusion was to convince people of his own greatness."

She noticed that the central table was clear in the center, as if a large object had been set upon it. Quite possibly a body. Peering through her lorgnettes she discerned small stains that were in all probability blood. The floor was free of such blemishes, however. She wondered at this. The only remnant of the hapless sorcerer had been a part of his innards. And if innards became outards there was usually a fair amount of gore to show for it. It was almost as if the murderer had taken care in obtaining the body part. How then had he, or she, actually killed the victim? If indeed the victim had been killed. Gretel had to keep her mind open to the possibility that the insurers were right, and that the disappearance of Ernst Arnold was the consequence of bungled magic.

She strode about the room, looking for clues. Few presented themselves. The door had been found locked, according to Widow Arnold; the window remained closed and unbroken. Gretel kept in mind what Frau Arnold had told her of discovering her husband's remnant and nothing else. When she had received no word of reply from him through the door, she explained, she had fetched the spare key from her jewelry case and gained entry. It must have been a terrifying moment when she realized what she was looking at, and that the rest of her beloved husband was nowhere to be seen.

There were no signs of struggle or violence of any sort, save for the patches of dried blood, which were no more than might have been produced by a minor nosebleed. If someone had taken the trouble to murder the sorcerer, remove and leave behind his appendix, and take the body away, they had done so with considerable care, and without, it appeared, causing any panic or thrashing around on the part of the victim. A fast-acting intoxicant, perhaps? A swift blow to the head? But delivered by whom? And for what reason? Experience had taught Gretel that motive provided the biggest clue of all. At that moment, those with a possible reason for such an action fell into three categories: clients, colleagues, and everybody else. As the last of these groups was the most difficult to tackle, Gretel decided to start with the first and work through the second, hoping that there would be no need to contemplate the third.

She was at the point of leaving the magicarium when she experienced a strong feeling that she was being watched. She stood very still, listening hard, casting her glance about the place, trying to ignore the ticklish sensation of the hairs at the nape of her neck rising. She could neither see nor hear anything that might be capable of gazing at her, if you didn't count the four eyeballs in a jar on the top shelf over the window, which she chose not to. She waited a moment longer. Nothing appeared, yet the unpleasant sensation did not diminish. At last she decided it was of no significance and left the room with a harrumph. She made her way across the garden, where the August sun beat briefly upon her head, and into the house. She obtained from Frau Arnold her husband's engagement book, which recorded all his clients' names and details, along with occasions on which he carried out work for them. She also asked for the most recent yearbook of the Sorcerers' Circle. She was on the point of leaving when the surprisingly sensible and commonplace door knocker announced the arrival of Kingsman Kapitan Strudel. He stepped into the hallway and greeted Gretel with his customary warm scowl.

"What are you doing here, Fraulein?" he demanded.

"I am doing my job, Herr Kapitan, as no doubt are you."

"Kingsman's business is not your business," he snapped.

Gretel held the books behind her back. If she knew Strudel, which she did, he would have them off her in a minute. It was a constant source of irritation to the Kingsman that Gesternstadt's famous detective single-handedly solved more crimes than his entire department. Gretel knew that if he thought she was withholding useful evidence he would make her suffer for it. In her opinion, there was a time for sharing, and this was not it. Edging sideways toward the door she treated him to a deferential little bow, which should have aroused his suspicions, but he was too busy feeling flattered.

"I shall not keep you from your important duties one second longer, Kapitan," she promised, reversing out of the door and hurrying away.

The day had stepped into its stride and become hotter than Gretel had expected. She found that her clothes were unsuitably warm, causing her to glow in a way she liked to think looked becoming, but feared would move on to hot and bothered very shortly. She clucked loudly to herself at the annoyance of August. She had endured quite enough stifling days, forced to shelter beneath parasols and broad-brimmed hats to prevent her face from having the look of a laundry maid about it. Heat did not suit her, and she looked forward to the gentle embrace of autumn. She welcomed crisp, cool air, and the more flattering garments it called for. For now, she must contend with unhelpfully high temperatures that would bring about sweating and chafing and a rustic high color she did not care for.

It was in this mood, then, that she set forth to find the first of the sorcerer's clients. Gesternstadt was a small town, and she was all too familiar with its every street and corner. As she strode beneath the floriferous window boxes and stepped around the prettily planted barrows and urns that people of a fluffier disposition insisted on placing at their doors, she tried to ignore the cheeriness and quaintness for which the place was known. It grated upon her. It wore her down with its relentless joie de vivre. Did the townsfolk truly believe one could chase away the ills of the world and the terrors of the night with a few well-placed flower pots and a perma-smile? What was wrong with a bit of facing up to reality? If Gretel had something to smile about then she would smile and look rather elegant while doing so. She was not prepared, however, to face the world with an imbecilic grin come what may, and fervently wished others would stop it.

"Good morning, Fraulein Gretel!" called the apothecary from his shop doorway. "Another lovely day!" he exclaimed, as if she were incapable of assessing the weather for herself.

She grunted at him and moved on, but there were plenty more where he came from. From all sides, she was assailed with Good Mornings and Delighted To See Yous. Well-wishers and friendly neighbors blocked her path, arm in arm, to exchange syrupy pleasantries, or popped up like jack-in-the-boxes from behind a stretch of privet or picket fence.

Head down, Gretel did her best to elevate her thoughts to a higher level, and as she did so, the handsome, refined features of Uber General Ferdinand von Ferdinand came into the sharp focus of her mind's eye. She felt a new warmth spread through her that had nothing to do with the heat of the day. She had not seen Ferdinand since her time cruising aboard the *Arabella*, which seemed an age ago now. The memory of dancing with him was still vivid, however, and as she brought her mind to bear on recalling the feel of his strong arm about her waist as they waltzed around the ballroom, her irritation at Gestern-stadt, her neighbors, and mankind in general began to fade. She would go about her work in an agreeable frame of mind, and good results would surely follow.

TWO

Two hours later, her feet aching, her brow furrowed, and her hair frizzed from the heat, Gretel lay upon her beloved daybed, eyes closed, drawing comfort from the softness and plumpness of the many silk cushions thereon.

Hans came in from the kitchen. "A successful start to your investigations?" he asked.

"Not by any measure."

"Oh, not taking the case, then?"

"Indeed I am, Hans, for how else am I to keep you in weisswurst and ale this winter?" She did not allow him time to respond, but went on, "I accepted the brief from

Frau Arnold, along with names and addresses of those I must interview in search of information both background and foreground regarding the disappearance of the hapless sorcerer."

"Well, I'd call that a good start."

"Not if you were me, Hans. Not if you had trudged and traipsed the length of this wretched town knocking on doors that remained unopened, in search of people who were gone away, ill, or otherwise indisposed, resulting in not a single questioned asked nor answer obtained." She opened her eyes and sat up so that she might rub her stockinged feet. "I tell you, brother mine, you have not known discomfort until you have experienced the tyranny of cobbles beneath kitten heels. If I turned my ankle once I did it a dozen times."

"You could try wearing sensible shoes."

"Those two words do not belong together."

"How about a little refreshment? Might that put things in a better light?"

"It might, and it is most definitely worth trying."

"Right you are." Hans turned toward the kitchen and then stopped. "Oh, I have news that may cheer you."

"I doubt it."

"No, really, listen. Herr Mozart is coming here, to give a concert. How about that?"

"Mozart? The darling of Vienna? The most sought-after musician in all the land, coming to Gesternstadt? You must be mistaken, Hans."

"I am not," he fumbled in his trouser pocket and produced a crumpled flier, which he handed to Gretel. "Man in the Inn gave me this only last night. See for yourself."

She took the notice and read that a certain Herr W. A. Mozart would be conducting a new piece of music at the town hall in two weeks' time. Tickets were available now.

"Good Lord," said Gretel. "It does appear to be true." She did indeed feel her spirits rise, borne up on the waft of Viennese sophistication unexpectedly blowing her way. Such an event would call for a new gown. Would provide the opportunity to rub shoulders with what passed for society in the region. Might even offer the chance for a romantic evening. A thought that she rashly mentioned to Hans.

"I wonder if the Uber General would be free on that day?" she mused. "I believe he has returned to his duties at the Summer Schloss. He might enjoy escorting me to such a cultured event."

It was then that Hans made a curious noise. It might have started out as a coherent sentence, but it emerged as a garbled utterance devoid of actual language yet strangely still able to convey sentiment.

"What's that, Hans?"

"Nothing. I did not say a word."

"A word, no, but you clearly voiced an opinion, and one that seemed to contain the remnants of a *pshaw*!"

"I . . . er . . ." His face grew pink from the exertion of trying to think of something to say while clearly not daring to say anything. All of which served only to irritate Gretel further.

"You know something. Let's have it."

Hans took a gulping breath and then blurted out, "General Ferdinand has a girlfriend. Or so rumor has it. Though, matter of fact, not so much a girlfriend as a fiancée. If hearsay can be relied upon. Which of course it cannot be. Or should not be. And I know how you feel about gossip, and gossip this may be and nothing more. Though I got it from a man at the Inn, who has a sister who works at the Summer Schloss, who talked to a maid who did the very woman's hair, and saw her very engagement ring, and . . ."

He stopped. Gretel noticed him take hold of the doorjamb as if bracing himself for the full force of her fury. She was, in fact, undecided as to the appropriate response to this news. After all, Ferdinand was nothing to her and she nothing to him. After all, they had indulged in nothing more than a flirtation. After all, he was a handsome, eligible man, and had every right to become engaged to whomsoever he chose. After all, a few dances, a few glances, a few missed chances in difficult circumstances did not any manner of obligation make.

After all that Gretel felt suddenly drained. She had not the energy to raise herself from her daybed, let alone take to the streets once more to resume her investigations. All at once, everything felt pointless and colorless. She settled deeper into her cushions and closed her eyes again.

"What is there to eat?" she asked.

"You're not going back out, interviewing and whatnot?"

"No one ever solved a case on an empty stomach, Hans."

"Well, I did purchase some rather splendid weisswurst this morning, and I've just opened a new batch of sauerkraut, which looks particularly successful. Bottled it only last month, so a little young, but pungent, nonetheless."

"Bring it to me, brother mine, and do not stint on the mustard or rye bread or anything else you consider helpful. I shall dine, then I shall nap. I am more likely to find those I seek at home in the evening, in any case."

"I shall fetch a veritable feast!" Hans promised, hurrying out of the room with the light step of one who has just escaped a seemingly inevitable unpleasantness.

Gretel lay and waited for the food that she knew would revive her spirits. She could not permit herself to wallow. She was a woman of business, a woman who must make her own way in the world, and she could not afford the luxury of a tender heart. If Ferdinand wanted to marry someone other than her, there was little she could do about it.

⚜

By the time Gretel set out again dusk had fallen, softening the edges of the buildings, blurring the rooftops, and generally casting a fuzzy gloom. It suited Gretel's mood far better than the earlier sunshine. The only thing preventing her from wearing a scowl was the knowledge that such an arrangement of the facial features could lead to aging and unattractive lines in later life. Her pride might have been dented by the news of Ferdinand's betrothal, but her vanity remained intact.

Her first port of call was the home of one Victor Winkler, a cheesemaker who, according to Ernst Arnold's appointment book, had engaged the services of the sorcerer quite recently. The ledger did not contain details of the specifics of the work, so Gretel was wholly unprepared for the startling appearance of the man who opened the door to her.

"Herr Winkler?" she asked, as much to buy time to recover from her surprise as out of politeness.

"Who wants to know?" snapped the middle-aged man, who was of middling height and build, and mostly unremarkable aside from the one, unmissable characteristic that set him apart. Gretel had encountered hirsute men before, of course, and had known many who chose to wear a full set of whiskers and abundant beard. Victor Winkler, however, did not appear to have any choice in the matter of his facial hair, for he was entirely covered in it; every inch of his face—and for all Gretel knew the rest of his body, although this was a point she determined not to think about—bore a layer of thick, brown, luxuriant fur. He showed not a patch of skin, but only a sleek and soft pelt, much like a cat. The idea that he might *be* part cat caused Gretel to squirm. She forced herself to focus upon the reason for her visit.

"My name is Detective Gretel, and I am making inquiries regarding the disappearance of Ernst Arnold, on behalf of his widow . . ."

"That charlatan!" Herr Winkler growled. Gretel wished he wouldn't.

"I understand you were one of his clients."

"I paid him good money to work his sorcery on me. Very good money."

"The magic was not . . . successful?"

"Does this look successful to you?" Herr Winkler gestured at his own face.

"That rather depends," Gretel spoke cautiously, "on what you were hoping for."

"He promised me good results with one treatment. He swore he could work his magic and succeed where all others had failed to rid me of my affliction."

"But he did not?"

"*Magic*, indeed! That man had no more magic in him than your or I."

"I wonder, Herr Winkler, if I might step inside, so that we can continue this discussion in private." Here she glanced pointedly over her shoulder, though the street behind her was unhelpfully empty. Gretel was eager to hear more, and did not want this evidently dissatisfied customer of the sorcerer slamming the door on her in a fit of temper. "It seems to me," she went on, "you have a well-founded grievance against the late Herr Arnold, and I should like to know the details."

Gretel had played her hand well. She had judged that Herr Winkler had a lot to get off his chest—and here she tried hard to blank further furry images from her mind—and would not pass up the opportunity to offload the tale of his suffering onto a new recipient. He stood aside and beckoned her. Gretel followed him into a somewhat drab sitting room. She wondered if the dim lighting was to provide a cover for his appearance, and was not surprised at the total lack of mirrors in the place.

They sat on matching chairs of equal and unyielding ugliness on either side of an unlit fire and she took out her notebook.

"Tell me, Herr Winkler, when did you last see the sorcerer?"

"Two weeks ago. I had called him here so that I might show him the continuing extent of his failed *treatment*."

"Forgive me, Herr Winkler, a delicate matter, I realize, but I have to ask, what precisely were you expecting from Herr Arnold's magic?"

"To be rid of this excessive coverage, of course!" He appeared to be getting angry, but it was hard to read his expression under so much fur. "The sorcerer said he could get rid of it all, so that I would no longer have to endure daily the torment of jibes and laughter at my appearance. In point of fact he made it worse."

"Worse?" Gretel made notes.

"The cursed stuff grows thicker now than it did before his meddling!"

"And yet, as I understand it, Herr Arnold's reputation as a practitioner of sorcery was unbesmirched. He remained held in high esteem among his peers and clients until his untimely demise. You did not think to complain, to make public your dissatisfaction, or to take your complaint to the Sorcerers' Circle, perhaps?"

Here Herr Winkler grew uncomfortable and fidgeted on his uncomfortable chair. "I thought about it, yes, but then, well, Herr Arnold persuaded me to keep my grievances to myself."

"Persuaded how?" Gretel asked, though she was confident she already knew the answer.

"He refunded my fee, of course, and . . . added a little more. To cover my disappointment, and any inconvenience caused, etcetera, etcetera."

"He bought your silence."

Herr Winkler's frown deepened into furry furrows. "I was entitled to compensation! That sorcerer should have been stripped of the name."

"And yet you did not feel it incumbent upon you to warn others of his shortcomings?"

At this the man got to his feet. "I have told you what happened, Fraulein. The man was a fraud, that's all you need to know."

Gretel left the house with a much better understanding of Herr Arnold's situation than she could have hoped for. She had been right in her assessment of the sorcerer's home; he was not a wealthy man. Nor, it seemed, was he a capable magician. She had just encountered startling proof of his ineptitude, as well as evidence of the lengths to which he would go in order to protect his professional reputation. Gretel decided that more of his clients must be interviewed, and was fairly certain that they would reveal similar experiences of the sorcerer's work.

She moved briskly through the town toward the next address in the diary. It had become properly dark, and the streetlamps had been lit. Couples were walking, arm in arm, taking advantage of the pleasant evening to stroll and whisper and coo and even, heaven help her, kiss. The more she looked, the more examples of romantic activity she found. There appeared to be a smitten couple around every corner. Why was it that suddenly everyone seemed to have someone? Everyone, that was, besides herself. She brushed past giggling youths, blushing new brides, the happily married, and the enamored elderly. Even Widow Arnold had enjoyed a loving marriage up until the moment her husband had been so reduced. Gretel was aware that this sudden sensitivity was due to the news of Ferdinand's engagement. All at once she felt the sore point of her hurt feelings shift to something altogether more powerful. She began to experience a growing anger at the way she had been so summarily passed over for someone else. Why had the general seen fit to turn his back on her, to deny the burgeoning friendship that had been developing between them? And who was this Jenny-Come-Lately to steal away her man without so much as asking permission? True, no promises had been promised, no declarations declared. But still, they had danced together at the festival in Nuremberg, he had held her tight while they galloped across the sands on his black stallion on the isle of Amrum, and there had been lingering looks and meaningful glances aplenty.

"Well, engaged is not married!" she declared emphatically to the night, to a surprised couple on a nearby bench, and to herself. She decided then and there that she would not give up Ferdinand without a fight. She would complete the business of interviewing the sorcerer's clients and then it was straight to Madame Renoir's Beauty Salon, where she would submit to any and all treatments and tortures that might put her in the very best of shape for the battle ahead.

THREE

The treatment room at the beauty salon was one of the places where Gretel often managed some of her very finest thinking. On this occasion, as she lay upon the narrow yet comfortable bed, her body basted in fragrant oils and unctions and wrapped in the warmest and fluffiest of toweling, she felt ideas and inspiration were only moments away. Her hair was enjoying an intensive rejuvenating treatment, and was still swathed in layers of muslin and cotton. Her skin tingled, steeped in essence of juniper and geranium, stimulating and soothing in equal measure. She had earlier endured the unpleasant business of hair removal from areas which, in her opinion, hair had no business being, so that now only gentle and enjoyable processes lay ahead. Such as the beautification of her hands and feet. And an invigorating massage of the scalp. And a slathering of expensive creams upon her face. And a fitting of her newly ordered and custom-made wig.

While she lay thus, she allowed her brain to idle, to coast, to drift where it would, setting it free to roam the intricate chambers of her mind, where she was confident it would happen upon the elusive answers and shy solutions hidden there. She gave it a little nudge in the right direction by pondering one or two of the facts presented by the case of the errant sorcerer.

The first of these was that Herr Arnold had not been good at his job. On the contrary, by all accounts other than that of his widow, he had been utterly useless at any sort of spell casting, conjuring, ethereal fixing, or indeed magic in any shape or form. He had, it transpired, blundered from client to client, bodging and bungling, and then doling out dough to keep his failures secret. After interviewing the unfortunate Victor Winkler—whom no amount of depilation would render hair-free—Gretel had visited two more of the sorcerer's unsatisfied customers. One was a young man so stricken by shyness that it had taken him a month to summon the courage to call at the Arnold residence in the first place. If he had been reticent and retiring before the sorcerer's ministrations, he was downright reclusive afterward, so that Gretel had been compelled to conduct the entire interview through the letterbox of his firmly locked front door. Crouched awkwardly, her questions had been a little blunter than they might have been. The young man had quivered in his hallway, but, like Herr Winkler, he had welcomed the opportunity—now that the sorcerer was dead—to unburden himself of his secret. The magic he had paid for had not alleviated but worsened his condition, and Herr Arnold had paid him not to tell anyone of his experience.

The final client on Gretel's list was a woman who listened to her enquiry and then, without saying a word, led her into the kitchen of her home. There she indicated her husband, or at least, the vestiges of him. Gretel had known Herr Roth as an able baker, who had worked successfully in Gesternstadt for many years. She had, briefly some weeks ago, wondered at his absence from the market, and now she knew the reason. His wife's misfortune—and his own, indeed—was that he was a dour man, known for his grim countenance and gruff disposition. People forgave him this because he was an accomplished baker and his honigkuchen was second to none. Frau Roth, however, had grown tired of living with such a grumpkin and asked the sorcerer to make him more cheerful.

"You see how it is, Fraulein?" the wife asked Gretel.

Gretel did see. It was tragic. On this occasion, rather than amplifying the problem, the sorcerer's magic had worked too well. The once burly, round-faced man, with arms muscled from years of kneading dough and hefting bread trays, had been reduced to a stick-thin, flimsy husk of a thing, and all because he could not stop laughing. His body was wearing away from the effort of it. He gasped and guffawed and *hee*-ed and *haw*-ed ceaselessly, tears of joyless mirth streaming down his frail face, while he bent over doubled and clutched at his sides as he shook with unrelenting laughter. It was a pitiful sight. Shutting the door on him, Frau Roth had confirmed that she had taken money from the sorcerer in exchange for keeping the baker quiet. Or rather, keeping him at home, as clearly he could not go out in public without questions being asked about his condition. In fact, the Roths had received regular payments from Herr Arnold, who was the first to admit that the baker was no longer in any state to bake, and therefore could not earn a living.

Gretel's mind, cosseted and comforted as it was, brought forth a conclusion or two.

To begin with, the missing magician might have been a useless sorcerer, but he was a halfway decent human being, in as much as he had a conscience that did not allow him to shy away from the responsibility he had toward his hapless clients. He had made a mess of things, and he had been prepared to pay for his mistakes, at least in hard cash and to the best of his ability.

Furthermore, this was a state of affairs which could not have continued indefinitely. If the sorcerer was paying for rather than being paid for his own work, the law of diminishing returns suggested that he must have been fast approaching a state of bankruptcy. And such a state, in Gretel's experience, was apt to drive people to do Desperate Things.

Added to which, Herr Arnold had gone to considerable lengths—including financial ruin, it would seem—to protect his professional reputation, despite his chosen profession being one for which he was, evidently, singularly unsuited. Why would he bother? Why not simply find some other employment? Was the admiration of the Sorcerer's Circle so vital to his happiness?

"Ah, Mademoiselle Gretel!" Madame Renoir's cheery voice with its pretty French accent interrupted Gretel's thoughts. "You look beautifully rested, *ma cherie!* Come, let me assist you in the sitting up. I have the very finest oil from Morocco for your scalp!" she said, holding up a slender bottle of golden liquid.

Gretel allowed herself to be repositioned and relaxed once more as the beautician's fingers worked their magic.

"Mademoiselle, your hair will look exquisite after this."

"But not as exquisite as my new wig," Gretel countered. "When will it arrive?"

"Before the week's end. Oh! It will be something wonderful. The new method of weaving the hair onto a netted cap is *très, très belle!*"

"Not to mention *très, très* costly."

"But every coin well spent, *n'est-ce pas?*"

With this, Gretel could not argue. She had promised herself a new wig after her last one had taken a dunking in the sea off Schleswig-Holstein, and a new wig she would have. There was even greater justification for it now with the upcoming concert. The concert and Ferdinand's fiancée. For there was no doubt in Gretel's mind that they would both attend, such was the importance of the occasion, having such an illustrious composer as Herr Mozart in Gesternstadt. Well, Gretel would be ready. For the event, and for the competition. She would look her best, and the new wig would be the showpiece of her outfit. Ferdinand could not help but notice her, and she would make him consider what he would be giving up if he married this whoever-she-was.

"Tell me, Madame Renoir, what do you know of Herr and Frau Arnold?" she asked, attempting to keep her mind on matters of business. The beautician had proved a useful source of knowledge in the past, and this time was to be no exception.

"Of the sorcerer, very little at all, but of Evalina Arnold— well!" Here she paused to make a face of delight. "Such a pretty woman, and she was even prettier as a girl. She could have had her pick of the young men in Gesternstadt."

"Really?" Gretel struggled to marry the picture in her head of the somewhat ordinary hausfrau she had interviewed with a town beauty. But then, the woman had been grief stricken, and clearly not at her best. Perhaps she would scrub up well, and after all, a face could be transformed by a bright smile.

"*Mais oui!*" Madame Renoir insisted, "She had the very brightest of smiles."

"And a happy marriage, from what she tells me. Alas, she is now a sad widow and her sadness is of a tearful, off-putting nature."

"*Bof!*" Exclaimed the beautician as she ran more oil through Gretel's tresses.

"Bof?"

Madame Renoir gave a Gallic shrug. "I'll wager she will not remain so for very long. There is nothing more certain to restore a woman to glowing beauty than the flattering attentions of ardent men."

Pondering this for a moment, Gretel had to admit that there was truth in what the beautician said. A thought made itself known to her, jumping up and down and waving at the back of her mind. She brought it into focus and saw that it had merit and that it was pertinent to her enquiries. Prompted by it Gretel asked, "Was there, aside from her husband, anyone in particular who was enamored of Evalina Arnold?"

"*Bien sur!* There was one who was deeply, deeply in love with her, and his heart was so broken when he lost her to Ernst that he never took a wife, but lives as a lonely bachelor still. He is called Herr Voigt. The name is familiar to you?"

Indeed it was. It was written in Gretel's notebook: Herr Otto Voigt, Master Magician, Grand Wizard, and Head Sorcerer of the Gesternstadt Sorcerers' Circle.

⁂

The surprising thing about Herr Voigt's home was not its outward appearance, which was as normal as normal could be. It was a narrow town house, built of wattle, daub, and timber, with generous eaves, painted shutters, good-sized window boxes, and a smart, red front door. So far, so Gesternstadt. It was the interior that caused Gretel's freshly plucked and tinted eyebrows to rise. Unlike the abode of Herr Arnold, there was not one piece of wizard junk to be found here. No throne-like chairs, no crystal balls, no gargoyles, or stars, or dangling moons, or anything remotely sorcerous by way of clutter and furnishings. In fact, there was barely anything at all that could not be considered essential. The house appeared to be full of bareness. To be filled with empty. To be stuffed to the gunwales with lack and absence. It was not a style of decor with which Gretel was familiar, nor one to which she warmed.

She had the impression that Herr Voigt had been expecting her. He let her into the hallway with a curt nod of greeting, but when she offered him her hand he looked aghast at the idea of touching it. Instead he led her into a reception room that had evidently been equipped in the hope it would never have to receive anyone. There was a table at one end, with two books upon it, and a row of quills lined beside them. There appeared to be nothing so messy as ink anywhere in view. Three pictures—all of maps of the classical world—were attached to the walls at precise intervals from one another. There were four candlesticks, each bearing candles of perfectly matching height, as if the sorcerer demanded that even their burning was regimented. It was a resolutely cheerless space.

Gretel's heels rapped loudly upon the bare boards as she followed him to the only seating in the room: two spindly legged chairs, devoid of cushions, straight-backed and free from springs or padding. She sat carefully, but even so noticed her host frown at the way her skirts spilled—rather fetchingly, she had thought—over the seat, this way and that. She did her best to rearrange herself tidily, tucking her feet under the little chair. She took out her notebook, peering over it to quickly assess Herr Voigt's appearance. The first word that came trotting to mind was *neat*, quickly followed by *contained*, chased home by *fastidious*. His hair was precisely trimmed and tamed. His clothes were elegant and spotlessly clean. As were his fingernails. There was nothing at all to mark him out as a practitioner of magic and caster of spells. He had the look of nothing more exciting or unusual than a public notary, though with fewer ink stains.

Gretel pitched in with some warm-up questions. "How long had you known Herr Arnold?"

"Many years. We went to the same school, and we both trained as sorcerers at much the same time."

"And you found him to be a competent and successful man of magic?"

"He would not be permitted to remain a member of the Sorcerers' Circle unless that were the case," Herr Voigt pointed out.

"Quite so, but what was your personal opinion of his professional capabilities?"

"I had no personal opinion of the man."

"Truly? And yet I understand you and Evalina Arnold were once quite . . . close?"

Opposite her, the man underwent a swift transformation. His features, which had been to this point exemplars in the art of masking any emotion, sprang into life, as though cut free of unseen bonds. A smile as broad as the Danube spread across his face, and the coldness in his eyes was replaced by a remarkable warmth. Gretel was astonished at such an alteration. It was but a transient glimpse into the sorcerer's heart, however, for as soon as he became aware he had let slip his façade he regained stern control of himself. Nonetheless, Gretel had the answer to the unaskable question: *Are you still in love with the woman?* So there was a motive for murder, and yet, and yet . . .

"That is," Gretel continued, "I believe there was once the possibility that she might not have married Ernst Arnold, but have become Frau Voigt instead?"

"I fail to see what such ancient history has to do with the . . . unfortunate situation regarding Herr Arnold." As he spoke he kept his gaze cast down, and repeatedly smoothed the fine wool of his breeches over his knees.

"Jealousy can be a vicious master," said Gretel.

"Which is why I freed myself of its rule years ago." He looked up and met the searching eyes of his interlocutor. "I am not a man to act upon rash impulse, Fraulein. Furthermore, if, as you seem to be implying, I was determined to rid myself of Ernst so that Evalina would be free, why would I wait all these long years to do so?"

Long lonely years, Gretel thought. "A fair point," she agreed, and one she had already considered herself. She began to feel that anything useful she would glean from Herr Voigt would be picked up from what he chose not to say, rather than the crumbs of information he was prepared to offer up. She needed to test a newfound theory. She got to her feet and began roaming the room. "What a very . . . discerning eye you have for decor, Herr Voigt," she declared, pausing to scrutinize one of the maps, then moving on toward the desk. The sorcerer leaped up and followed close behind, watching her every move with anxious eyes. Gretel lifted her lorgnettes and peered at the neat stack of books. "And a lover of mathematics, I see," she said as she flicked through the pages of the first volume before pushing it to one side, leaving it open, moving on to the next, deliberately dislodging the row of quills as she did so.

Herr Voigt began to breathe heavily. When one of the quills fell to the floor he snatched it up, setting it down quickly in the exact spot it belonged. Manners restrained him from actually tidying and organizing the books as Gretel was perusing them, but he was in hot pursuit.

"Yes, a fine home you have here, Herr Voigt. Still, do you not feel the lack of a woman's touch? A silk cushion here, perhaps?" She indicated a bare windowsill, dropping her lace handkerchief on it to make the point. Her host scurried after her and removed it. "A bowl of roses there, maybe?" she asked, circling back to the desk to sweep aside the books so they crashed to the floorboards, the quills following, scattering and bouncing in all directions.

The effect upon the Grand Wizard was pronounced. With a gasp he pounced upon the fallen items, gathering them up, whereupon he returned them to the desk, his visitor utterly forgotten as he placed them with regimental order. When the task was completed he remained visibly dissatisfied and raised his hands, uttered a spell, and tweaked the arrangement minutely. At last, content that order had been restored, his breathing returned to near normal. It was then that Gretel leaned forward and laid her hand upon his in a gesture of reassurance.

"I see you are a man fully able to manage his own house," she said.

But Herr Voigt did not hear her words. He was staring in horror at her hand upon his, her flesh contacting his own. For an instant he appeared unable to move, and then he wrenched his hand from beneath hers, taking out his own spotless kerchief with which to rub at it.

Gretel smiled a small smile to herself. She now knew all she needed to know about Herr Voigt. Her interview complete, she bid him good day and went on her way. The facts she had collected from his strange home were these: he was still in love with Evalina Arnold, which gave him a motive for murder (for jealousy kept beneath the surface for so many years does not extinguish but burns hot as lava until it must burst forth); and he was incapable of the physical contact, the disorder, not to mention the sheer brutal messiness, such a killing as that of Ernst Arnold would have involved. There was, of course, the possibility that he might have used magic as a weapon precisely to avoid touching anyone or anything, but still Gretel could not imagine the man so disrupting the space around himself, so engaging with chaotic violence as to actually do away with another human.

All of which meant that she was no further forward in her investigations. All she had convinced herself of was that a whole list of people were *not* the sorcerer's murderers. Which meant back to square one. And square one, in this case, was Ernst's magicarium.

Gretel took a deep breath, ignored the rumbling of her nearly-empty stomach, and resolved to return to the sorcerer's place of work and the scene of the crime and not to leave until she had at least one sensible, tangible, concrete and useful lead. She determined she would stay there all night if need be, though by the time she had hobbled over the cobbles of the town again she was fervently hoping that Evalina Arnold would provide her with a soft chair, a cozy blanket, and at the very least a bite or two of supper while she worked. She might have reminded herself that blessed is she who expecteth nothing.

FOUR

Two hours later Gretel sat on a hard chair in the chilly magicarium, painfully aware of the rate at which her mental capacity was dwindling due to lack of food. Hans trudged disconsolately around the room lifting objects at random.

"Remind me why I am not sitting by the fire at the Inn at this very moment with my favorite stein full of my favorite ale in my hand?" he asked.

"Because two can search more quickly than one."

"Even when neither of them knows what it is they are searching for?"

"Especially then," Gretel insisted. She had intercepted her brother on his way to an evening of drinking and pressed him into accompanying her to the sorcerer's home. Her reasoning had indeed been that many hands made light work, and that Hans's hands were as good as anyone's for rifling through the muddle of the cluttered shed in search of Clues. What she would never admit to him, and could barely admit to herself, was that sometimes, just sometimes, her sibling had a way of unwittingly nudging her in the direction of theorems and postulations that proved helpful in her investigations. And she certainly needed some manner of help if she was to make any progress in this case, it seemed. So far no one had presented themselves as a probable murderer. At one point, the Head Sorcerer had looked like a prime suspect, but having met him Gretel had all but crossed him off her list. That he might benefit from the death of Herr Arnold was undeniable. That he had had anything to do with it seemed unhelpfully unlikely.

"My word!" exclaimed Hans, peering into a jar of something slimy. "This place is filled with things I can't put a name to."

"Best if you don't look at that shelf," said Gretel, gesturing at the label over it that declared the collection to be *Eyes, teeth, essential organs, and other body parts.*

Hans recoiled. "I had no idea magicians had any use for that sort of thing."

"This one did, apparently. Though by most reliable accounts, even such extreme ingredients did not improve his wizardry."

"Where did he get all these, d'you suppose?"

"As I said, best not to dwell upon the contents of those particular jars."

"But they might contain Clues. How do we know they don't?"

"We don't know, we just hope." Gretel dragged herself to her feet to resume her own search. "We hope that a Clue, when we see it, presents itself as such loudly and clearly and sends us in a direction we might actually wish to go." She stood next to her brother and followed the line of his appalled gaze. It came to rest on something greenish-blue and wobbly that bobbed about in a yellow liquid. "And *that*," she said, pointing, "is not a direction I wish to go in my worst nightmares."

They continued to hunt in hungry silence. Despite the heat of the day, the sorcerer's shed was grimly damp and cold as evening descended, having no sunshine or fire to cheer it. The room was so stuffed with artifacts and paraphernalia that looking for anything was slow and difficult work, let alone looking for something that might not be there. Or if it was there, might not be as willing to reveal its importance as Gretel hoped.

"I say, look at this!" Hans held up a dusty crystal ball. "Perhaps we could peer into it and see the future."

"Seeing the sorcerer's body would be more useful."

"That too. Shall I give it a rub? No, wait, that's for lamps and genies."

Before Gretel could respond to this there was a rustling on a ledge above their heads, just beneath the ceiling. Scrolls and packets and bundles were dislodged by Something, so that they rained down upon the seekers. The Something that had done the dislodging then flew about the crowded space, swooping and flapping in a manner that immediately set Hans squawking and flapping, while Gretel issued stern commands for him to calm down and stand still. The more he flapped and crashed about, knocking things over with every panicked movement, the more the Something zipped back and forth with increasing alarm until at last it caught its feet in Gretel's hair, from which it dangled, trembling, silent, and terrified.

"Don't move, sister mine! There is Something stuck in your hair!"

Gretel ground her teeth but kept otherwise perfectly still. "Yes, thank you, Hans. I had noticed that."

After the sudden frantic activity there followed a tense, silent stillness.

"I wonder, Hans," said Gretel softly, "without troubling yourself to get up, are you able to tell me what exactly that Something is?"

After his flailing about, Hans had washed up, supine, atop a pile of sacks filled with heaven knew what, and righting himself would have been a clumsy task. Gretel had no wish to startle her passenger further, for who could tell what it might do next?

"It appears to be a small bird. No, not a bird . . . a bat! It's a tiny bat. Aaah, quite a charming little thing really. If you don't look at its piggy nose. Or those rather beady eyes. Or . . . those teeth."

"A tad more detail than I required, but thank you again, Hans."

At that moment the door opened and Frau Arnold arrived carrying a tray bearing two steaming mugs and a plate of biscuits. Hans, galvanized by the sight of food, hauled himself upright. The resulting noise—much of it puffing from Hans— caused the bat to struggle, so that its feet became ever more tightly ensnared in Gretel's hair.

"Oh!" cried Widow Arnold, "I see you have found Jynx. I have not seen him since poor Ernst . . . left us. I had thought him lost forever too." With great tenderness, she untangled the shivering creature, stroking it and speaking soothing words to it until it became sufficiently calm to perch, like a miniature pitch-black parrot, upon her shoulder.

"Jynx was my husband's dearest pet. He was never without him. He would even encourage the little thing to assist him in his sorcery." Evidently sitting upright did not come naturally to Jynx, for he quickly flopped forward to hang upside down from Frau Arnold's lace collar.

Gretel frowned at the furry creature. "Most magicians choose a fluffy rabbit or a snowy white dove . . ."

"Oh, Ernst had no interest in domesticated beings. He loved nature, all things wild. He found Jynx on one of his walks." The widow's eyes filled with tears once more. She looked up with a quivering lip. "Oh, but this is proof indeed that my poor dear husband is dead, for he would never have gone anywhere without Jynx!" She fell to weeping again, so that the bat was forced to tighten its grip while sobs racked the woman's frail frame.

"Let us not come to hasty conclusions," Gretel said, and then, in an attempt to divert Evalina's thoughts from sadness she went on, "I see you have brought us some refreshment. How very kind."

"Oh, yes. I thought you might be in need of it after so many hours in here."

Hans brightened. "Exceptionally thoughtful of you, Frau Arnold," he said, taking the mug and sniffing its contents.

"Warm milk," the hostess explained. "And some oatmeal biscuits I baked myself."

"A nip of something reviving in there, perhaps?" asked Hans hopefully.

The widow shook her head and resumed her sobbing.

Hans made a face at Gretel, who made one back. He attempted to bite into a biscuit but it would not yield to his teeth. He set to dunking it in his drink in the hope it might be rendered edible. Gretel felt her own appetite fade. She turned back to Frau Arnold.

"Let's just suppose," she said as gently as her patience would permit, "just for a moment or two, let us suppose that Ernst is living still. Is there anywhere special to him, other than his beautiful home, naturally, anywhere else he loved that he might go if he was distressed in any way? Somewhere he went alone?"

"Oh, we always did everything together! Ernst used to say that an hour spent apart from me was an hour without joy. We would go away to charming little towns for weekends, and once he even took me to Munich, though that was quite a long time ago, and was very expensive, and anyway Ernst said there was more beauty and delight to be found in our own dear home than any city in the world." She paused to give a little hiccup of sadness. Gretel waited. At last Frau Arnold fetched from the fluffy, marshmallow realms of her mind another spoonful of information. "Though of course I never went with him when he was gathering things for his work. He always made those trips alone. He said I would be bored, and too much of a distraction for him because he would always be gazing at me and holding my hand when he should have been paying attention to his work."

"A highly perceptive and considerate man," Gretel said, raising her pencil over her notebook to write down what she was sure would be the very place where questions would be answered. At last, something that could be called a lead! She would get herself there as swiftly as possible, and was confident her investigations would then bear fruit. And therefore payment. "And where, pray tell me, was it that the good sorcerer took himself off to on these . . . work trips?" Behind her she heard a squashed, cynical sound emerge from Hans. Fortunately Widow Arnold was deaf to its implications.

"Always the same place," she said with a flat sigh, as if her husband's guess that she would be bored there was being borne out. "The woods."

Gretel hesitated, pencil poised. "The woods? You mean the forest to the west of Gesternstadt?"

Hans made another small noise, this one involuntary and provoked by the very mention of the place of his childhood trauma.

"Yes," said Evalina, "Ernst went there to gather the special items he required for some of his magic."

Gretel suddenly found the magicarium rather airless, and the stays of her corset rather tight. She tried to take a steadying breath, but little by way of air could be found.

"Herr Arnold foraged for herbs and fungi, perhaps?" she asked the widow. "Along the perimeter, one assumes."

"Oh, no. He would be gone for days. He said that the things he needed could only be found deep, deep, deep inside the woods."

Hans echoed with a squeak, "Deep, deep, deep . . ."

"That's right," she went on. "In the very darkest of dark parts."

"Darkest of dark . . . ," Hans murmured.

"And he always made these forays alone?" Gretel tried to write something down, but found her hand was on the shaky side for good penmanship.

Frau Arnold nodded. "Except for Jynx," she explained with a wan smile. "His faithful companion always accompanied him. Always," she repeated, the smile crumpling into a grimace of woe. Excusing herself, she hurried out of the shed, the bat detaching himself to flit back to find a beam from which to hang.

For a moment neither Hans nor Gretel spoke. There sat between them, fatly and heavily, their shared horror of the woods. This abhorrence was so very fat and so very heavy, that, given the space already taken up by the siblings, it pressed up uncomfortably against both of them. At last Gretel shoved it aside and resumed her search.

"What are you looking for now?" asked Hans. "There are no Clues here, I am certain of it, and after what Frau Arnold said about the deep, the dark, the you-know-what, well, that's that, isn't it? I mean to say, you have your work to do and all that, but you can't go . . . *there*. You wouldn't countenance going . . . *there*. Would you?"

"I must go where the trail leads me, Hans."

"Yes, but the deep . . . the dark . . ."

"Even there. If the sorcerer vanished into the forest, then into the forest I must go after him."

"But, Gretel, so much deep darkness, so much dark deepness."

"Will you stop that. You are no help to me if you fall to pieces. I shall, of course, do my utmost to be safe. Believe me, brother mine, I am not in a hurry to risk my neck or my sanity if it can be avoided. No, what is needed here—to minimize risk—is planning. Clearheaded thought. And as much information as possible." Gretel sifted through a pile of papers upon the table as she spoke. "What would assist me most would be some manner of directions; some details regarding the precise spot visited by the sorcerer; something resembling a map," she explained.

There exists, of course, a natural bond twixt sister and brother that binds them through all the trials and tribulations of life. That bond is strengthened tenfold should they endure particular hardships and calamities while young. So it was with Gretel and Hans, which meant that even with her gaze averted, even with her back to her brother, even with Hans's best efforts to appear casual and nonchalant—or perhaps precisely because of those efforts—she was able to detect a subtle shift in his stance, a tiny twitching of his nose, a minute flickering of his eyes that gave away the fact that he was Hiding Something.

She turned to face him, hands on hips. "Let's have it," she said.

"Have what?"

"Whatever it is that you have just this moment attempted to conceal with your ample posterior. A good try, and a fair chance you might have succeeded, given your rear end could probably bring about its very own lunar eclipse if the need arose, but you can't fool me, Hans." She held out a hand. "The Whatever, if you please."

Hans resisted for only a matter of seconds, knowing that he could not outwit his sister once she had found him out. He shifted away from the workbench, reached behind himself, and pulled out a faded, folded, ragged, and worn sheet of paper, marked with drab colors and smudged lines and points.

"This?" he asked, his face a study in innocence.

Gretel took it from him and shook out the folds. "Yes, Hans," she said, still maintaining a stern glare, without even lowering her eyes to look at it. "This thing that so resembles a map that it is, in fact, a *map*."

Hans watched her as she peered at the chart through her lorgnettes. "I was only trying to do what's best for you, don't you know? Trying to protect you. As a brother should. I mean to say, we haven't fared well in woods in the past, you and I. And the worry is, *my* worry is, that if a person is handed a map, and once they have that map in their hand, then they oftentimes take it into their heads to follow the thing wherever it directs them. Which in this case is somewhere . . ."

"Hans, I swear, if you utter the words 'dark' and 'deep' . . ."

"Wouldn't dream of it."

Gretel spread the map on the table and traced a wobbly line with a determined finger. "Your concern is touching but unnecessary, Hans. The way is clearly marked. Herr Arnold must have used this to guide him to his secret destination many times."

"Well, if he did, and it's here, and he isn't, then how is he there without it?"

"Presumably the route is now so familiar to him he has no more need of it."

"So you do believe him still alive and gone to this . . . place?"

"I believe it possible. Possibly even probable." She refolded the map and gently but firmly pushed it down her cleavage so that it nestled securely in the tight embrace of her corset. "What is more, it is the only real lead we have. Whatever drew the sorcerer into the woods, whether he be there now or not, will reveal to us the truth about what happened to him. I am convinced of it."

"So you are going then? Into the forest."

"Not I, Hans. We."

❖

Gretel was a firm believer in a firm hand when it came to managing her brother and his more expensive habits. Not the least of these was his propensity for whiling away evenings that turned into whole nights at the Inn. There he would drink and gamble, and depending on the cards, the company, and the quality of the ale, he might come home having made a gain, or—and this was more likely—he would return with empty pockets. Time and again Gretel had impressed upon him that his talent for poker, and indeed all games card based, was compromised by his talent for drinking. The Inn, unfortunately, promoted the pursuit of both at the same time. Given their parlous financial state, she would ordinarily have ushered Hans home after their work at the magicarium, directing him to their own brandy bottle and then the kitchen. However, these were not ordinary times. Gretel was all too keenly aware of the terror with which her brother regarded even the shallowest and palest of woodland glades; to ask him to go with her into the heart of the gloom on a quest for who-knew-what was to test his mettle and his loyalty both. It seemed to her, therefore, that to allow him to scuttle off to the Inn for the remainder of the evening was both fair and politic. He had seized the opportunity and the coins offered, and hastened away before she could think better of her generous gesture.

The streets of Gesternstadt were still pleasantly warm, and as Gretel made her way home she saw, to her dismay, that there were numerous couples still strolling arm in arm. She was just muttering darkly to herself about people not having anything more worthwhile to do when she noticed a particular person of a particular build and a particularly dashing burgundy cape (with gold silk lining), walking toward her. Ferdinand. She would face him. She would speak plainly. They would not converse, she would merely tell him what opinion she held of men who played fast and loose with the affections of women they had begun to give particular ideas. But then she saw again how handsome he was. Noticed anew the attractive curve of his calf. Started to feel the same blend of fuzzy warmth and sharp thrill that she always experienced in his company. Her resolve collapsed like a cheese soufflé whipped too fast from the oven. She would no doubt have humiliated herself then and there on the Grand Strasse had not a tall, slender, young woman emerged from a doorway to take General Ferdinand's arm.

Moving more quickly than she had done for many a long moon, Gretel darted into the cover of an alleyway. She peered out. The couple strolled on. Arm in arm. They chatted. They smiled. They laughed! The laughter was the pin in the balloon of Gretel's composure. The second they had moved out of sight she bolted from her hidey-hole and strode across the square, turning sharp left, not toward her own door, but in the direction of that of the dressmaker. The next time she saw the Uber

General, she promised herself, she would be resplendent not only in her new wig, but in a new gown. She would be the most glamorous, most sophisticatedly turned out woman at the concert when the day came, and no flippety-gibbet slip of a look-at-my-tiny-waist fiancée would be able to hold a candle to her.

FIVE

The next two days were filled with rather too much activity for Gretel's liking. Having studied the map, she spied a small dwelling indicated at a point she calculated to be less than a day's walk from where the stagecoach would drop them. This calculation was based on nothing firmer than a vague hunch, propped up by an uncertain feeling, and further supported by a desire for it to be so. Gretel had sent a letter to the occupant of the cottage requesting food and lodgings for one night, with the promise of fair payment and heartfelt gratitude. Beyond that, they would have to camp. The notion was a depressing one. Gretel was a connoisseur of life's little luxuries, and the least of these she believed to be good food and a comfortable bed. Camping, from what she had heard, seemed to be defined by an absence of both these things.

Perversely, Hans had brightened at the thought of, as he had put it, "slumbering beneath the stars!," so that his view of the whole expedition had altered considerably. His sudden enthusiasm for outdoor living, campfires, whittling, and all things similar had led him to gather quantities of equipment, the like of which Gretel had not known existed. The sitting room was home to a great mound of the stuff. There were flints and knives and balls of string and sheets of canvas and metal trivets and fish-hooks and snares . . . Gretel had been forced to call a halt to the acquisition of so many supplies, pointing out that they would soon spend more than the case could possibly earn, and that anyway, they would be unable to carry it all. In fact, her primary reason for inviting Hans to accompany her was to utilize his talents as a packhorse. She didn't want him taking so much paraphernalia that she would be forced to transport her own luggage, or else what was the point of putting up with him?

One of the few upsides of the mission was its low cost. Previous cases had seen her travel to such places as Nuremberg, and while she would rather have been there for her own enjoyment, it was a ruinously expensive place. One night's bed and breakfast, followed by a few days under canvass, on the other hand, would cost very little. On the matter of money, Gretel had thought long and hard. If, as she strongly suspected, the sorcerer was alive, and she found him, the life insurance company would not need to pay out. As she had already established that the man was all but broke, it followed that she would not then be paid her fee. Much as she would delight in seeing Frau Arnold's joy at being reunited with her husband, delight did not pay bills or buy winter wood. After careful consideration, therefore, Gretel had contacted the insurers and secured promise of payment by them if she brought back proof of Ernst Arnold's continuing existence.

But was he alive? There was still the disturbing evidence of the appendix to be explained. Could they be certain that it had, in fact, belonged to Herr Arnold? Gretel had taken the bottled body part to the apothecary, who was, with the help of Otto Voigt's sorcery, going to run a number of tests that should, he assured her as she handed over his outrageous fee for the work, provide the provenance of the remnant.

But even if the sorcerer was minus his appendage, he could still be living. The truth was that Gretel would go into those woods not knowing if she was looking for a mutilated corpse or a living, breathing sorcerer with a story to tell.

After another restless night, Gretel sat up in her bed, blinking at the sharp dawn light that was forcing its way through the gaps in the shutters. It was horribly early to begin her day, but there was little use chasing sleep now. She clambered out from beneath the tangled covers and slipped a peignoir about her shoulders before descending the stairs. The sitting room presented an unappealing place to sit with the abundance of camping equipment at its center, so she continued to the dining room and sat at her desk. She plucked a sheet of paper from a dusty pile, dipped a somewhat blunt quill into the watered-down ink, and scratched out a letter to Frau Arnold. In it she outlined her planned journey, what expenses she was likely to incur, and how long it might all take, and gave an assurance that she would return as soon as was humanly possible with news of her husband, and an invoice. Given that the only way the insurance company would pay out would be if his disappearance could demonstrably be shown to be murder, it was hard to put a cheerful slant on the letter. She thought about expressing her view that the man was in fact still alive, but did not dare raise the woman's hopes at this stage.

The front door was flung open and Hans fell through it. He lay upon the Turkish Kilim, face down, apparently in no hurry to get up.

"Have you been at the Inn all night?" Gretel asked.

"Hgmmnff," said Hans into the rug.

"Thought so. Well don't expect me to take pity on your fragile state. We must leave this day, whatever condition you are in."

Hans managed, with some difficulty, to roll onto his back. The flattened stub of an unlit cigar was still clenched between his teeth. He waved away his sister's concern with a pudgy paw.

"Best thing for a hangover, bit of fresh air. A brisk walk will soon set me right. After a feed, of course," he added, continuing his roll so that he might push himself up to his knees. He then sat back on his heels. A fuzzy grin settled upon his overly pink features. He stayed in this position for some time, resembling, Gretel thought, nothing so much as a large, happy pig sitting in a mud wallow.

"It will be something more than a brisk walk, Hans. We will be gone for days, and there is all that camping apparatus to be carted hither and yon. And firewood will need to be gathered, tents set up, some manner of meals prepared. Not to mention the need for sharp-eyed map reading if we are ever to arrive at the right place."

"Fear not on that front. Any of those fronts," said Hans, his diction still slurred from drink. At last he rose to his unsteady feet. "I have good news from the Inn."

"That seems unlikely, but go on, I'm listening."

"Well, I was talking to a fellow, who knows a chap, who has a cousin . . ."

"So far so much like every other evening at the Inn."

". . . who once went on an exhibition. Expectation." Hans paused and gave a shake like a dog ridding itself of water before continuing, "An expedition, yes that's it . . . he went off on a camping adventure somewhere wild and dangerous . . ."

"Was he running from the law?"

"What? No, don't think so. His idea of fun, far as I can gather. Anyway, point *is* he had a guide. Wonderful bloke, by all accounts, goes by the name of Cornelius Staunch. He is a true specialist in these things."

"These things?"

"Camping, hiking, building fires, catching food, all that. A man at home in the wilderness, fearless, resourceful . . . and the best thing of all? You'll never guess what. Go on, try, guess!"

He stopped, and Gretel realized with a weary heart that he was building up to a Big Moment, and that in order to get to whatever point he was trying to make she would have to play the game.

"He wrestled a bear with his bare hands?"

"More than likely, but that's not the best thing," Hans was growing ever pinker as he suppressed giggles.

"He found a crock of gold at the end of a rainbow?"

"Now you're just being silly."

"For pity's sake, Hans, just tell me so that we can both get on with our lives."

"I sent word asking him to help us, and a message came back saying that he would!"

"What?"

"I have engaged his services," Hans declared, "to assist us in our work. You in your work. However you want to look at it. He has agreed to meet us in the you-know-where a couple of days from now, and take us on to where we want to go, looking after us all the while."

Gretel was astonished to find that this was indeed good news. An experienced outdoors person, who could presumably light a fire and read a map, would make the whole unedifying task far more bearable. She could not quite bring herself to congratulate Hans, however, as he was now looking so insufferably smug.

"And how is he going to find us, on day two or three? Even we don't have a firm idea of which route we will take."

"But Gretel, he's an expert tracker. He has hunted animals and humans and others all over the globe. He will surely be able to follow our tracks. He would have joined us sooner, but he's dangling off an Alp somewhere just now."

Gretel was forced to concede that Hans had done well. She offered him words of a bolstering nature, which ended in her suggesting that one of his own delicious meals would be the very thing to set them up for their journey, and wouldn't he like to make the most of his beloved kitchen before he was parted from it? He needed no further encouragement to scurry off in search of bratwurst and pig's knuckle.

No sooner had he vacated his space on the rug in the hallway than a sealed note was pushed through the letter box, from where it floated briefly this way and that, riding a dusty little sunbeam to the floor. Gretel bustled from her perch at the desk and picked it up.

"Ah," she said to herself upon reading its contents. And then, more thoughtfully, "Aah." The letter was from the apothecary, and it confirmed, beyond doubt, that the appendix had belonged to none other than Ernst Arnold. Did this make it more likely he was dead? Gretel found that she was no more certain than she was uncertain. Still, the information was a fact, and facts were what would, ultimately, reveal the truth.

She had taken no more than two strides from the hallway when there came a hammering upon the door. She opened it, ready to berate whomever it was who saw fit to come thumping before she had taken breakfast. Her mood improved, however, when she found one of Madame Renoir's Salon girls standing on her doorstep. The young woman held out a large box tied with cerise silk ribbon.

"Your new wig, Fraulein Gretel," she said. "Madame insisted it be delivered to you the very moment it arrived."

Gretel took it with trembling hands. There was little that could induce the fizz of excitement she experienced at the prospect of wearing a brand-new, highly fashionable, exquisitely crafted, and tailor-made wig.

"Thank you, my dear," she said and then gasped as she heard the tinkling of miniature chimes.

"Oh, Fraulein, those will be the extra silver bells you requested," the girl explained. "They look divine!"

Both women beamed at each other, lost for a brief moment in shared wonder at the beauty of the world and everything in it.

Gretel's joy turned to sadness, however, at the thought of having to leave her new prize behind the very day she got it. It seemed cruel of life to arrange things this way.

"One thing," the girl spoke earnestly, "the wig must be broken in before it can be worn out. That is to say, you must take every opportunity to wear it, as if breaking in a new pair of shoes."

"Every opportunity, you say?"

The girl nodded. "Otherwise it will not fit at its best for its intended occasion. Madame was most insistent on this point."

"Indeed." Gretel gave the girl a coin for her trouble and contemplated the box. The wig had been an expensive indulgence; a reward to herself from herself after the success of her previous case. It seemed only right that she should do it justice, to make the most of her investment. Which meant, if it was to be in tip-top shape and fitting perfectly come Herr Mozart's concert, she would have to wear it whenever possible before the date. It struck her then, how helpfully secret forests could be. She would take the wig with her. She would wear it for a short time twice a day, away from the prying, envious eyes of the women of Gesternstadt, away from dashing generals and their unsuitable fiancées, so that there would not be another to match it come the day of the performance, both Herr Mozart's and her own.

❖

Two hours later, she and Hans arrived at the stagecoach, somewhat out of breath due to their haste in order not to miss it, and the awkward weight of their baggage. The warm weather continued, so that the morning sun added to their discomfort. Gretel was already questioning her choice of outfit. She had stared long and hard into her capacious wardrobe, waiting for the perfect clothes to present themselves, but none did. It had felt as if her beloved gowns and ensembles were reluctant to venture into such an uncivilized place. She had tussled with the opposing forces of practicality and flair. She must choose sturdy footwear, and yet she knew her spirits would be depressed by such ugliness. She should select garments that were heavy-duty, and yet how she would miss the sigh of silk against her skin. She ought to take only dark colors to disguise the ordure and grime of the woods, but her heart beat a little faster at the shimmer of pale blue or the fresh glow of mint green.

In the end she had settled for a linen gown the color of pressed blackberries (or, according to Hans, a bad bruise, but the day Gretel took any fashion advice from Hans would be the day she took to her daybed forever), with a cream bodice and matching bolero jacket. She had pinned a wide-brimmed, black-fringed hat to her hair, as she felt the shade might be useful. It was also made of a crepe that would allow it to be folded small and packed away when she was wearing her new wig instead. For it was Gretel's plan to break in her new adornment while walking, as soon as they were out of sight of the town, and when there was the protection of leafy shade for both it and her. She had forced herself to push her feet into a pair of stout ankle boots, knowing that anything more delicate would be ruined by all the tramping. At least there would be few people to witness her lack of kitten heels where she was going. But still she appeared to be wearing the wrong thing, for the day was uncommonly hot, and the linen unhelpfully thick.

"I say," said Hans, "this striking out and striding forth is more than a little heating."

"We have not yet begun," Gretel reminded him. "The walk to the stage post is one you have made many times before without breaking a sweat."

"Ah, but I have adopted the gait of the hiker, sister mine. See? See how I swing my legs and arms, the better to take up a rhythm that will cover the leagues swiftly and surely." Although they had arrived at their destination, Hans insisted on marching up and down to demonstrate his new technique. Gretel watched her brother with a mixture of pity and irritation. Not for the first time she wondered how she could be of the same blood as a man who leaped (puffing) at the opportunity to wear lederhosen. He had chosen his felt hat and toggles from the wide selection that filled his wardrobe, and now, with a bulging rucksack, rolls of bedding and canvass, and tin mugs a-dangling and clanking as he moved, he cut a ridiculous figure, as she surely would if she walked beside him. She would be forced to tell herself frequently, over the coming days, that Hans's uses were not, never had been, nor ever would be, of the ornamental variety. His broad shoulders and biddable nature were what counted now.

"I would conserve your energy, Hans," she told him, indicating the stagecoach that was now ready to take on passengers. "Heft our belongings aboard quickly and there may be time for a quick snack before we reach the start point of our trek proper."

"Right you are!" Needing no more motivation, Hans set about his task.

Gretel was on the point of getting herself inside the coach when the familiar, nasal tones of Kingsman Kapitan Strudel halted her in her tracks.

"Leaving town in the middle of a case, Fraulein?" he asked.

"As you see, Herr Kapitan."

"Not your usual modus operandi. Are you, perhaps, conceding defeat and abandoning your investigations?" He circled Gretel slowly as he put his questions to her, his thin neck and scrawny limbs and all over flimsy physique giving the appearance of one who had been filleted earlier in the day and was now held up only by gristle and bad temper.

"I have never found the case yet that would force me to give up, as I am certain you know."

"Oh? Then I must deduce that you are traveling on matters to do with the case."

"The people of Gesternstadt are indeed fortunate to have you in charge of their security," Gretel told him.

"Ahah!" The Kapitan gave a yap of triumph. "Which means you must have information pertinent to the case of the missing sorcerer, and that information you cannot keep from the kingsman of this region. For if you do you will be charged with obstructing kingsman's work, withholding evidence, hampering official investigations, and obfuscating facts pertaining to the ongoing enquiry!" Strudel was quite breathless with glee at his own cleverness.

Gretel regarded him coolly. The man was an idiot, but he was what passed for the law in Gesternstadt, and he could make difficulties for her if he had a mind to. Which was, by all accounts, the only manner of mind he ever had. Tempting as it was to goad him into a frothing state before delivering some withering riposte, she knew she must resist. Public humiliation tended to bring out the worst in minor officials, and was apt to get them issuing warrants and having people dragged away, locked up, and subjected to all sorts of inconveniences. She tried a smile that would not quite take but only twitched at the corners of her mouth.

"I promise you, Kapitan Strudel, if I find anything relevant, anything at all, you will be the very first to hear of it. After all, this is, as you have so astutely identified, a difficult case. Nothing is dearer to me in this world than my professional reputation, and for the sake of it I will put aside pride. How much more likely to solve the case will we both be if we pool our knowledge?"

Strudel narrowed his narrow eyes at her. "You say that, but how do I know you do not already have pertinent information?"

"If I had, do you really think I would be entering those deep, dark woods?" she pointed out. "It is precisely because of the lack of clues or leads that I must cast my net wider. You must surely know that it is at no small personal cost that I venture to the scene of my childhood nightmare."

This threw the Kapitan. Painful experience had taught him that Gretel was almost always playing him for a fool, but he so liked the idea that the fearless detective was actually admitting to being *scared* that he could not resist believing her. Gretel watched him attempting to sift truth from fiction. His eyes suddenly widened (which is to say they came close to achieving something beyond their customary small proportions). He had evidently taken an idea into his head, a place where, after all, it had ample room to roam.

"You!" He called Hans over, crooking a crooked finger at him. Hans came, mopping his brow with a disturbingly gray kerchief. Gretel at once saw the man's plan. If you want a simple truth, simply ask a simple question of a simple person. Ideally a simpleton, should one be available.

"Phew! Hot work, all that hefting," said Hans. "How can I help you, Herr Kapitan?"

"I see your sister has you well employed. Tell me, where is it you are headed?"

"Haven't a clue," said Hans. "Nor has Gretel, truth be told. Clueless, both of us. Ha, ha, not good for a detective, but there it is. Can't win 'em all, eh, sister mine?"

"You don't actually know where you are going?"

Hans shook his head emphatically.

"Then tell me this, who is it you are going to see?"

"Ha! Would all be a great deal easier if we knew the answer to that one. These questions of yours, Herr Kapitan, dashed tricky. Teach you all this stuff at some manner of academy, I suppose."

"So, you don't know where you are going, or who you are going to see? Then what do you hope to gain by going into the deep, dark woods?"

Gretel held her breath. The mention of the unmentionable might just have been enough to shake Hans's composure and have him blabbering and jabbering all manner of things she did not want Strudel hearing.

"Well," said Hans, paling just a shade beneath the rosy glow of exertion and heat, "Gretel hopes to find out some sort of something, from some sort of someone, which might lead some sort of somewhere, so that we can present Frau Arnold with some sort of answers and then get paid. I just go where I'm sent and do as I'm told. Such is a brother's lot in life, Herr Kapitan."

It was convincing because it was, after all, the truth, truthfully told.

Strudel treated them both to a cheery sneer, pivoted on his heel, and strode away.

Gretel patted her brother's arm. "Help me into my seat, Hans. And then snack, I think."

"Snack!" he echoed.

SIX

Gretel was not a fan of stagecoach travel, but this was one occasion when the journey went unnervingly swiftly. All too soon they had reached the point in the road where they could easily access the fringes of the forest, and were being handed their luggage. It was early afternoon, and the heat of the day was setting the air like jelly about them, so that it no longer felt fit to breathe. It was with damp underarms and clammy backs that the pair stood on the gritty verge and watched the coach tear away from them until the very last puff of dust had dispersed.

"Well," said Hans, "here we are."

"Here we are," Gretel agreed. They turned to face the forest. The outer edges consisted of a variety of trees, in fetching shades of green, broad-leaved and not too closely set. "It really looks rather pretty, Hans. Quite light, verdant, full of charming flowers and pleasant scents, I shouldn't wonder."

Hans's silence suggested she might have over-egged the pudding. "Come along, then," she said, picking up the small vanity case in which she carried her beloved wig. "Let us to work!" So saying, she strode forth, following the dry, narrow path that led away from the dazzling sunshine, and into the dappled shade of the trees. Hans followed close behind, his bulky backpack clattering and clanking as he moved along.

The interior immediately provided a very welcome respite from day's sunshine. There was indeed plenty of light, falling in fractured beams upon the loamy floor, over which trailed tiny white flowers, twisting around the glossy leaves of wild garlic and short, wiry grasses. Birdsong serenaded them as they walked, and small birds of the harmless and attractive type flitted this way and that among the boughs of the oaks and birches. And Gretel had been correct in her expectation of delightful aromas of the herbs and plants around them. There were even butterflies, and Gretel at her most grumpy could not deny the appeal of lepidoptera.

"See, Hans? It is really not so bad. Before you know it we will be accustomed to the place, we will follow the map, becoming fitter and more confident with every stride, and we will reach the cottage of Frau Burgdorf in good time for supper. All we have to do is stick to this," she explained, slipping her bag strap over her arm so that she could take the map from her pocket and unfold it as she walked. "It is all perfectly clear. We proceed along this path, which is marked thus . . . ," she held the tattered paper beneath his nose for a moment, ". . . for approximately half an afternoon. After which time we should reach a small stream, which may be the ideal place to take a little refreshment."

"Oh?" said Hans, in a small but less-scared-than-he-thought-he-was-going-to-be voice.

"And from there it is only a short distance more, with a gently upward incline, through a more rocky region of the woods, until we reach our first overnight stop."

"Well, that all sounds very manageable," Hans agreed. "I could grow accustomed to this exercise business, take it up as a new habit perhaps," he announced, and the two of them fell into a companionable silence as they walked on, save for the soft squeak of Hans's lederhosen.

Two hours later, having made splendid progress through what continued to be picturesque, fragrant, and charming woods, Gretel studied the map again and signaled to Hans to stop.

"We should be very nearly at the stream," she told him. "Time for our picnic."

"What?" He turned toward her and cupped his hand over her ear.

"Picnic!" she found herself yelling.

Hans shook his head. "It's no good," he bellowed back. "I can't hear you over that roaring noise."

Gretel had been hoping the unsettling rumble she had been hearing for a few hundred strides now was all in her own head. Alas, this was not so. She walked on and rounded the next bend to find herself toe to edge with a deep, wild, fast-flowing, rock-filled torrent. It was not wide, but too wide to jump. The speed of the water had carved a gouge into the forest floor that now formed a steep-sided gully, through which the white water raced. Most of the roaring came from the waterfall just upriver, over which countless quantities of peaty water charged before swirling past.

Hans came to stand beside her. "Ah," he mouthed soundlessly.

Ah, indeed. Gretel shooed him back with flapping hands and they made their way farther down the bank to a grassy knoll where the noise was less and speech was at least possible.

"How on earth are we to cross?" Hans asked, somewhat unnecessarily, in Gretel's opinion.

"Have you nothing in that pack of yours that might assist us?"

"I shall look but . . ." He shook his head and sucked air through his teeth in the manner of one pronouncing something a hopeless case. He slipped the rucksack from his back and dug deep. "No, that won't help . . . no . . . no. Oh, nice bit of weisswurst, we might gain strength from that." He paused to hand Gretel the sausage and then resumed his digging. "Oh, maybe . . . but no." He pulled out a bedroll and canvas sheet. There was rope, but it was thin and short and meant for constructing an awning or hammock, not hauling large Bavarians across fast-flowing water courses. Hans straightened up, defeated. "Nothing," he said flatly. "But a stout stick would help, wouldn't it?" He pulled a folded knife from his pocket. "If we wade across . . ."

"Wade! You are suggesting I step into *that*."

"It will be perfectly safe. We will form a human chain, with me at the fore, testing the way with my trusty staff." He bounded off to assault a blameless hazel bush. "This is the very stuff, nice and springy, d'you see?" To make his point, he bent back one of the taller, whippier offshoots of the little tree. Unfortunately, his palms were sweaty, so that the branch slipped through his grasp, springing back to smack him smartly in the eye. "Ow!" he yelped, hopping around, clutching his face.

"Hans, stand still and stop making such a fuss." Gretel put her hand on his arm. "Let me have a look, I'm sure it won't be . . ."

But it was. It was every bit, and then some more. As Hans revealed his eye Gretel felt her stomach turn over. The whole socket was already a bloody, swollen mess.

"The good news is," she told him as calmly as she was able, "that your eye is still where it should be. The cruel wood has not removed it."

"Good news indeed," gasped Hans. "And the bad . . . ?"

"It may . . . smart a bit for a while. But think of this," she added, searching for words of encouragement, for they could not afford to lose momentum, "you will have a rakish scar once it has healed up, and there is nothing that says 'bravery' like a rakish scar."

"You are right about that, sister mine!" Hans squared his shoulders manfully. "I will endure."

"That's the spirit. Although, if you are willing to sacrifice your kerchief, I think it would be a good idea to cover it up." She was relieved when he agreed to a makeshift bandage, as the look of the thing was quite revolting. "There!" she assured him, "Attractively piratical."

"You think?" Hans cocked his head this way and that, blinking out from his one good eye. Suitably encouraged, he chopped off a good-sized hazel stick. The pair then removed their boots and stockings, which they hung around their necks. When the moment could be put off no longer, Hans took Gretel's hand, and together they clambered down into the river.

"Hell's teeth!" cried Gretel as her feet met the bone-chillingly cold water. "Has no one told this torrent that it is summer?"

"Snowmelt from the Zugspitze!" Hans gasped by way of explanation.

They inched their way forward. Each step was slipperier and more perilous than the one before it. The rocks upon which they must tread were coated with slimy algae, and the force of the water against their ankles, then shins, then knees, caused them both to wobble and teeter. Gretel felt the hems of her hitched up skirts and petticoats become quickly sodden and heavy, so that they dragged against her wish to go forward. She had to push hard to make her legs lift and move through the river.

"Keep going!" Hans cried, probing with his stick, which was in fact proving a boon. "It's working. We shall soon be across!"

Pride might come before a fall; blind optimism—or in Hans's case, half-blind optimism—also often precedes a painful and humiliating upending. Just as they were within a stride of the opposite bank; just as Hans gallantly handed his sister past himself and guided her toward the other side; just as he allowed himself a small smile of pride, and even Gretel was summoning up some minor manner of congratulation, Hans's feet were swept from under him. With a shout, he fell backward, his own considerable weight crucially tipped by the not-inconsiderable pack still strapped to his shoulders. Down he went, flat on his back, into the water. Fortunately, the water was not deep enough to drown him. Unfortunately, it was sufficiently deep and plentiful to saturate and ruin every vulnerable item of their camping apparatus. The blankets. The bedrolls. The food. All were soaked and rendered twice their weight and half their usefulness in the time it took Hans to let out a "Gadzooks!"

After a great deal of puffing and gasping and much by way of muttered curses, Gretel was eventually successful in hauling her brother from the river. They lay panting on the bank for some moments before they felt able to continue. At last, Gretel cajoled and nagged Hans into getting up and getting along. The day was fading fast. Soon it would be dusk, and neither of them wished to be wandering through the woods in the dark. They forwent their picnic in order to reach safety before nightfall, settling for nibbling disconsolately on a bit of wet wurst as they went. The squeak of Hans's lederhosen had been transformed into a squelch.

As they walked on, Gretel noticed subtle changes in their surroundings. The trees were closer together, the undergrowth denser, the forest canopy blocking out more of what was left of the sun. In what remained of the heat of the day, Hans steamed gently.

"I say, Gretel, how much farther?"

Glancing at the map, she said, "Not far at all."

"Good thing. Wet leather chafes, you know."

"A passing discomfort only. Soon we will be in the cozy embrace of the little guest house, where no doubt a meal is being prepared as we walk, and you will be able to change into dry garments."

Gretel was doing her utmost to show everything in its best possible light, but even so she could not deny to herself a creeping sense of unease. She told herself it was nothing more than a long-buried memory struggling to the surface, and should not be paid any heed. Nevertheless, one reason for her disquiet simply could not be ignored, and that was the strong impression that they were being watched. Or possibly followed. The word "stalked" pounced into her mind, but she batted it aside. Of course there were woodland creatures thereabouts. Naturally all sorts of small animals would be curiously observing the strange interlopers in their midst. She was too big and too bold and too old to be spooked by a few squirrels. She squinted at the map through her lorgnettes.

"If I am not very much mistaken, the cottage should come into view about . . ."

". . . *now!*" Hans finished her statement in such a tone as caused her to stop in her tracks, as he had done, and look up to see what it was that had made him express so much in such a little word.

The cottage was indeed in plain view, but there was nothing plain about it. It sat in a charming clearing, its garden flower filled, its little cobbled path twisting from a dear wooden gate attached to a white picket fence. The forest stood aside, as if held back, to allow this pretty space for human habitation. But the cottage was not an ordinary cottage. It had windows where windows should be, and a chimney where a chimney should be, and a front door at the front of it. But . . .

Gretel and Hans stood and stared. Gretel knew she was holding her breath and was certain her brother would be holding his too. Neither of them spoke. Neither of them moved. For her part, Gretel was aware of just about the only time in her life when she had ever had an almost overwhelming urge to run. But that urge was canceled out by the bowel-loosening terror that was now taking hold of her. In the end she could do nothing but stand and stare at what was before them, for their accommodation was no more or less than the most detailed, most artfully constructed, most colorful, most elaborate, most splendid example you ever did see of a gingerbread house.

SEVEN

Hans recovered sufficiently to about turn and attempt to flee. Gretel took hold of his collar.

"Where do you think you are going?" she asked.

"Away from here. Away from that!" he replied in a stage whisper.

"It is just a house."

"You know full well what it is," said Hans as he squirmed beneath her grasp.

"You are overreacting. It is a traditional style of house. It's not really made of . . . gingerbread."

"How can you tell?"

"Look closer. Go on, look."

He forced himself to squint at it with his one available eye.

"Well," he allowed, "it does appear to me a real house. Just made to resemble . . . food."

"As I say, a tradition, part of the vernacular architecture hereabouts. Only you and I would read anything else into it."

"All the same, I don't believe you want to spend a night in it any more than I do."

"I certainly don't want to spend a night out here. Think of our situation: you have had a soaking, and so has our bedding and our food. Night is almost upon us. We are booked in to stay here. I received a very pleasant letter of confirmation from the proprietress, Frau Burgdorf, who sounded as sane and hospitable as the day is long. I refuse to let ghosts drive us away from comfort and a good meal, and toward privation and hunger."

"Well, when you put it like that . . ." Hans steadied enough for Gretel to risk releasing him.

"It is tradition, Hans, nothing else."

"Fair enough. But I give you fair warning, if anything remotely resembling a witch comes out of that house . . ."

At that moment, the bright red door with the painted details that looked so very much like piped icing slowly swung open. A figure emerged from inside the house.

Hans gasped.

So did Gretel.

There stood before them a woman of striking elegance and beauty. She was tall and slender, with golden hair piled atop her head, as if done effortlessly and casually, and yet resulting in something truly sophisticated. Her gown was all flowing lines and slinking satin. Not exactly high fashion; more something for wearing at home for a soiree. Gretel took in at once the daringly high heels and the tasteful emerald earrings and ring, as well as the narrow, plaited gold bangle and matching brooch. She could not help but admire any woman who so clearly knew how to accessorize. The apparition of loveliness blinked a little against the low sunlight, shielding her eyes with her hand.

"Hello? Oh, darlings, is it you? Are you here at last? Welcome! Welcome!" she called out in a voice that contained not a trace of crone, but an unmissable, sexy purr. As she spoke she held up a long-stemmed cocktail glass to toast their arrival.

"I say!" said Hans, in an altogether different kind of whisper to the one he had been using only moments earlier. "I say!" he repeated, for no particular reason.

Gretel gave him a shove forward and then strode up the path herself to offer their hostess her hand. "We are very pleased to have found our way to your door, Frau Burgdorf," she said.

"Oh, call me Zelda, for heaven's sake, darling, *please!* Everybody does. And anyway, every time I hear 'Frau Burgdorf' I look around for my mother-in-law! Ha, ha!" She ignored Gretel's proffered hand and leaned in close to deliver a noisy kiss on each cheek. "Your turn!" she squealed at Hans, who allowed himself to be similarly welcomed. "My, but you are a strong fellow! And whatever have you done to your poor eye? Come along in, and I'll see to that for you. But first, who's for a cocktail?" She slipped her arm through his and fairly waltzed him over the threshold. Gretel followed on.

Where the exterior of the house was an homage to Bavarian culture, the interior was something quite other. It was open and spacious, filled with chaises longues, settees, fur rugs, silk throws, and more cushions than Gretel could count. Though she did try. The whole effect was of leisure, and of luxury. It was Bohemian, yet refined and somehow not so fancy. Gretel felt suddenly that she had gone beyond her limits of tiredness. Whether it was the march through the hot day, the lack of food, or the sight of such seductive comfort, she could not be sure. She knew only that she must recline at once if she were not to fall over.

"Forgive me . . . Zelda, but I must sit for a moment."

"Oh, but of course! You must both be exhausted. It is such a long way to the stagecoach stop. Now, Fraulein Gretel, you sit just here . . ." She led her to a green velvet sofa that Gretel all too happily sank onto. "Perfect. Kick off your shoes, my darlings, relax. You are in Zelda's home now, and I desire nothing more than to see my guests happy and taking their ease." She guided Hans to a high stool beside what looked like a bar of some sort. "You sit there and mix us all some lovely drinks. Here," she pushed an armful of bottles of jewel-colored liquids, a shaker, and an ice bucket toward him. "I believe you are a man who knows a thing or two about drinks. Am I right?" When Hans mumbled and nodded happily she clapped her hands together in delight. "Wonderful! I shall fetch water and a bandage for your poor, dear eye, and then we shall sip our cocktails, and when you are recovered I will show you to your bedchambers to change for dinner."

She swept out of the room.

"I say!" said Hans again, staring at the closed door after she had gone as if he might be able to see through it and watch her some more. "Not a hint of witchiness there, eh, sister mine?"

"Maybe not, Hans," Gretel agreed, pulling her damp boots off her damp feet. "But have a care: charm can undo a man quicker than a sharp knife."

Zelda Burgdorf continued to ooze charm for the entire evening. And very irresistible it was too. Gretel herself soon succumbed to it. After lurid-colored cocktails of Hans's own invention, they were shown their own small but comfortable rooms where they were able to change, wash, and dress in the few dry, clean clothes they had left. Most things had received a dunking in the brook and so had to be hung up by the kitchen stove to dry. Their host kindly provided them with curious flowing robes and housecoats, prompting Hans to declare as they went to the table that they resembled nothing more than a party of artists and poets. There followed a delicious meal of trout stuffed with cream and almonds, served with minted potatoes and green beans, and then a pudding of treacle sponge. All the while Zelda regaled them with tales of her glamorous past.

"You have lived in so many fascinating and faraway places," Hans observed, dabbing brandy from his chin. "How came you here?"

"Oh, a girl can tire of the city," Zelda told him. Which is to say she told him nothing.

Gretel fought to resist the effects of food, drink, and the soothing environment. She must see if the woman knew anything about the sorcerer, without, of course, giving away too much about her own reasons for venturing into the woods. Which Zelda had not asked about at all. Which either meant she was extremely discreet and well-mannered, or something else. Besides which, much as Gretel wanted to enjoy her hostess's company and relax both mind and body, she could not shake off the niggling sense that something was amiss. And niggling senses that could not be shaken off should not be ignored. They were, experience had taught her, tenacious for a reason.

"And what of Herr Burgdorf? Is he . . . not here, your husband?" Gretel asked, deliberately leaving the question as open as possible.

Zelda gave a shrug and took another gulp of her viridian cocktail. Despite serving two types of wine with supper and now a good cognac, she herself never drank anything else. "No, none of my husbands is here," she said.

"How many were there?" Hans wanted to know. Thanks to Zelda he had a fresh, neat dressing over his eye, but the bruising the hazel stick had inflicted was spreading out to blacken and blue half his face. The other half was its more customary after-dinner pink.

"Four. Poor lambs, I couldn't keep any one of them for long. The first stepped into a bear trap—oh, he was such a fine, handsome young man! The second drowned in Lake Como on our honeymoon—he was a weak swimmer, you understand. The third," she paused to drink a little more, "the third was rather elderly. A beautiful mind, so insightful, so clever, that was what I loved about him. And a lover of fine art. We traveled to so many places to view masterpieces."

"What happened to him?" Hans asked.

"He took up painting, wanting to emulate his heroes. Then one day he mistook his turpentine for his water glass and . . ." she made a rueful face and shook her head. "So very sad. His paintings were getting really rather good, poor dear."

"And number four?" Gretel asked.

"Ah, my true love! My fourth husband was a dealer in diamonds. Oh, what times we had! Amsterdam, London, the Orient . . ."

"And he is not living still?" Hans ventured.

"Alas he is not. Fell down a mine shaft. It was so deep they could not recover his body. And he'd only owned the mine a few weeks. However," she said, brightening a little, "they did find two very large diamonds down there when they were trying to reach him. Poor dear lamb must surely have been trying to get one for me. See here?" She extended an elegant hand and I saw that the emerald ring of earlier had been exchanged for a large diamond solitaire.

"A fine memento," Gretel said.

Zelda gave a sigh. "I suppose it is. But a memento won't keep a girl warm at night."

To her left, Hans's color deepened and he gave a little cough.

"Tell me," Gretel pressed on, "have you ever had a guest staying here by the name of Ernst Arnold?"

"I don't believe so. But then, guests do not always give their real names. I pride myself on running a discreet establishment, Fraulein. Their business is not my business."

"A laudable sentiment. I wonder then, might you have noticed a sorcerer among your clientele ever?"

Zelda's face was inscrutable. She sipped her drink some more, running a long finger around the rim of the glass. "Sorcerer? No. No, I think not."

Gretel nodded and swirled her brandy in its snifter. It was possible the woman was telling the truth. What seemed to undermine that possibility, however, was her complete lack of interest in the subject. It seemed only human nature, having been asked about a particular man with a particular name and a very particular profession, to wish to know more. Why did Zelda not ask even one question about why Gretel was looking for him, or why she thought he might have stayed at her house? Such a lack of interest struck Gretel as suspicious.

"You live quite a solitary existence now, Frau Zelda, if I may say, compared to your earlier years. Do you not find life in the woods a little quiet?" Gretel asked.

"Darling, I'm done with all that running around!" Zelda insisted, dunking another olive in her cocktail. "No, it's the simple life for me now, although as I say," here she paused to pass a scrutinizing eye over Hans, "a girl can want for male company now and again."

Hans drained his glass.

Gretel rolled her eyes. All she needed was her brother getting into some sort of romantic entanglement with a merry widow. She hauled herself to her feet and took Hans by the arm.

"We have an early start. Thank you for a fine meal and a pleasant evening. We will bid you good night."

She steered Hans to his room and then went to her own. It was small, low-ceilinged, and cottagy, but the furnishings were, like those of the downstairs, plush, lush, and just a touch decadent. The bed looked particularly inviting, with its satin-edged velvet quilted cover and feather pillows. Still wearing her borrowed clothes, Gretel pitched forward onto it and, medicated by cocktails and brandy, and without bothering to extinguish the candle on her bedside table, she was soon sleeping deeply.

This blissful rest did not, however, last more than an hour. She awoke from a disturbing dream, in which she was once again ensnared in the gingerbread house of the witch of her childhood. She came to, clawing her way out of the nightmare, sweaty and breathless. For an instant, when she opened her eyes, the room was transformed from being the small but sumptuous bedchamber she had entered earlier into a pokey, bare room filled with dust and cobwebs. The image was fleeting, but unsettling. Brushing it off as a remnant of her dream, Gretel got out of bed and threw open the shutters. It was a clammy night, so that little by way of fresh air was to be had. She sat at the dressing table and pulled toward her the vanity case she had so devotedly carted so many miles. A tiny shiver of excitement ran through her at the thought of what lay within. On an impulse, she opened the case and lifted out her wonderful wig. It felt soft and luxurious and expensive in her hands. She took a brush to it and repaired any flattening brought about by its being confined and conveyed. Then, with great care, she set it upon her head, pushing her own wayward locks up underneath it, and securing it with several hairpins. She considered the results in the looking glass. For a better view, she dropped the chain of her lorgnettes over her head—taking pains not to snag the wig or its adornments—and lifted the glasses to her eyes.

"Splendid!" she said to herself. "Simply splendid."

But as she looked she glimpsed, just for a fraction of a second, something that caused her heart to skip a beat. It seemed that the room behind her, as reflected in the mirror, was again altered to the version she had seen in her nightmare. She whipped around, but all was as it should be, velvety and lovely. The candle had burned down to a short stub, so that it gave off a feeble and unreliable light. Rubbing her eyes and silently chastising herself for giving in to her overfed and over-stimulated imagination, Gretel decided she needed to freshen up in order to feel better, and hopefully to get back to sleep. Her borrowed shift dress was clinging to her uncomfortably, and her throat was unpleasantly dry. She needed water, and her own nightdress, which should by now have dried out.

Taking the candle and tiptoeing so as not to wake the household—and still wearing her wig—Gretel left her room and descended the narrow stairs to the kitchen, where the wet garments had been put to dry. The room was still messy with dishes and leftover food, but was otherwise as one might expect, with simple wooden furniture, a dresser of jars and bottles of preserves and pickles, bundles of herbs and onions hanging from the beams, and a large, black stove with a size-able oven in which, no doubt, the evening meal had been cooked. Gretel found her clothes on the wooden rack. Her nightdress was perfectly dry, so she changed into it, taking care not to dislodge her wig as she dropped it over her head. She found her short, green woolen cape that had been in Hans's pack, and that too appeared to be free of river water. She pulled it around her shoulders for ease of carrying, and pushed her feet into her nicely warmed boots. Feeling restored a little already, she fetched a cup of water from the pail beneath the window and then headed back to her room.

As she climbed the stairs she began to feel a building cross-ness take hold of her. What ought to have been a simple walk over a few miles had left them battered and bruised, particularly Hans, with ruined supplies and equipment. They had both drunk more than was good for them, which meant they would both be traveling under the weight of headaches the next day, a fact that would not be helped by her lack of sleep, and to cap it all, Frau Burgdorf had not only been unforthcoming about the sorcerer, she had been downright secretive. Why, Gretel wondered?

In her chamber, she unfolded the map once more and squinted at it in the candlelight. Tomorrow would see their trek begin in earnest. Without any further information as to Herr Arnold's whereabouts, they had no option other than to rely on the map and trust it to lead them to him. With a sigh of irritation she folded the thing up and stuffed it into her cape pocket. She was at the point of flopping into bed once more when a curious noise snagged her attention. She cocked her ear. There it was again. It was something between a snigger and a cry, and appeared to be coming from one of the other bedchambers.

Stepping onto the landing and hearing the sound a third time, she identified its source as Hans's room. Perhaps he too was experiencing a bad dream. As the thought formed in her mind, Gretel was certain she saw the purple and scarlet rug under her feet fade to nothing, revealing bare boards, worn and splintery instead. She blinked hard and clutched at the handrail of the top of the staircase to steady herself. But her palm landed not on a polished walnut balustrade, but a broken chunk of rough-hewn pine, crumbling from the work of the woodworm that inhabited it. The guttering light of her candle threw out jagged shadows, upon the edges of which half-glimpsed forms jumped in and out of her vision. She began to feel a dark foreboding churn her stomach.

She thought of calling out to Hans, but something made her hold back. She crept to the door of his room and pushed it open so that she could peer inside. What she saw made her quail. Her brother was sitting up in bed, sporting a black eye patch, and wearing a pair of borrowed red Chinese silk pajamas and a dopey grin. Zelda, wearing a feather-trimmed chiffon chemise barely long enough to cover her embarrassment, was dancing seductively around the room. Such a scene would be naturally disturbing, given that she was witnessing erotic goings-on involving her own sibling, but that was not the worst of it. Her vision continued to register two versions of everything, slipping from one to the other as if the house was under some manner of spell. And that spell appeared to be losing its hold, so that the glimpses of the darker, scarier reality it was designed to obscure were becoming more frequent and more prolonged. As she watched, Zelda herself altered from the glamorous, winsome woman of a certain age to an ancient, hook-nosed, toothless, wart-ridden crone. Her soft, lithe body revealed its true self to be bony and saggy and mottled. It was clear Hans was only seeing the pretty version, for even half-drunk he would have screamed and fled in terror had be realized the nature of what was now climbing onto the bed with him.

Gretel flung wide the door and hollered, "Hans! Hans, get up! You are being deceived!"

"What's that? Dash it all, Gretel, a little respect for a fellow's privacy . . . ," he gasped, coyly pulling the coverlet to his chin.

"She is not what she seems!" Gretel insisted.

Zelda the Terrible let out a furious hiss in her direction before turning back to Hans, simpering in her guise as Zelda the Tantalizing.

"Your poor sister is just jealous, Hansie. She is a lonely woman, don't let her spoil your fun," she cooed, tickling Hans under the chin as if he were an oversized pussy cat.

Hans all but purred. "Yes, go away, Gretel, do," he begged, flapping a hand at her.

Gretel knew she had to get him to see the real Frau Burg-dorf. She searched her mind for what she could recall about witches, but everything was deeply buried. It was not a subject she wished to think about. She forced herself to remember all that she had learned after her childhood trauma. Witches were dangerous largely because they were experts at beguiling, and Hans was, at that moment, just about as beguiled as a person could get. She ran through all the witch tests she could think of, but there was no time to strap the woman to a ducking stool, or feed her witch cakes, and the chances of getting her to agree to some sort of intimate search seemed slim.

"Hans, I tell you it is all a glamour, a spell, an enchantment! She is not what she appears to be!"

"Do go back to your own room, sister mine. You are evidently still feeling the effects of those rather wonderful cocktails."

At that moment there was a disturbance in the air about Gretel's head. Sensing movement, she turned just in time to see something dark come flying through the doorway, whiz past her wig, and speed into the room. It turned and swooped close to her face long enough for her to see that it was a small, fast, apparently agitated bat.

Zelda noticed it too. She let out a furious shriek as it flew toward her. It was only then that Gretel recalled that witches, though they take all manner of creatures as their familiars, won't touch a bat. Certainly Frau Burgdorf seemed to hold a fierce antipathy toward the things, for she swiped and swatted at this one as it swooped and swooshed around the room. Not only did this cause the woman to break off from seducing Hans, it also adversely affected her ability to maintain the spell of illusion she had placed upon herself and her home. Which meant that even Hans could now see what she was.

Gretel had heard her brother utter many strange sounds over the years. Some had been drunken expostulations. Others had been gleeful exclamations (usually prompted by food). Others still had been strangled cries uttered in the midst of some perceived danger. However, never, *never* before had she heard anything like the scream of horror that now came forth from him. And as he screamed he leaped up from the bed as if fired from a slingshot. Zelda was busy with the bat, which seemed to be making a point of tangling with her. It broke off to fly close to Gretel for an instant, so that she could stare right into its bright little eyes, and then it went back to attacking the witch. Gretel suddenly grasped that this was not any old bat, it was Jynx, the sorcerer's bat. She had no more time to ponder this point, however, as Hans was forcing her out of the room.

"Run, Gretel! For pity's sake, don't just stand there. Can't you see what she is? What *that* is?"

Indeed she could, for now, her trickery exposed, the witch dropped the pretense of the illusory spell, and all and everything was revealed in its true state. The house was no longer an inviting, sumptuous Bohemian retreat; it was a fetid, dank, and filthy witch's lair. As Gretel and Hans charged down the stairs they could hear the witch cursing them and giving chase. The stairs wobbled and shook, as if trying to trip them up. The kitchen, which had looked so warm and kempt while ensorcelled, was now a stinking space, piled with rotting food, all of which crawled with maggots and worms. Hans screamed again, and Gretel might have joined in, had she breath for both shrieking and running, which she found never to be the case. As they sped for the back door she had the presence of mind to grab Hans's rucksack from its airing place next the stove. She thrust it at him.

"Take this!" she yelled, "and stuff it with anything else useful. Hurry!" She could hear the witch's footsteps thundering along the landing. Although slowed by the redoubtable little bat, she would soon be upon them. Gretel could not imagine what the woman's intentions were, but she herself had no intention of waiting to find out. She bundled Hans toward the exit.

"Wait!" he cried, "I haven't got the . . ."

"There's no time. Go on!"

She wrenched open the door. Outside the dense canopy of trees blocked out all moonlight, barely allowing a blinking star, so that all was Stygian gloom. Gretel felt herself hesitate, balking at the awful blackness. She was still clutching her candle stub, but it was a pitiful glowworm of light against such darkness. She would later consider that it was that hesitation that nearly cost them everything.

Hans shouted out, "My hat!" and dashed back into the room for it, his rucksack slung over one shoulder.

In that second, Zelda reached the bottom stair and sent a swift spell to slam shut the door, flinging chairs before it to form a barricade.

Gretel realized that they were trapped. She and Hans—him clutching his rucksack and beloved hat—backed up as far as they could against what had only seconds before been their escape route. Zelda, eyes flashing, clawlike hands outstretched, advanced slowly and surely across the room toward them.

EIGHT

Now I have you!" cried Zelda.

"But why ever do you want us?" asked Gretel, hoping to play for time with talk while she thought of a way to flee.

"Especially me!" Hans piped up. "Why would you want me? I mean, really, I'm no use to anyone. I can understand you wanting Gretel, of course, mind like that could come in handy, but me . . . ?"

Gretel stepped sideways to tread firmly on his toes. As she was in her boots and he was barefoot this resulted in an *ooph* followed by silence.

"What an opportunity!" Zelda went on. "Couldn't believe my luck when I got your letter. All these long years I've tried to think of a way of luring you here, and then you write asking if I have a couple of rooms available for a night. Ha!"

"All these years?" Gretel frowned.

Hans found his voice again, though it was somewhat squeakier and quite a bit more trembly than when he had last had it. "You don't mean to say . . . You can't mean to tell us . . . You cannot possibly be . . . ? Can you? Are you? Tell me you are not!"

"Of course she isn't, Hans, don't be ridiculous."

"But she might be!" He recoiled back against the stacked chairs at the very idea. "I mean to say, we never saw the you-know-what actually die, did we? She might have survived. She might have."

Zelda gave an exasperated shout. "Of course she didn't! You push a witch into an oven and slam the door, doesn't matter how good she is at spells, she's going to end up crispy and dead. My poor darling sister didn't stand a chance."

"*Your sister!*" chorused Gretel and Hans.

"That's right. That's who you so cruelly, cold-bloodedly murdered."

Gretel drew herself up. "We acted in self-defense, no more, no less."

"Says you."

"We were children!" she pointed out.

"Who can be vicious, deceitful creatures. Everyone knows that."

"As opposed to sweet, harmless, truthful witches, I suppose?" Gretel asked.

"Not all witches are wicked," said Zelda.

"True, but your sister was. She kept us prisoner, mistreated us both horribly, and was planning to feast upon Hans, as soon as she had him fattened up a bit."

At this point all eyes turned to stare briefly at the hugeness of Hans. It was hard to imagine a time when he had needed fattening up.

"We only have your word for that!" Zelda cried. She had begun to prowl back and forth in an agitated fashion, and Gretel noticed the worms and spiders and slugs and now rats that evidently shared her home start to gather behind her like a small, loathsome army. "For years I've had to watch you two made into heroes. Money from King Julian, stories in the paper, a free house, on and on and on about how clever you were and how terrible my sister was."

"I'm sure she had her good points," Hans ventured.

"Shut up, Hans," Gretel hissed at him over her shoulder. "And start dismantling that barricade while I distract her. Go on!" She waited until she was sure he was cautiously removing one stick of furniture after another, stepping forward with her tiny candle so that his actions were hidden by the gloom. She reasoned that they were dealing with someone not entirely rational who was clearly harboring a grievance, and moreover resented all the attention she and Hans had received as children. Attention that, no doubt, she would have preferred for herself.

"I can see how that must have been galling for you," Gretel said, taking a step or two toward the restive witch. It took all her nerve to do so, when her mind, body, and soul were screaming at her, quite convincingly, to run in the opposite direction. "I don't suppose anyone spared a thought for a grieving sibling."

"Indeed they did not! My only living relative, but did that matter? No! Was I offered any compensation for my loss? I was not! Cast out and shunned as the sister of a would-be murderess, and forced to move away."

"Hence your globetrotting life since?"

"Oh, the idiots I had to marry in order to support all that traveling, when all I wanted to do was come home."

Gretel was puzzled. "But this is not the same house, nor the same spot . . . ?"

"Of course not. I'd never have been allowed to return there and build a new one. When I finally got rid of husband number four . . ."

". . . ah, the conveniently deep diamond mine."

"Fool shouldn't have been so trusting," Zelda dismissed Herr Burgdorf with a rude gesture. "By then sufficient time had passed, and I had amassed a sufficient fortune, to be able to settle here."

"And take in guests?" Gretel was mystified.

"I was biding my time," Zelda explained with a smile that was far more terrifying than her scowl.

"For a way to get to us," said Gretel. "An interesting cover, the lonely luscious landlady."

"The enchantment was wearisome, and alas its range limited. Gesternstadt was beyond it, so that I could not appear at your door, no matter how much I wished to do so. Instead I had to wait, and to suffer such tiresome clientele."

"One of whom was the sorcerer, Ernst Arnold, was it not?"

"He might have been," said the witch, clearly reluctant to help Gretel in any way, however small, however late in the day.

"Well, if it hadn't been on his map I would never have found your pretty little trap. He must have been here, else why would he have so clearly marked it?"

The witch's smile broadened, treating her visitors to a view of teeth so ruined and blackened Gretel deduced the woman must have been nibbling on sugar candy and gingerbread every day of her life. "He had a sharper brain than you, it seems, for he encoded his chart beyond your deciphering."

All at once Gretel saw the truth. "The mark of the cottage on the map—it was not a recommendation but a warning!" She silently chided herself for her own stupidity. Stupidity that had lead them into such terrible danger.

"I might have known," Zelda was crowing now, "that you'd bungle your way here eventually. You and your oh-so-clever detective work. Pah! All I had to do was set my snare and wait. And wait I would, however long it took."

"I don't know whether to be astonished or flattered that you should go to such lengths, that you should carry such a grudge for so long. I think I am both."

"I want revenge!" Zelda shrieked, which set up a screeching and squeaking from the rats, as well as a bit of sobbing from Hans.

The witch raised her arms and started muttering a hex beneath her breath. Gretel knew she had to act fast, but her options were limited. At that moment Jynx entered the kitchen and flew at Zelda, interrupting her spellcasting. Gretel hissed at Hans, "Get that door clear!" and was about to set to helping him when her candle stub disintegrated, spilling hot molten wax over her fingers.

"Ouch!" she yelped, dropping the burning remains of the candle. It fell not directly to the floor, but into the folds of her dress where it hung on the airer in front of the stove. She was alarmed by the ferocity of the flames that burst forth when the flame met the fabric. The whole garment went up in a leaping, smoking *woomph* that instantly ignited the clothes draped next to it. Suddenly the room seemed filled with fire. And screams, not the least of which were her own.

She turned and pushed Hans at the doorway, the two of them with their untied terror barreling through the remaining items of furniture and batting the door out of the way. They fell out into the darkness.

"Run, Hans. Come on, get up and run!" she cried, hauling him to his feet.

Behind them the whole cottage was engulfed in flames with unnatural swiftness, as if the wicked magic that coated it was the most combustible material there could ever be. The gingerbread and barley twists might not have been real but still the air was filled with the smell of burned sugar. From inside the house came the sounds of Zelda screeching and cursing. Something sped through the crumbling doorway toward them. For a moment Gretel feared it was the witch riding her broomstick, but it was the sorcerer's bat, his fur a little singed. He flitted round in wobbly loops, clearly suffering from the effects of the heat and smoke, before landing on Gretel's wig, where he latched on tight to the strings of silver bells with his tiny claws.

Things began to explode inside the cottage. Gretel took Hans by the hand and the two of them ran for the cover of the trees. It was not until they were both utterly out of breath and unable to take another step that they sank down behind a fallen oak, crouching low, and turned to witness the final moments of the gingerbread house. The inferno lit up the black night, sending multicolored sparks and tongues of flame bursting high into the inky sky. It was a wonder the forest itself did not catch fire. Even the smoke was of a sinister and uncommon variety, stinking of burning candy and smoldering decay, mottled green and purple against the blaze. As they watched, the building fell in upon itself.

"Good heavens!" Hans gasped. "That has surely finished her!"

Gretel wanted to agree with him, but she had just noticed the darker smudge of smoke in a singular shape that escaped from the chimney seconds before the collapse of the cottage. It might have been nothing more than the contents of the kitchen going up. It was probably that, she decided, and not worth mentioning to Hans.

Deciding it best not to venture far without properly studying the map and regaining their wits, the duo trudged in what they hoped was a straight line until they could no longer smell the fire nor hear the crackling of the flames. They found a hollow tree, clambered into it, and passed the remainder of the night in fitful, dream-peppered sleep.

Gretel was awoken by a painful crick in her neck and the sharp light of a summer dawn. She unfolded herself from the tree, scrambling out to sit on a mossy rock. Hans puffed his way out after her, leaning back against the trunk of their makeshift boudoir.

"I say," he rubbed his eyes as he spoke, "the birds in these parts kick up quite a racket. Bit early for such chirpiness, I'd have thought."

"They have the advantage of heads free from the aftereffects of cocktails," she pointed out.

"Well they might show a little consideration for the rest of us." He groaned as a tuneful blackbird landed beside him and began welcoming in the new day.

Gretel pointed at the sagging, not to say squashed, rucksack still attached to her brother's back. "What did you grab?" she asked. "Let's see."

He shrugged the thing off and delved inside, pulling out treasures one at a time. "Pack of cards . . . cigars . . . oh good, my lighter," he said, pausing to test it out, then flinching as the flame reminded him of their narrow escape of the night before. He went back to rooting through the bag. "Some black bread . . . a bag of toffees, glad I thought to bring those . . . another pack of cards . . . and this," he declared, emerging to hold up a loop of wire.

"Which is what, exactly?"

"The thing that will catch us breakfast, sister mine: a snare!"

"I see. And how many times have you successfully set a snare?"

"Well, none. Point of fact, I've never set one *unsuccessfully* either, which could be seen as giving me a 100% success rate. All a matter of how you view it really."

"I view it realistically, Hans. Which means that black bread and those toffees are all we have between us and a diet of woodland herbs and water."

"Don't be so defeatist. I shall soon have us a plump young rabbit."

"Oh? And how many of those have you seen since we entered the forest?"

"Well, none. But we wouldn't, would we. I mean to say, they are shy creatures, born to move with stealth and guile and general all-around cleverness."

"Which won't keep them out of one of your expertly constructed snares?"

Hans gave a harrumph and selected a cigar from the box, leaning back, eyes closed against his sister's disapproval and their difficult situation both.

Gretel took stock of their situation. They were lost in the woods, both dressed like imbeciles, without their precious camping equipment, and decidedly rattled after their encounter with the witch. She lamented the loss of her lovely linen dress, and then recalled how quickly it had become ablaze. What manner of dye did they use in modern fabrics, she wondered? She looked down at her nightdress, which was splattered with dust and filth from the cottage, and mud and woodland detritus from their night spent alfresco. Her poor lorgnettes were similarly encrusted with dirt, but otherwise undamaged. Her short cape at least provided a little modesty, and the map was still snugly in its pocket. Her boots, for all their ugliness, were a godsend. She put her hand up to test her wig. It appeared to have withstood the ordeal well, and was still in good shape, complete with all its bells and bows, and the addition of one small, slightly sooty bat. Hans, in his Chinese silk pajamas and Bavarian hat, looked like a lost player from an amateur opera group. Their supplies were pitiful. She had with her neither comb nor powder. Things had, on the face of it, come to a pretty pass. Still, there was the map, Hans's lighter for starting a fire, and food enough for half a day.

She unfolded the map, laid it on another mossy stone, and smoothed out the worst of the crumpling. After wiping her lorgnettes she was able to scrutinize the finer details the sorcerer had drawn and noted. The general area of the forest was plain to see, with its points of ingress and egress. The main path was marked clearly, along with tributary routes and dead ends. There were worryingly vague patches bearing words like "tight" or "boggy" or "tricky," and rather good sketches of wolves and bears at irregular intervals. She looked again at the witch's house. It was depicted as a simple woodland cottage, though now that she examined it more carefully she noticed a curious symbol drawn upon the door. Presumably it would have meant something to someone of a sorcerous ilk. Tracing their journey with a finger she worked out that they were not, in fact, far from the path, and could rejoin it a little way on. They would then be able to continue in the direction marked. She estimated that, with luck and a following wind, they had three days' marching ahead. They would have to sleep where they fell, and hope that Cornelius Staunch's tracking skills were up to finding them before they succumbed to hunger. The endpoint on the map was cloaked in mystery, with swirls and curious emblems the significance of which she could not fathom. After the revelations regarding the witch's cottage, these took on a sinister aspect to Gretel's eyes. But the point was evidently important to the sorcerer. It was, she was certain, where he would have gone on his secret sojourns. It was, she was equally certain, where she would find either the man himself, or the answer to the question of his fate.

She got stiffly to her feet. "Come along," she said firmly. "We have a job to do, Hans. And if we want to eat proper food and to ever get out of these woods, this map, and this case, are the things that will deliver us. We go on!"

NINE

Fifteen minutes of struggle through the undergrowth did indeed see them reunited with the main path, which gave Gretel hope that they could, after all, navigate accurately with Ernst's map. The day was hot, so that neither of them felt the absence of proper clothes particularly, but Hans was suffering the hazards of walking without shoes. His progress was punctuated by cries and yelps as he trod on thistle or nettle. Soon, however, he learned his painful lesson and scanned the ground ahead for safe places on which to step.

Jynx, after the exertions of the previous night, slept inverted, dangling from Gretel's wig. However much she disliked the appearance of the thing against the pale beauty of her head-dress, she could not deny that he had been instrumental in their escape from the witch. It seemed he too wanted to find the sorcerer, and had decided that sticking with Gretel—or possibly with the map—was his best chance of being reunited with his master.

As they walked on, Gretel noticed the character of the woods begin to alter. The trees were planted closer together, blocking out more of the summer sun. There was a predominance of pine, spruce, and larch now, with the broader-leafed trees fewer and smaller. The flower-filled glades disappeared altogether, and with them the smell of roses and small, sweet flowers. Instead the pungent smell of pine began to catch in the back of Gretel's throat.

They ate the bread and most of the toffees during the first two hours of walking. At one point Hans happened upon a briar and filled his hat with juicy blackberries, which sustained them for a further two hours, and left them both with purple-stained mouths. They drank from brooks and springs when they came upon them, with Hans bemoaning the lack of ale and Gretel dealing with the growing urgency of needing an impromptu water closet of some sort. Eventually she had Hans stand guard while she crouched behind an ivy-clad tree.

"Who am I guarding you from?" Hans asked.

"Not *who* but *what*."

"What?"

"Bears perhaps. Or wild boar. Or wolves," she explained.

Hans gasped. "Is that when they get you, wolves and whatnot? While you are so indisposed? Seems like unfair play to me."

Gretel emerged from behind the tree, hoping the leaves she had used in place of paper did not turn out to be poison ivy. "I doubt such animals have been taught the rules of polite society, Hans. We are beyond any such etiquette here."

"But do you really think there are bears? I mean, one hears tales . . . but . . . if there are, how are we to defend ourselves?"

"I understand there are two schools of thought on the matter. One says that humans are not natural prey for either wolves or bears, and that if you make sufficient noise, and make yourself big enough, they will run in the other direction. The other wisdom is that you must make stealth your friend, move silently through your surroundings, by so doing neither alerting the hungry beasts to your presence nor provoking them into an attack."

Hans chewed over this information as slowly and carefully as if it were a mouthful of bony fish. At last he gave a shrug. "I believe we both will be better at large and loud than invisible and silent. That should be our tactic."

"So long as you promise not to sing."

"Sing, no. But whistle, I shall. And I will thrash with this," he decided, plucking a long stick from a wiry tree next to him. "The sound of me beating back nettles and such will give anyone listening the message that I am a man of action; determined, vigorous, and not to be tangled with."

Gretel regarded her brother in his grubby red silk, with his eye patch, berry-stained face, and bare feet. She feared he looked as if he had already been tangled with quite extensively. Still, if it made him feel better . . .

"Thrash away, Hans. Let us settle on another two hours' march before we make camp for the night." As she spoke she was all too aware of how meager and uncomfortable that camp would be. They had not beds, nor bedding, nor anything with which to construct a tent. They had nothing to cook in, on, or with, and not so much as a medicinal swig of brandy between them.

"Look!" Hans sang out cheerily. "Wild garlic. We must have some." He tugged at the bright leaves until a muddy bulb emerged. Barely bothering to dust off the soil he chomped into the thing, munching happily. "Mmmm! Quite refreshing. Want some?"

"I prefer mine cooked. Let's take some with us, that way you can render them more tempting once we have a fire lit."

The idea of being in charge of firelighting and cooking cheered Hans, as Gretel knew it would, so that he whistled and thrashed on, nibbling a little garlic now and then, his breath alone a fierce deterrent for any would-be predators. They had traveled quite some distance before he began to plead for them to stop and set up camp. Gretel was able to cajole him a little further in search of the perfect campsite—level ground, a bit of a break in the trees, preferably by a stream. She let him think she was eager to be on with the hunt for the sorcerer, which indeed she was, but he did not realize that she was also keen to put a little more distance between themselves and whatever remained of Zelda. For all the time she had spent convincing herself that the witch must surely be dead, she could not shake off the uneasy sense that they were still being followed and watched.

At last he would be driven no further. They selected a spot that conformed to their requirements fairly comprehensively, and both gathered twigs, leaves, and fallen boughs with which to construct a fire. Given how easy it had been to set the witch's cottage ablaze, they were dismayed at how impossible it now seemed to be to light a simple campfire. Gretel wished she had another garment to sacrifice to the cause, but neither of them could spare any clothing. Hans bent low beneath the ambitious construction of wood and kindling, blowing as good as any bellows might into the smoky smoldering his lighter caused at the base of the thing, but not a single flame burst forth.

"Really, Hans, I thought you knew how to do this."

"The wood is damp. This forest is so dense, nothing dries out properly." He set to puffing and blowing harder.

"We must have something we can use to get it going. How about your cigars?"

"My best Havanas? Never!"

"Well then what about some of those cards of yours?"

"My playing cards?!"

"Why not? You have two packs. I think the likelihood of us rounding up a four for canasta is slim, don't you?"

"But Gretel, my cards, they are the tools of my trade."

"They are combustible. Don't you want a cheery fire to rest your poor feet by? And light in the darkness? And hot roasted garlic?"

Hans opened his mouth to protest further but another sound silenced him. It was a long, low, wailing howl. When it stopped there was a charged silence, and then it began again. And when it did, a second, chilling, primeval howl joined in. And then a third. And a fourth.

Wordlessly, and with shaking hands, Hans snatched the cards from his pile of belongings and held his lighter to one after the other until they had properly caught and the twigs atop them had done the same. After that he became entirely focused on feeding the fire with as much wood as they could find. Neither of them uttered the word "wolf" for where was the need when the creatures were serenading them? Once he had convinced himself the fire was steady and that the wolves would not come near it, Hans took the remaining garlic bulbs and buried them beneath the embers to roast. Gretel felt it was something of a backward step, putting the things into the earth when they had gone to the trouble of taking them out of it only hours earlier, but she thought this might not be the moment to criticize. At one point Hans got a little carried away with his alfresco cooking and leaned in overly close to the heat of the fire, losing his exposed eyebrow in the process. The removal of this reliably expressive, bristly adornment to his brow left him with a permanently surprised expression, which rather suited him, as if life was constantly astonishing him. Which it often was. When he pulled the baked bulbs from the fire, with a deal of *ooch*ing and *ouch*ing and burned fingers, he handed two on a dock leaf to his sister with great pride. Gretel was hungry enough to have eaten them raw and muddy by this point, and so was delighted to find that they tasted quite delicious. Warm food in her empty tummy sent goodwill and hope coursing through her veins.

"Could have done with a little salt, Hans, but otherwise very good indeed. I knew there was a reason I brought you along."

Jynx became quite lively as dusk fell and zipped about feasting on flying bugs.

"Gosh," said Hans, "if only we could catch our supper with such ease."

They rounded off their meal with the last of the toffees. Having stoked the fire up as much as they were able, they elected to slumber sitting up, back to back, leaning on each other. That way, they reasoned, they could not be snuck up upon by anything given to sneaking. Gretel feared she would not get more than five minutes sleep in such a position, and said as much to Hans as she leaned against his broad back and closed her weary eyes.

Judging by the depth of the darkness, several hours had passed when Gretel came to with a jolt. The fire was still going, but had consumed nearly all its wood, so that it was now nothing more than low embers, and a similarly low glow. She realized that she was no longer sitting up, but lying flat on her back on the leafy ground. She turned to lean on her elbow and squint into the gloom. A moment's staring was all it took to establish the awful truth: Hans had disappeared.

For a full two minutes Gretel stood beside the dwindling fire and hissed "Hans!" into the darkness. No answer came. It was a ridiculous thing, to try to make oneself heard while at the same time trying not to. She repeated his name in the hope that her brother would respond to it, whereas an Undesirable Other—particularly of the furry variety—would not. In fact, no one and nothing responded. She considered the possibilities. He might have crept off to avail himself of the woodland water closet, i.e., the privacy of a tree a little way off. But then he would have heard her insistent nagging and answered. He might have gone on a somnambulant meander, in which case he could have fallen into a bog, a hole, or a deep sleep some way off. He might have been (she hesitated to form the thought) taken. By something. Or someone. But surely this would have involved such resistance and noise and commotion as would have been impossible for her to sleep through. She dismissed this explanation and settled instead upon his having woken, bleary-eyed, and wandered from the camp for some Hans-like reason only to lose his way. More than likely he had succumbed to sleep once more, and she would find him sleeping like a log, possibly next to a log.

There was no choice but to go in search of him. She repacked their few possessions, including her wig, and shouldered the rucksack. Jynx fluttered about beside her, a little piece of darkness moving in the darkness. Gretel found a longish, thinnish bough and persuaded the end to catch fire. This smoky torch would have to serve as both light source and protection. It didn't feel like much of either. She scoured the ground for signs of which way Hans might have gone, reasoning that someone of such a robust stature must surely have left a trail to follow.

There were indeed clues. Squashed plants. Broken twigs. Crushed areas of moss. A dozen strides along she found his pocket kerchief. Trying hard not to imagine what might lurk in the gloom beyond the reach of her torch, she pressed on. Here and there things scuttled and scratched. An owl hooted. There was, mercifully, no more howling, so that she was able to convince herself there were no wolves close by. Every now and again she risked calling out and then strained her tired ears for a reply. She began to feel irritation building within her. Why could he not be relied upon simply to stay put for a night? Or not to fraternize with witches? Or fall into streams? Or all but put his own eye out? She had brought him along largely to carry their camping paraphernalia and now they had none, and she was carrying their remaining luggage herself. Things had not, it could be said, gone according to plan.

The path she was following became narrower and twistier, the trees on either side closing in tight to the edges, so that she wondered how Hans had been able to fit through. She found several snagged silk threads on the trunks of the larches that now lined the way, suggesting her brother's progress had been something of a squeeze. And then she began to hear curious noises, faint at first, but growing ever more distinct. She made a mental note to question Hans, at the earliest opportunity, about how he and strange sounds seemed to be so often connected. Gretel crept on cautiously in the direction of what she now recognized as some manner of music. There were bells, and a light drumming, and something that could have been a harp. It was all rather tuneful and pleasant, which went some way to removing her apprehension. When she was sure she was almost upon the source of the music, she got down on her knees and shuffled to the top of a small hillock, from where she was able to peer down into the dingley dell below.

What a sight greeted her eyes!

There was a clearing at the bottom of a gentle slope, and in it a party appeared to be taking place, attended by miniature people. There were two central fires, around which these little beings sat or danced as the band played with gusto on their suitably small-scale instruments. Tiny lights dotted the low branches of trees and bushes, and by using her trusty lorgnettes Gretel identified these as glowworms hung in jam jars. The atmosphere was one of jollity and fun. Indeed the little people danced and drank and feasted in their bright clothes as if the woods were the safest and loveliest of places to be. And in their midst, lumbering and stumbling, danced Hans. If he had been taken by force and was being kept against his will he certainly showed no signs of it. He seemed to be having quite the time of his life. A self-confessed nondancer, he was doing his best to keep up with a lively jig, though it was only the nimble footed-ness of his hosts that prevented them from being inadvertently stamped upon by him.

As she watched him he looked up and saw her. "Gretel!" he cried, waving cheerily, evidently delighted to see her. "Come and join us, do! Look, everyone, it is my sister, come to join in the merrymaking."

Gretel made a second mental note to discuss with her brother his penchant for trusting people of brief acquaintance. She stood up, brushed off her cape and nightdress as best she could, and descended to join the throng. Immediately she was surrounded by the curious small people. They darted and jumped and dashed about in a way that might have been unsettling, but they all wore such broad grins or beaming smiles it was not possible to feel intimidated by them, even though they numbered quite a few.

"Here!" Hans grabbed her hand and pulled her onto what passed for a dance floor. Gretel saw that his patched eye had been stuffed with some manner of herbal poultice. It smelled rather strongly, though not unpleasantly. "You have to try this, sister mine. More fun than any dance you've danced in your life before, I promise you." He held onto her and wheeled her about with an energy and enthusiasm she would not have thought him capable of, particularly given his lack of sleep, food, and shoes. She noticed tiny tankards made of nutshells around the place, and a larger one fashioned from a piece of bark that could only have been for Hans.

"Who are your new drinking companions, Hans? How was it that you left me to come here with them? Did they threaten you?"

"Threaten? Good gracious no! The very idea," he laughed as he spoke, but then found he could not also dance, for want of breath. At last he stopped whirling them both across the trampled earth of the forest floor. "No, I got up to, well, you know, do what a person must do when he has spent the day drinking spring water . . . and on my way back I encountered a little group of these wonderful folk. They were on their way here for the party and invited me to join them. It seemed churlish to refuse."

"And it never crossed your mind to wake me up?"

"Didn't want to disturb you," he explained with another guffaw of laughter. "Thought I'd come back later and then I could introduce you." He swept an arm wide and slow to indicate the entire company. "These, sister mine, are the woodland pixies, and a jollier, happier band of people you could not wish for."

Gretel frowned at him. "What are you drinking?" she asked, forced to raise her voice above the crescendo of music, cheering, and laughter. "It seems very potent."

"Marvelous stuff!" Hans agreed, snatching up his vessel to offer to her. "Never come across anything quite like it, have to say. Here, be my guest."

Gretel sniffed it suspiciously. She could drink even her brother under the table if she had a mind to, but there was something unfamiliar about the liquor at this party. Something not entirely alcohol based, she decided.

"Thank you, no," she said. "I prefer to drink with people to whom I have first been introduced."

"Then let us rectify the situation at once!" Hans insisted, moving in a manner that suggested focus was not currently his strong point as he searched for someone in the crowd. Gretel observed that while Hans was dancing with the pixies, he had become most definitely pixilated.

TEN

The pixies were reduced versions of the more common humans. They were identical to, say, Gesternstadt folk in every aspect save their size, which was that of a garden gnome, and their slightly rustic attire. Most wore garments that seemed to have been fashioned from the very woodlands they inhabited, all leafy greens or earthy browns, spun or weaved from the flora that surrounded them. Here and there adornments of beetle wings or tiny polished stones lifted their outfits, and Gretel could not help but be impressed at the skilled tailoring and needlework that must have been required to produce such minute, detailed, and sturdy clothing.

"Here, I say!" Hans attracted the attention of an adult pixie, a male, who sported a fine beard and a ready smile. "Come and meet my sister."

"Greetings!" exclaimed the little man, extending a hand while keeping a tight hold on his tankard with the other. His grip was firm, though Gretel noticed as she shook it that he had an unsteady gaze that wavered as he made eye contact with her. Again she wondered what it was they were all imbibing.

"I am pleased to make your acquaintance. . ." She waited for Hans to introduce her properly, and when he did not was forced to prompt him. "Hans? A name?"

"Oh, he doesn't have one," Hans explained. "None of them is called anything. It's the way things are done here; friendly, casual, each man equal to the next. I find it rather refreshing, have to say."

The pixie nodded. "We are all friends here. No need for formal Mr. This or Missus That."

"But," Gretel felt compelled to ask, "how do you know whom you are talking about?"

"Ah, we don't encourage that," the pixie told her. "Doesn't do to talk about people who aren't present. Might be misconstrued. Could be thought of as tittle-tattle and contain hurtful words. Wouldn't do at all. Not here."

Hans beamed "I do so like these little fellows!"

Gossip was a pet hate of Gretel's, but even so, she found the concept the pixie was putting forward more than a little problematic. "No one is more in agreement with you than I on the matter of malicious whisperings, believe me, and yet, how can you identify a person when you have a need to? If, for instance, you wish to locate a specific person, or engage the services of another? Both cases might require the discussing of those persons with another party."

"That's easy, we just use the thing that is distinctive about that person, say his job or a standout feature."

"And if they have no job, nor any . . . standout feature?"

The pixie took a thirsty swig of his drink and raised his eyebrows. "Can't imagine why you'd want to seek them out if that were the case. But, supposing you had your reasons, we just use the relation that person has to another person, until we get to one who has something worth noting. So, say you wanted to ask for that person over there . . ." Here he paused while Gretel followed his pointing finger to see a youngish male pixie of medium height and unremarkable appearance, "you'd just ask for the son of the man with the talent for singing."

"I see. And this can be applied to anyone, however dull their family?"

"Course it can. Just keep going. All identities radiate out from someone worth mentioning, so you can step back to them if need be."

This seemed to Gretel to be an unnecessarily complicated way of going about things. It also made her worry that she would end up being referred to as Sister of Drunken Simpleton. "Tell me," she asked "how then do you address one another in person?"

"Oh, some friendly way or other. Helps if you add a little detail. Most people hail me with Friend Middling Tall, on account of my height, which is neither great nor completely insignificant. That old lady down there . . . see? Everyone hails her with Grandma How Old?! because of her great age." He drained his tankard and peered blearily into the carousing throng. "And over there I can just see Friend One Too Many. He's the one under the table."

Hans laughed. "Marvelous system, isn't it? And the absolute best thing about it is that you don't have to remember anyone's name. Isn't that sensible? I mean to say, when there is so much merrymaking going on, who wants to be bothered with struggling to recall names, when you more or less just call people by what is most obvious about them? Dashed clever, ain't it?"

Gretel was aware there were times during her brother's drinking bouts when he was hard pressed to remember his own name. Given that the pixies seemed to share his love of intoxicating brews there was an element of good sense to their system. She wasn't sure, however, she wanted to be called by the most obvious thing about her, given that she had slept in the open, had not so much as put a brush through her hair for days, was still dressed in her grubby nightgown and cape, and could only imagine the shiny, blotchy nature of her face after all she had been through of late.

"I do believe, sister mine, that I have found my soulmates here."

"Hans," she spoke in a whisper she hoped could not be overheard. "You are not in control of your senses."

"But, Gretel, look about you." Here he waved his tankard, sloshing pungent pixie ale over his bare feet. "What fun! What merriment! What a way to live!"

"A party is a party the world over."

"Not for woodland pixies. They live like this every night. Days are just to be got through as gently as possible, doing the very bare minimum that must be done, finding food, brewing ale, and so forth. The remainder of the time they drink and share goodwill and let the rest of the world go by. I tell you I love these little fellows. They are my natural brethren. My people," he insisted, somewhat tearily.

"Indeed, Hans? And this despite the fact that you weigh the same as a small bullock, while your diminutive friends could be fatally squashed by a carelessly sitting spaniel?"

"Must you always see the downside? Here," he grabbed a beaker of ale from a nearby log stool, "what you need is a little of this. You'll be amazed at how your cares just slip away, slip away, slip away . . ." And with that he twirled on his filthy feet and teetered back to join the dancing.

A passing female pixie took pity on Gretel and led her to a soft, mossy corner beneath some honeysuckle where she might rest. She provided her with a blanket knitted of thistledown, rabbit fur, and owl feathers, a beaker of what she promised was nothing more potent than spring water, and a plate of food. Gretel experienced a moment's unease when she recalled how hospitable the witch had been, but she comforted herself with the thought that all she need do to protect herself from the elves was set Hans to roll among them. She sat and nibbled at the surprisingly tasty morsels, which were of necessity many, being so small. She detected nuts and berries and seeds, with a type of unleavened bread and pastry, and carefully avoided anything that resembled a mushroom. Her stomach full at last, she reclined beneath the woodland coverlet, closed her eyes, and, despite the continuing music and dancing, was soon asleep.

The next morning she woke up to a scene that put her in mind of the aftermath of some historic battle or other, although with the smell of barbecued food and sweet beverages rather than gunpowder. There were little bodies strewn hither and thither in attitudes of having collapsed in the middle of dancing or drinking or possibly both. Some pixies snored softly, others hiccupped, and a few more muttered in their presumably dream-filled sleep. Hans lay at the center of them, a beached whale to their sprats. Gretel sat up and pushed her flattened hair out of her face. Two young girl pixies came trotting up to her. She noticed that as they moved their tiny feet appeared to scarcely touch the ground at all. This lack of contact meant they could move in almost complete silence, and of course, they would leave no tracks. Gretel wondered if the sense of being watched that had been with her since entering the woods was because of the pixies after all. Could they have been following her and Hans and waiting their moment to make their presence known? She sought to identify what it was about Hans that had caused them to wish to reveal themselves to him. She was fairly certain it had to do with their recognizing a fellow drinker when they saw one. She would wait to see if they all continued to be so relentlessly cheerful when they were sharing the delights of a hangover.

One of the young pixies offered her some blackberries. "Are you hungry, New Friend Exceeding Large?" she asked sweetly.

Gretel did a quick mental maneuver that allowed her to accept this nomenclature with good grace. She was, after all, a new friend, and compared to even the biggest pixie thereabouts, she was undeniably large.

"Thank you." She took the proffered fruit. As she did so she noticed a vivid scar running down the arm of the pixie. It began above the elbow, traveled over the joint, and halfway to the wrist. The young pixie self-consciously moved her arm back.

"An unfortunate accident?" Gretel asked.

The girl nodded. Her companion spoke up. "Sweetling Climber fell from a tree. Again."

The two exchanged rueful glances.

"And sustained a bad break, by the look of it," said Gretel.

"I did, New Friend Exceeding Large. Mother was furious."

"People often are when they find they have narrowly but safely escaped their greatest fear," said Gretel. "It must have been dreadfully painful."

Sweetling Climber shook her head, "Oh, we have things to take away the pain," she explained. "It was the healing that took so long. I wasn't allowed to climb anything! Not even a bush!"

"May I see?" Gretel held out her hand and the pixie let her examine the injury more closely. "A serious break like that can heal badly, but this looks as strong as ever it was. It was expertly set. You must have a fine apothecary or bonesetter among you."

"We do not," said the girl.

Her friend agreed. "Old Elder Knit-bone does his best, but his eyes are not as sharp as they were."

"I was so very fortunate. There was a stranger in the camp. Passing through. He stayed only a couple of nights. He was here when I had my fall, and it was he who set my arm. He was so clever, the stitches so neat, and the bone mended better than anyone had hoped it could."

"That was indeed great good fortune," said Gretel, her mind whirring into action, pulling together disparate facts, sketching hypotheses, drawing conclusions. "This stranger, he was not a pixie?"

"Oh no, he was from outside the forest, like yourself and your brother. Only . . . narrower."

"Some are," she conceded. "So he might well have had a name?"

The girls both laughed at this and Gretel instantly recognized her mistake. Not being a woodland pixie it was certain he did have a name, but it was equally certain none of them would have bothered to ask for it. She tried a different path toward the answer she sought.

"Someone who did you such a great service, you would of course remember very well. What can you tell me about this mysterious stranger?"

Sweetling Climber smiled at the memory of her savior. "He was tall. That is to say, not just next to me, but *very* tall, taller than you and your brother. He had a kind face, with soft eyes, and a nice way of speaking. Always pleasant. Cheerful in all he did and thought. He fit in here well. Apart from his clothes!"

The pair giggled. "Long, flowing robes, deep purple they were, with a hat to match, all embroidered with stars as if a piece of the night sky had come down to join our party!"

Now it was Gretel's turn to smile. "Such a man would have been invited to visit often, I imagine."

"Certainly! Friend Mends All is welcome any time. He likes to call on us to make merry, and to see how I am," she added, an endearing blush coloring her tiny face.

Gretel felt excitement rising inside her and slapped it down. It was too early in the day for displays of triumphant joy, particularly without having properly breakfasted. "One more thing, when was the last time you saw this fine fellow?"

"Why he was here for the Berryblasted Feast. He stayed for the whole of the festival—three days and three nights—before moving on, and we were so happy to be able to treat him as our very special guest."

"The Berryblasted Feast sounds quite an occasion. On what date does it fall?"

"It is a moveable feast," the pixie told her, beginning to skip away, her interest in the visitor waning along with her patience for questions; such is the temper of youth. Already her friend was trotting off along the path.

"Wait!" Gretel called, scrambling to her feet. "When did it fall this year? When did you last see Friend Mends All?"

But three young male pixies chose that moment to spring from the undergrowth and chase the squealing girls away. The noise woke others in the camp, Hans among them, who came mumbling and stumbling into consciousness.

"Dash it all, Gretel, is there any need to shout?" he asked, rubbing his head. His silk pajamas had bits of moss and fern sticking to them. There were twigs in his hair, but rather than pluck them out he merely jammed his hat on top. Beside him Friend Middling Tall woke up, looking remarkably fresh and cheery. Indeed, Hans appeared to be the only partygoer who was suffering any ill effects after such a deal of drinking. Whatever their ale was brewed from, the pixies were clearly accustomed to it.

"Good morning, New Friend Exceeding Large," chirped Hans's drinking partner. Gretel tried to ignore the depressing fact that he had seen the same obvious thing about her the girls had seen. A point not helped by his turning to her brother and greeting him with, "Hail, New Friend Stout Hearted! What a bright, lovely day it is. Let us take breakfast and a stroll so that we are in fine fettle for more merrymaking tonight."

Hans gave a little groan. "Highly decent of you, but I rather think I might sit the next one out. That ale of yours packs a punch. And even more so the morning after, have to say."

Friend Middling Tall gave him a cheery slap on the back—having leaped on a fallen log to be able to reach—laughing away such an idea. "But to begin again is the best remedy! Why, soon you will be drinking like a true woodland pixie."

Gretel butted in. "I fear we must depart before such a useful life skill can be honed."

"Depart? But you've only just arrived!"

"We are not in these woods for our own entertainment, alas. If we were we would wish for nothing more than to stay here and be the guests of such excellent hosts." At this flattery the pixie puffed himself up happily. Gretel pressed home her advantage. "We are searching for someone, and that search is urgent and of great importance on many counts, which sadly I am not able to discuss. However, you may be able to assist us . . ."

"In any way we can! Always delighted to help a fellow drinker."

Gretel gave a nod of thanks. Hans looked as if he would have done the same if the action would not have been so painful. He was still rubbing his temples.

"I wonder," Gretel asked, "could you tell me when Friend Mends All last dropped by?"

"Friend Mends All? Marvelous chap. You should see what he did for Sweetling Climber."

"I have seen. Marvelous indeed."

"Welcome here anytime he likes. Always happy to share a beaker of ale with him."

"And you last did so . . . when, can you recall?"

The pixie frowned, evidently searching his memory.

"I understand he was here for the Berryblasted Festival." Gretel attempted to help him.

"Was he? You're probably right about that. Thing is, there are a lot of festivals. Hard to remember who was here and who was not."

"Perhaps it would be easier just to tell me the date of the festival."

"Ah, yes, I can do that. Always on a Tuesday."

"Good . . ."

"Unless there's been a late full moon, in which case it's a Wednesday, obviously."

"Obviously."

"Though I don't think the moon was late this year. Or maybe it was. Ha, goodness! How the old memory lets a person down!"

Gretel could not help thinking that the old memory was not helped by being pickled every night of the year.

"Anyway," their host continued, "I know it was after Summer Fayre, because it always is, and that's in . . . May. June! Yes, definitely June. And . . ." He thought so hard beads of sweat formed on his tiny brow. Suddenly he smiled broadly. "And it was before you came! So there we are! Yes, there." He nodded brightly, pleased with his own powers of recall.

Gretel was less impressed. "So you're saying he visited sometime between June and now? Wonderful. You've been so very helpful. Come along, Hans, we have miles to go. Time to move along."

Hans let out a whine. "But, Gretel, we still have no camping stuff. And no food, and do we really know where we are going? And my head hurts. And perhaps I should just have a little nap, and . . ."

"Hans! We don't have time for your hangover. We still have the map, so yes, we do know where we are going, even if we are uncertain as to how we will get there. We also know the sorcerer was here . . ."

"We do?"

"Yes. While you have been partying and sleeping, I have been continuing with my investigations. Which, may I remind you, is the reason we are here. Helpfully, I have found out that he often visited and that he mended the broken arm of a young pixie. Unhelpfully, no one here can remember when they last saw him. Which is frustrating in the extreme."

"It is?"

"Yes, of course it is! The date would give us definitive proof of Herr Arnold's continued existence. As it is we have merely a strong possibility, or maybe a probability given the progress of healing on the arm, that his latest visit was recent. How recent, we cannot yet know."

"Fixed a broken arm, eh? I thought you said he was rubbish at magic," Hans pointed out.

"He was. Is. Whichever. But I've seen that arm and it is has been expertly mended, somehow. Now, come along, we will prevail upon these good pixies for some food and then be on our way."

ELEVEN

The pixies did indeed furnish them with freshly baked breads, pastries, and fruit and nut cheeses, as well as another poultice for Hans to apply to his eye later on. Much to his amazement they also presented him with a speedily made pair of boots, constructed of plaited vines, bark and moss, which he declared most comfortable. They gave Gretel a present of the feather and thistledown blanket, for which she was exceedingly grateful. Friend Middling Tall consulted the map with her and made sure they were set back on the right path for the direction in which they wanted to travel. He explained that pixies were territorial beings, and liked to stick to their own region of the forest. This being the case he had never ventured more than a day's walk from their home, so could shed no light on what the travelers might find beyond that distance.

Jynx reappeared from his night's hunting and clutched onto the strap of Hans's pack. The unlikely trio was waved off cheerily, with Hans giving a few wistful looks back, and a number of heartfelt sighs as he left his new merrymaking friends behind. Gretel promised him they could visit again one day, but she made sure he had not hidden any bottles of pixie ale in the rucksack.

The weather continued to be fair. A little too fair, in fact, for Gretel's liking. There was a heaviness to the air that suggested the accumulating heat would soon spill over into a thunderstorm. They had no shelter other than the trees, which she had a vague notion was a Bad Place To Be if there was lightning about. After two hours of walking they paused for a brief lunch, during which Gretel had the devil's own job preventing Hans slumping into a snooze that could have consumed the rest of the day. They trudged on. The forest closed in tighter and tighter around them as they walked.

After a further two hours Gretel called another halt so that she might put on her wig. She had not forgotten that it needed more "breaking in," and when Hans commented on how ridiculous she looked, given the rest of her ensemble and their current location, she argued that it boosted her morale to think of the concert, and dressing up in finery, and doing something sophisticated and not mud-based. Jynx clearly agreed, leaving his perch on the backpack and choosing instead to settle upon Gretel's wig. The effort of arguing had defeated Hans completely. He sank to the ground, declared himself unable to take another step without a restorative nap in which to sleep off the rest of his hangover, and pointedly lay flat with his hat placed firmly over his face. Gretel recognized the signs of a man who would not be pushed another inch. In truth, she too longed for respite from all the marching around and the privations. Not the least of which was the absence of a water closet. She left Hans snoring tunefully and went in search of a small, private place where she might do what had to be done and could be put off no longer.

Despite the denseness of the forest and the abundance of cover, Gretel found it hard to settle on a spot that felt secure. This was due in no small part to the fact that she still was dogged by the notion that they were being watched. This idea was even more disturbing now than it had been before, as now she could not reasonably imagine the pixies might be following and observing then. So then, who? Or indeed, what? In the end she had no choice but to lift her nightdress and squat inelegantly among the pine needles and brambles. No sooner had she lowered her posterior than an incongruous sound reached her ears. It appeared to be music. Not of the woodland merrymaking variety, rather something almost orchestral. A brass instrument, she decided. A horn. A hunting horn!

"How thrilling!" Gretel declared to the woods. An image flashed through her mind of the glamour of a hunting party. There would be sleek, prancing horses, ridden by brave and sporty men, no doubt turned out smartly. Perhaps they would be accompanied by ladies in sumptuous riding habits wearing fetching veils, their cheeks flushed attractively but showing not a jot of fear as they cantered gracefully after the hounds. There might be a dozen of those black and tan dogs, eagerly tracking the scent of their prey, baying with excitement. It might even be a royal hunting party! In which case there would be handsomely uniformed soldiers, and the horses would be tacked in the very finest leather, trimmed with brass or silver. And there would be more than a simple bugler; there would be extra musicians, and courtiers, and minor members of the royal family, and no doubt a whole entourage following on with an elaborate picnic for after the hunt.

"Marvelous!" Gretel announced, standing up and craning her neck to listen better. There was the horn again, and even the shouts of the huntsman urging on horses and hounds. And now she could clearly make out the hungry cries of the pack as they picked up the scent of some poor creature. As she listened the sounds grew louder. And it was just as Gretel experienced a fleeting moment of pity for the animal that was being tracked, just as she briefly but vividly imagined the hounds upon it, sending it to ground, leaving it no escape, just then that a terrible, queasy thought took hold of her. And would not let go. For a terrible thought that has its roots in truth and fact and the inevitability of a chain of events that will lead to an unavoidable conclusion will not easily be shaken off. And that thought was that that prey was . . . herself.

There is nothing like fear to lend wings to the heels of even the most reluctant runner. Gretel tore through the woodland undergrowth, heedless of the brambles that clawed at her or the nettles that stung her, so focused was she on getting as far away from those now-terrible toothsome hounds as possible. She tried to tell herself that they were not trained to hunt people, and so would not, ultimately, tear her limb from limb. But at the same time she knew she must smell of nothing so much as a woodland creature herself by this time. And a terrified, sweating one at that. And was it not the smell of fear that drove hunting animals to a frenzy of bloodlust that would be sated by nothing less than a kill? Or would training prevail, and the dogs be brought meekly to heel by the huntsman? It was too great a risk to put the theory to the test. She could not trust someone else's skill, nor the fickle nature of any animal whose natural will had been bent to suit man's wishes. She had no choice but to run and to keep on running. It soon became clear to her, however, that she would not succeed in outrunning the pack, no matter her head start. She must outwit them. Spotting a brook she recalled the knowledge that scent could not be tracked through water and flung herself into the stream. It was not, mercifully, the swift torrent of earlier in their journey, but shallow and tame. The cool water revived her a little as she splashed through it, seeping its way into her boots. She was aware of Jynx bumping about on her wig as he held fast while she ran.

The horn was sounded.

The hounds were in full cry.

The huntsman hollered *view-halloo!*

The water dragged at Gretel's ankles even as she pulled herself up the bank on the far side. For a moment she lay panting on the riverbank, her wet nightdress gathering a coating of dusty soil that turned to mud upon it. She lurched to her feet and ran on. Glancing over her shoulder she saw the rich dark colors of hounds' coats in the frighteningly close distance, and fragmented glimpses of colorful riders between the trees. At that moment Gretel was not sure which fate would be worse: to be savaged by the pack, or exposed to the scorn and ridicule of the hunting party.

She was horrified to hear the sound of the paws splashing through water. Her subterfuge had failed. Gasping, she looked around for some other means of escape. A twisty tree presented itself, one of the few that, not being a narrow, towering pine, offered its low, broad branches as if a ladder. She grasped the lowest boughs and hauled herself upward. Her boots enabled her to tread boldly on the knots and rough bark, but her nightdress and short cape gave scant protection, so that her limbs were soon scraped and scratched horribly. Her sweaty fingers slipped as she tried to grasp a smoother branch, and she only succeeded in pulling herself up onto it on the third attempt. With the pack now circling the base of the tree and leaping and snapping at her, she was at last able to straddle the chosen bough and sit, clinging tight, praying that the hounds were poorer climbers even than she was. She had only ever before seen hounds from afar, streaming picturesquely across the landscape. Up close, with the sharp end pointing at her, they were nothing more nor less than slavering beasts intent on murder. She wondered when they had last been fed. Or if the wretched things were fed at all. Perhaps they relied upon killing their prey if they were to eat. Even so, it was hard to feel sympathy when they were viewing her as dinner.

The huntsman's shouts preceded him into the small clearing. He called to his pack with a firm voice that seemed to calm them a little. He was accompanied by another rider, a member of the hunting party, riding a glorious black stallion, wearing the uniform of one of King Julian's personal guard. A uniform that included a cape of rich burgundy. With a gold silk lining.

"Not now!" Gretel muttered to herself. "For pity's sake not here!" For she knew too well the broad shoulders, the slim hips, the long legs, and the shapely calves in their fine leather boots, even though from her perch it was hard to see the rider's face. Only one man had such a figure and sat a horse so well. Only Uber General Ferdinand von Ferdinand.

"Fraulein Gretel, can it be you up there?"

Evidently he had a better view of her, more was the pity.

Gretel sat up as straight as she could, mustering what remained of her battered dignity. She lifted a hand to straighten her wig and felt the furry softness of Jynx still nestled there. She told herself silently that it is not what you wear that matters, but how you wear it. A philosophy she had never, in fact, subscribed to before. Now, however, seemed a good time to start. Her supporting branch chose that moment to sag unhelpfully low. The hounds increased their snarling and snapping, bringing forth words of stern rebuke from the huntsman.

"I am investigating a case," she told Ferdinand. "I am working in secret, not wishing to reveal my identity," she added, in the hope it would explain her outlandish appearance.

"Indeed? You certainly look like something in disguise."

The bough dropped suddenly another arm's length. Gretel held on tight.

"I wonder if you would be so good as to tell your man to call off his hounds . . . ?" she asked.

"But of course." The general gave the command, and the huntsman, somewhat reluctantly, Gretel noticed, gathered his pack and took them back in the direction of the party.

"Thank you so much," said Gretel. She made no attempt to get down, knowing how undignified her descent was likely to be. Looking back through the trees she could see elegantly dressed ladies and gentlemen seated upon their pretty horses, waiting to see where the chase would take them next. She willed them to stay where they were. Any closer and she would be discovered by the entire gathering. To compound her discomfort, she spotted Ferdinand's fiancée among them, riding a snowy white horse with pink ribbons plaited through its mane. She was wearing a habit of the dreamiest sky blue, which set off her golden hair coiled beneath a matching veil to perfection.

Gretel had always made it a policy not to waste time and energy hating someone she had never met, however terrible their misdeeds. Ferdinand's intended, it had to be said, had not committed any misdeeds, as far as Gretel knew, but that didn't stop a boiling hatred stirring within her breast. She became aware Ferdinand was watching her.

"Are you acquainted with the Countess Margarita?" he asked.

Gretel ground her teeth. A title was just about the last straw.

"As I said earlier, I am here on business, going about important work in my capacity as a private detective. I do not have time for chitchat and small talk with . . ." She searched for a description that would not put her forever beyond the pale, but that would make her feel better having used it, ". . . people," she finished lamely, feeling considerably worse for being so feeble.

The general smiled his infuriatingly handsome smile. "Of course, I understand entirely."

"Do you?" she snapped. "I don't think that you do."

"Oh, I am not as slow on the uptake as I look."

"Now you are fishing for compliments."

"Fishing and hunting at the same time?" He laughed. "I'm not *that* clever."

"No? It is as well you have found yourself a clever bride then, isn't it? Together the two of you will be almost as clever as . . ."

"You?" He continued to smile.

Gretel could only manage a scowl.

"Please, Fraulein, allow me to assist you in getting out of that tree."

"There is no need."

"Truly? You look a little stuck."

"I am not. I am perfectly comfortable. I am up here the better to survey my surroundings and observe points and facts salient to the case upon which I am working," she told him, fervently wishing that she had not been interrupted by the hounds mid-pee.

"I see. So, you don't want me to help you down."

"Thank you, no."

There was an awkward pause.

She looked down then and met his gaze, and her already weakened knees weakened further, for he was looking at her with what she believed was true tenderness and warmth.

"Fraulein," he began, then, more softly, with some yearning even, "Gretel . . . I have wished to speak with you for some time. I would not want you to think . . ."

But what he didn't want her to think would remain a mystery, as at that very moment came shouts and cries and a great clamor and commotion from the hunting party.

"The king! The king is hurt! King Julian is injured! Fetch the apothecary! The king, the king!"

Ferdinand's expression turned grave. He looked over toward the hunt and then back up to Gretel.

"I'm sorry," he said, "I must go. The king . . ."

"Yes of course. You must. Go, go!" she dismissed him with a wave and what she hoped was a brave-but-touchingly-forlorn-and-I-don't-care-if-you-know-it smile.

He wheeled his horse around and urged it forward. Gretel watched him plunging through the woodland, galloping to the aid of his master.

TWELVE

Gretel did not attempt her descent from the tree until she was certain the royal hunting party had departed. Fortunately they were entirely taken up with getting their injured king back to the Summer Schloss and therefore not in a mood to tarry. From overheard shouts and commands Gretel gathered King Julian had dismounted to stretch his rather frail and creaky legs and one of the more excitable horses had trodden on his foot. Not a sufficiently terrible injury to bring about a change of royal backside upon the throne, but enough to send everyone into a flap, not least the rider of the errant horse, whose future was less certain. Gretel slid from the bough as carefully as she could but still sustained further scrapes and bruises. At least her own blundering tracks were easy to spot and retrace, taking her back to where she had left Hans.

"There you are!" he cried upon seeing her. "I was on the point of setting out to search for you."

"So I see," Gretel replied, looking pointedly at the fire he had going and the pixie pastries warming upon it.

"Well, I thought about trying to find you, and about not knowing which way you might have gone, or why, or how far, etcetera and so forth, and then I thought, No, Hans, you are cleverer than that!"

"You did?"

"Yes, I deduced . . . see? You are not the only one to be able to do that, sister mine. I deduced that you would not have strayed far from camp, for it was nearing snack time and you wouldn't want to miss that. I further deduced that you hadn't raised the alarm, therefore there was nothing to be alarmed about."

"Brilliant, Hans."

"And my final deduction led me to action . . ."

". . . which was to start cooking?"

"I knew that the smell of good food would bring you back."

Gretel wanted to pull her brother's reasoning apart and stick pins in all the pieces, but she was too weary, too battered, too tired, and too cast down to be bothered. Instead she lowered herself gingerly to the ground close to the fire. "Your investigative methods may be suspect, Hans; happily your culinary skills can be relied upon." She waved at the steaming pastries. "Pass me one of those before I lose the will to live, would you?"

Hans pushed his rather misshapen hat a little farther back on his head and leaned over the low flames, expertly retrieving a pastry with two hazel twigs. He had at last been able to remove his eye patch, thanks to the poulticing, which stopped him looking quite as peculiar as he had, but he now sported spectacular bruising and swelling, such as might have been sustained in a boxing match. With a sigh Gretel realized that she probably looked no better than he did, with her disheveled hair, sullied wig, wholly improper (not to mention soaking wet) attire and now scratched and bruised limbs. What was more depressing was the fact that she could not see a way their situation would improve, either easily or soon. They would simply have to plod on, stick to the map, and find the place she believed the sorcerer would be. Unless the man was a complete idiot (and there was still room for doubt and hope on this score) he would be holed up in a modicum of comfort, and therefore might be able to obtain clothes for them, at the very least. Their situation was not helped by the increasingly sticky weather. The air was now thick with the promise of a thunderstorm. While a freshening-up of the day would be welcome, Gretel knew they were not equipped to withstand heavy rainfall.

"Here you are," Hans handed her a leaf platter bearing two pastries and some apple chutney. "Those pixies know a thing or two about food. Though it would be better washed down by a flagon of their rather splendid ale, have to say."

"We are making slow enough progress as it is," Gretel pointed out, taking the food from him. "Last thing we need is for you to be intoxicated again. How's your headache?"

Hans gave a rueful smile. "Still with me, but nothing that can't be improved by a snack and a nap." He lifted his hat the better to rub his brow. Instead of replacing it on his head, however, he uttered a mild oath as he dropped it into the fire. He snatched it up, dusting off ash and cinders. "Good heavens! Gretel, look at this," he said. He held it up to show her the slim wooden arrow that had pieced the green felt and now adorned the thing like an oversized hat pin.

Before Gretel had time to utter a warning, another arrow whooshed through the space between them, plunging into the trunk of a nearby spruce tree. Hans threw himself on the ground. A third arrow thwacked into the earth not a hand's breadth away from where Gretel was sitting.

"We have to move!" she cried. "Come on, Hans, get up, but keep low."

"How is a body supposed to do that? Dash it all, Gretel, I am no circus contortionist." He puffed as he attempted to run while crouching, only managing a few strides before falling facedown upon the loamy ground. Gretel ran around behind him and gave him a shove. She felt rather than heard an arrow whiz by her head. Jynx flew past in loopy circles, presumably the better to avoid being pinned to a tree.

"Keep going! We are still in range."

"But who is shooting at us?" Hans gasped as they lumbered deeper into the tangle of trees and undergrowth.

"The *who* is not of paramount importance at this moment. Look for somewhere to give us cover, but for pity's sake keep moving!"

At that moment there came a loud rumble of thunder. The sun disappeared behind a heavy cloud, so that the forest became a dark, murky place, strewn with half-visible obstacles.

"Ouch!" Hans squawked, pushing aside a whippy branch that he had run into. "It's too gloomy to move through this stuff at speed. I can't see where I'm going or what I'm running into."

"Take comfort in the fact that we too will be obscured. Ah, here!" She grabbed his sleeve and hauled him to one side, dragging him through the dense flora.

"We can't run through this."

"Don't have to. Shhh!" She flapped a hand to indicate they must be silent and dropped to her knees. Crawling forward, ignoring the thistles and sharp stones that dug into her, she led Hans under a fallen tree that had wedged itself a couple of feet from the ground. Ivy and other plants with a tolerance for gloom had enmeshed themselves around the tree, providing a curtain behind which the pair was able to hide, with the timber as their roof. There was only just enough space, so that they had to squeeze themselves in. As they did so, Gretel's wig was knocked from her head. It was not until they were wedged in their hideout that she saw it, sitting large as life, silver bells glinting merrily in the slender rays that here and there penetrated both canopy and cloud. Gretel cursed silently. It was too late to drag herself back out and retrieve the thing, but it might easily be spotted and give them away. They had no choice but to wait and hope.

There was another growl of thunder, much closer this time, followed by a startling flare of lightning that lit up the whole forest and made them both wince and gasp with the loudness of its accompanying crack. And then came the rain. It did not so much fall as hurl itself down from the leaden sky. It bounced off every leaf and branch and plant, forcing its way through the gaps in their shelter to spit and splash upon them. Gretel's heart constricted at the sight of her beloved wig sitting unprotected beneath such an inundation. Instinctively she began to crawl toward it, but Hans grasped her arm.

"Don't go out there!" he hissed. "They might be waiting and watching still."

Gretel had to admit he had a point. She sat back, ignoring the dripping water that was finding its way down the back of her neck while she could do nothing but witness her wig's gradual destruction.

It was hard to measure the passage of time spent beneath the fallen tree, so hypnotic was the pelting of the rain, the aural assault of the storm, the body-numbing effects of the cramped space, and the high level of fear induced by having a murderous archer at large. Gretel had time to ponder her brother's not unreasonable question: who was shooting at them? And why? Something struck her at once: either their assailant was a poor shot—in which case why had he tried to stick them with arrows in the first place?—or he was an expert shot and had not meant to kill them, only to scare them. In which case, job done, but again, why? The pixies had been friendly and surely had no grievance against them. The witch? Could Zelda be living still and out for their blood? It was a possibility, but even if true, Gretel could not imagine the witch using anything so pedestrian as a bow and arrow with which to hunt them. No, such a choice of weapon suggested a pursuer who wished to remain at a distance, to remain unseen. Could the sorcerer have received word that he was being tracked and be out to prevent the progression of Gretel's investigations? It was a thought that could not, at this point, be dismissed. And yet how would Herr Arnold (assuming he still lived) know of her plans? And again, such a weapon, such a method of deterrent, did not fit with what she knew of the man. So who, then? And why? And what was to be done? For they could not stay huddled in their damp, gritty hiding place forever.

After an interminably long time, which was not enough to bring nightfall, but more than sufficient to render Gretel's left leg completely insensible and her wig all but melted into the leafy forest floor, there was a subtle easing of the rain. The storm itself had moved on, leaving only the irregular fall of raindrops from the leaves above, and allowing the return of sunlight fractured through the boughs overhead. There was a strong aroma of wet woodland: pine bark, nettle, earth, and fungi. Gretel was about to suggest that they emerge, before all feeling was lost in her other leg and she became unable to do so, when there came the sound of footfalls. They listened hard. The footsteps came closer. At last, a pair of feet, clad in tough, sensible boots, strode into view. The owner of the feet came to a halt beside the remains of the wig. The figure crouched down to examine the soggy mass of hair and silver. As Gretel and Hans held their breath, a young, lithe man stooped further to peer in at them. A smile as cheery as a sunflower spread across his handsome face.

"Fraulein Gretel?" He held out a hand. "Cornelius Staunch, at your service."

Having extricated themselves from their hiding place and observed the briefest formalities of introductions, Gretel appraised their new traveling companion of the fact that they had come under attack.

"Jolly nasty it was too," put in Hans. "Had to abandon my hat. Most likely ruined. Shall not see its like again."

"We have all lost something dear to us," Gretel told him, picking up the sorry remains of her wig. Madame Renoir would have to work a miracle to save it. "However, we escaped otherwise unscathed, and for that we should be grateful."

"But if our unknown assailant should return . . . ?" Hans shook his head gloomily.

Herr Staunch put a steadying hand on his shoulder. "In times like this, we pull together," he said in a voice that was at once both calming and bolstering. "It's the challenges we face, the tests we overcome, that make us strong. And that strength will see us through, have no fear." He was a pleasant-looking young man, fresh-faced and vigorous, with a cheerfulness about him that managed to be perky without being tiresome. A rare and fragile talent, in Gretel's experience.

"Yes, but what are we to do to defend ourselves?" Hans asked.

Cornelius dropped flat to the floor to sniff the ground like a bloodhound. He spent so long with his nose pressed into the leaves that Gretel and Hans exchanged baffled glances. At length, he picked up some of the soil and rubbed it between his fingers. Next he sprang up onto his feet again and bounded off into the trees. Gretel and Hans stood and watched and waited, and moments later he reappeared, clutching an arrow. "Looks like our fellow has gone back the way he came." Here he gesticulated with the arrow. "His tracks lead south, and he was moving slowly, not chasing or searching, merely trekking out."

"How can you tell?" Hans asked, rubbing his bruised eye, which had set up a near constant itch as it healed.

Cornelius gave a shrug. "Depth of the footprints. Spread of the disturbed undergrowth. Distance between the footfalls suggesting the pace he was traveling. Simple stuff. No, I don't think he'll be bothering you again today."

Gretel gave a nod of respect. "I see you are, like myself, a person who uses facts as the foundation for deductions. A method of investigation of which I wholeheartedly approve. Now, my brother and I are a little damp and weary. Would you be so kind as to assist us in constructing some sort of shelter so that we might rest, and perhaps a fire to dry out our damp bones?"

"Nothing better for raising morale than a good fire!" Cornelius declared. "Gotta keep morale up. A strong mind and a strong heart mean a strong body. That's where true strength comes from," he tapped the side of his head. "Here, and here!" He placed his hand firmly upon Hans's chest above his heart. Hans's expression was that of a patted dog.

They returned to their camp of earlier, where they were able to retrieve Hans's hat, which was in a considerably better state than Gretel's wig. The fire had been extinguished by the deluge, and the food ruined, but they found the rucksack and its contents untouched, clearly not being of any interest to their attacker.

"We can rule out theft then, sister mine," said Hans. "We were not shot at by highwaymen after our loot."

Gretel didn't think the highwayman existed who would trouble himself to steal Hans's soggy playing cards, even soggier cigars, and a few bites of pixie pastry, but she resisted saying so. Cornelius was right. It was important to keep spirits up. She didn't want Hans getting ideas into his head about assassins creeping around in the night, or the possible reappearance of witches, or he'd be off scurrying for home as fast as his legs could carry him. They needed to rest, recover, and resume their quest.

Cornelius proved to be the capable adventurer Hans had promised. He laughed gently at their choice of campsite, pointing out its many obvious flaws and disadvantages, led them a short distance to an altogether superior spot, and then set about building a fire. He and Hans gathered armfuls of wood, but it was all so wet Gretel could not imagine it ever burning. Cornelius assured them it was only wet on the outside and would soon dry out in the heat of the flames. He eschewed Hans's lighter in favor of demonstrating how wood twiddled in the hole of another bit of wood could produce first smoke and then fire. Hans clapped with delight and declared it better than any magic trick. Gretel couldn't help thinking there was a bit of showing off going on, but then the man had to prove his worth.

He did so splendidly. Within an hour she and Hans were seated on log stools beside the cheeriest of fires. Within another hour Cornelius had strung up three hammocks, all situated beneath a roof woven of leafy branches, security against any further downpours. Satisfied with their accommodation, he came to join them at the fireside.

Hans smiled at him, completely won over. "I say, Herr Staunch, you certainly know your stuff. Beds all ready and set."

"Preparation is key to survival, every time. Get prepared for the night in good time. Good sleep is paramount to good humor."

"Can't argue with that," said Gretel, though she was beginning to feel she might like to.

Cornelius dug inside his own capacious backpack and pulled out a tin pot, which he proceeded to suspend above the flames. From a flask he tipped water into it, and then from a tiny tin caddy spooned dark grains.

"Coffee!" exclaimed Hans, breathing in the aroma. "What a treat."

While they waited for it to brew, Cornelius handed around food from his supplies, which consisted of strips of dried beef and chunks of stale but filling black bread. Hans had rescued some of the pixie chutney, and they all chewed happily for some time, reveling in the warmth of the fire, the gentle steaming of the woods around them, and the abundance of tolerable food.

"Tomorrow I'll show you how to catch meat for the fire," Cornelius said. "The satisfaction of catching your own food, the joy of a hot meal, and that protein hit," he closed his eyes briefly at the thought of it, "nothing like it. Gives you steel in the blood and iron in the will," he assured them.

As they ate, and eventually savored the simple but delicious coffee, Gretel outlined her plans to their new guide and help-mate. She was careful to give him only information necessary for him to be of the utmost assistance to her. It was not her habit to share the details of her investigations with another, particularly when they were at an early stage. She reasoned that Herr Staunch would have little interest, in fact, in the minutiae of the case, and had no need to concern himself with details not pertinent to their journey through the forest. Even so, he did have one or two questions of his own.

"Do you, perhaps, have a theory, Fraulein Gretel, about who might want to kill you?"

Hans inhaled his coffee.

"We don't know he was trying to kill us," said Gretel quickly.

"He nearly got me with one of his nasty little arrows!" Hans wailed.

Cornelius nodded, "He loosed off quite a number of the things."

"My point exactly. He skewered Hans's hat, but otherwise missed us entirely, while placing arrows frighteningly near. I believe he was not a poor marksman but a skilled one, and that his purpose was just that: to frighten us."

Hans gave a harrumph. "Well, he certainly did that. Never run so fast in my life. Well, not since we were chased by that murderous witch, of course. Showed a fair turn of speed on that occasion too."

Herr Staunch raised questioning eyebrows at Gretel. "Murderous witch?"

"Her grievance was an old one," she told him. "Nothing to do with the case."

"But she was still trying to kill you?"

Hans choked on a bit of dried beef, recovering noisily.

"She won't bother us again, I assure you. Do not concern yourself with what is in the past, Herr Staunch. It is important for my investigation that we keep moving forward."

"Always a good plan," he agreed. "Keep up the momentum. Keep the energy flowing. Keep confidence high and push on through."

"Quite." She held out the tin mug he had provided for a top-up of coffee.

"So why did somebody go to all that trouble just to frighten you?" The man was quite dogged in his questioning.

"I assume he was attempting to put us off our pursuit of the sorcerer's possible hideout, whereabouts, or whatabouts."

"And who would want to stop you?"

"Who indeed, Herr Staunch? Who indeed."

THIRTEEN

That night, after the startling effort required to climb into and stay in the hammocks, Gretel fell into a fitful sleep. Although tired enough to slumber through a bugle call, she stirred at every owl hoot and badger snort, her subconscious on the alert for danger. She told herself that being shot at by a mystery archer can do that to a person. She further told herself that it was not a natural state, for her, to spend so much time outside, and that sleeping in the forest was not conducive to a peaceful night. The place was full of sounds, not all of them easily identifiable. She told herself very firmly that the witch was dead, the archer was gone, and now they were guarded by the alert senses and boundless energy of Herr Staunch.

While she had her own attention, she told herself that, contrary to appearances, her investigations were progressing, so that success, and crucially payment, remained likely outcomes and recompense for her current discomfort. What she failed to tell herself, what herself would not have wished to hear, was that her state of disturbance came not from her wild surroundings, not from concerns regarding the case in hand, not even from the possibility of imminent attack. No, what was keeping her from her much-needed sleep was in fact her preoccupation with Ferdinand. Every time she closed her eyes, there he was. Ferdinand on his proud black horse. Ferdinand smiling his handsome smile. Ferdinand close enough for her to smell the sandalwood cologne he wore. Ferdinand racing off to help his king. Ferdinand galloping through the woods, burgundy cape flying, his new, slender, young, beautiful, titled fiancée floating along beside him elegantly seated on her snowy white horse.

"Hell's teeth!" Gretel muttered into the night air, causing Hans to snortle mid-snore and Cornelius to sit bolt upright in his hammock for a few seconds. When all had settled down again Gretel lay staring into the darkness, cross with herself for wasting precious sleep over a man. Particularly one who had clearly chosen someone else over her. She had work to do. She would do it. She would return to Gesternstadt, submit to the ministrations of Madame Renoir, and then make her entrance at the concert of Herr Mozart. Until then it was really no good at all dwelling on the matter. "No good at all!" she told Jynx as he swooped past.

❄

The next day the sun was up early, setting the woods to steam. Gretel tried to leave her hammock in a dignified manner but the only discernible way to dismount the thing seemed to involve a sudden tip that threw her to the ground. She found Hans there, having been similarly ejected from his own swinging bed.

"Morning, Gretel."

"I am surprised to see you up so bright and early, Hans."

"I am far from bright, but I do smell coffee," he said.

Cornelius had rekindled the fire and already the pot was simmering atop the flames. The three of them breakfasted on coffee and more cured beef and berries. Hans soon revived beneath the warm sunshine of Cornelius's disposition, but Gretel found such enthusiasm for life and living it a little wearying at such an hour. She sipped and supped in surly silence, nurturing the faint hope that a brisk walk and applying her mind to her work would improve her humor as the day matured.

What she had envisaged as a purposeful but undemanding stride though the forest, however, Cornelius saw as an opportunity to impart his many skills to his new charges. Not content with reading the map and keeping an eye out for risks, hazards, or unwelcome company, he seized every chance to demonstrate some talent or other, and encouraged both her and Hans to have a go themselves. Gretel demurred, but Hans took up each and every challenge with gusto. While Gretel trudged, muttering darkly about schedules and objectives, the two men set snares, walked up gorges, dug up tough roots and declared them food, plaited vines to make rope, and even presented her with a grub the size of her thumb and suggested she might like to snack upon it. It was a tiresome day indeed. It occurred to Gretel that they were not moving with anything approaching stealth, and could be followed by the most inexpert tracker. She actually started to comfort herself with this thought, deciding that any would-be attacker would surely have made his move by now, they had made themselves such an obvious target.

Which only demonstrated, she was later to think, how wrong a person could be. Cornelius had engaged her in a conversation regarding the merits (few, in her opinion) and demerits (clearly many) of feeding oneself on the insects of the forest, and Hans had gone trotting off ahead, infected with his new guru's enthusiasm to the point of fever, when there came a loud shout of alarm.

"Hans?" Gretel called after him. "Hans!"

She and Cornelius hurried along the path and rounded the corner, whereupon Cornelius grabbed hold of her.

"Don't take another step!" he warned. "It could be booby-trapped!"

This assumption was not a wild one. Here the path widened a little, and in the small clearing the leaves, needles, and twigs upon the ground had been scuffed and disturbed in an unusual pattern, suggesting sudden and unusual activity. The result of this was the unusual sight of Hans, suspended twenty feet in the air, his feet ensnared in a rope that had caught him and whipped him up to dangle undignified and breathless above them.

"Hans! What in the name of all that is sensible are you doing up there?" she demanded.

"Erm . . . spinning, currently."

Cornelius crouched low, inspecting the ground around them. "Nothing else here. Looks clear. Hans must have stepped into a single trap. A simple rope and spring mechanism. Common type of thing. Straightforward and effective."

"All the blood is running to my nose," Hans informed them.

"We'll get you down," Gretel called up to him, and then, more quietly to Cornelius, "How will we get him down?"

"Not a problem," he assured her. He took a loop of rope from his backpack and shinnied up the tree trunk with the ease of one who might have been born in its boughs. He sat upon the branch from which Hans swung, tied a knot in his own rope and then secured the other end to the tree. Lowering it down he instructed Hans to take hold and put it under his arm. There was a fair amount of struggling on Hans's part, but eventually he was securely tied. Much to his alarm, Cornelius then scooted along to the rope that had him by the feet and took his large knife to the knot.

"I say!" Hans called up. "Are you certain that's wise?"

He didn't get an answer and was not in a position to protest further, as suddenly his feet were cut loose, causing his body to right itself with some speed. He *ooof*ed as Cornelius's rope took up the slack to bear his weight. Cornelius was then able to slowly lengthen the rope and lower him to *terra firma*.

Gretel picked up his hat from among the leaves and handed it to him. "What happened, Hans? Did you see anyone?"

Hans stooped to untie the rope from his ankles. "Sister mine, I did, but you will not believe me when I tell you who . . . or rather *what* I saw in the seconds before I was so brutally taken up into the trees. Ouch, these are nasty rope burns, look."

"Hans, it is important you tell me who you saw."

"*What*."

"What?"

"Not *who*. I saw not a *who*, only a *what*. And what a what it was!"

Gretel started counting to ten but got only to three and a half before her patience snapped. "For pity's sake, tell me!"

Hans straightened up and looked her gravely in the eye. "It was terrible, sister mine. It was the stuff of nightmares. I shall never forget it. The cold, staring eyes! The wild, ferocious way it sniffed the air and glared at me as I twirled there, helpless as a babe . . ."

"Hans . . ."

"You won't believe me."

"I will!"

"You will scoff and ridicule and pour scorn upon my head."

"I will beat you about the head if you don't tell me this instant!"

"It was a werewolf!"

Gretel gaped at him.

"There!" Hans went on. "I've told you and now you will dismiss my testimony as the ravings of a man who has had his brains addled by being inverted. I knew it. Go on, pooh-pooh and make fun. Tell me there is no such thing as werewolves. Declare that I am making it up. Or seeing things that are not there. Go on. I knew you would not believe me."

Gretel shook her head slowly. "Oh, but I do, Hans. Oh, but I do."

They walked on until the sun began to sink in the sky, dipping below the treetops to signify the approach of twilight. Hans was keen to get as far away as possible from the creature that had ensnared him, and his traveling companions put up no argument against this. To take his mind off unpleasant things lurking in the undergrowth, Cornelius presented him with a rabbit he had snared earlier. When they eventually set up camp for the night, he showed Hans how to skin the thing, and then left him happily cooking it up with garlic and herbs. Gretel cornered him as he was fixing up the hammocks a little way off.

"Herr Staunch, did you hear what it was Hans said back there? About what he thought he saw?"

"I did." He patted her shoulder briefly. "Don't let it worry you. Fear and shock can bring about hallucinations. A bit of exercise, something useful to do . . . he's recovered well."

"I don't think he was hallucinating."

Cornelius paused in his knot tying. "You think he really saw a werewolf?"

"I think he saw what he thinks was a werewolf."

"A real wolf, you mean? Unlikely, in broad daylight, and alone. No. They stay in a pack and hunt at dusk or dawn. Unless it was injured or sick . . . But I didn't smell wolf anywhere close."

"Even so, I don't think he was entirely mistaken. I have my own theories, which I must keep to myself for a while longer. Suffice it to say, I believe he saw something real, rather than a creation of his imaginings. I further believe that we will come under attack again, at least once more, before this journey is over."

"Can you say what manner of attack that might be? We would be better able to defend ourselves if we knew our likely assailant. Fail to prepare and you prepare to fail . . ."

Gretel held up a hand, as much against his homilies as his questioning. "I can say no more. It is only a theory yet, and as such unproven. If we keep our wits about us we will not come to harm. I have studied the map again and I am hopeful we will reach our destination before nightfall tomorrow. Until then, we must be vigilant."

Cornelius reluctantly accepted this plan. "I'll take first watch tonight," he said. "We must not leave ourselves vulnerable to attack."

Hans surpassed himself with the rabbit stew. The hot food spiced with aromatic herbs revived them all and helped him to put notions of wolflike creatures far from his mind. He even succeeded in lighting one of his damp cigars, and was soon slumbering deeply in his hammock. Gretel thought it best not to disturb him, so volunteered to take his watch as well as her own. Later, in the depths of the night, she sat beside the fire, her pixie blanket around her shoulders, and peered out into the darkness of the trees. She was not afraid, for if her theory was correct their attackers did not, in fact, want them dead. She realized that she would almost welcome a third attack, as it would go some way to confirming her suspicions regarding the *who* of their assailants. The *why* was still a little unformed, but its hazy shape was something she felt confident would solidify and hold water by the end of the following day. All they had to do was withstand another attempt to turn them back, press on, and within a few hours they would arrive at the point on the map they had been slogging toward.

"And there we will find answers," she assured Jynx as he flitted past after a moth. "One way or another, we will find answers."

The following morning found Hans a little out of sorts. He might have appeared to have been sleeping peacefully, but he assured Gretel that he had spent the night being chased through imaginary woods by fearsome creatures that snapped at his heels, hour after hour, so that he awoke exhausted. Even Cornelius's coffee and bouncing cheerfulness failed to lift his spirits.

"Fear not, Hans," Gretel assured him. "We are nearing our goal. It might have come to feel as if we are doomed to roam these woods forever, but the end is almost in sight. And the end of a case, satisfactorily solved, brings with it payment and rest. Hold that thought as you march on and know that each footstep is taking you closer to that happy conclusion."

Even Cornelius appeared impressed at this little speech, pausing in his whittling to agree wholeheartedly. Gretel was grateful he didn't feel the need to start blabbing on about morale again.

She found that morning's trek particularly testing. She felt filthy and her clothes, such as they were, were in a dreadful state. What remained of her wig was wedged into the bottom of Hans's rucksack and she feared it might be beyond salvation. Her feet were rubbed to blisters by her wet boots, her hair was frizzed and matted so that it stayed up without pins, which was just as well, as they had all been lost during the events of the previous days. Hans was so jittery he kept seeing things among the trees, insisting that they halt while Cornelius investigated, so that their progress was even slower than usual. At midday they reached another deep, fast-flowing stream. Gretel and Hans stood and stared at it in dismay, but Cornelius became very excited. He rushed around collecting bendy branches and tying rope to trees on the river bank, constructing a system of pulleys and swings, while all the time explaining with breathless enthusiasm how safe and how easy it would be to cross with this contraption. He demonstrated how it worked, sailing across on the end of a swinging rope, yodeling with glee.

Gretel and Hans remained standing and watching.

"Enthusiastic sort of fellow, ain't he?" Hans commented.

Gretel agreed that he was, and then the two of them walked a little farther along the river bank and availed themselves of the sturdy wooden footbridge that was there.

It was as they were rejoining their ebullient guide on the other side of the river that a crashing sound from among the trees caught their attention.

"Did you hear that?" Hans asked urgently.

"I did." Gretel lifted her lorgnettes to peer between the trunks, but could see nothing.

The sound came again. The noise suggested something, or somethings, large and heavy and moving erratically.

Cornelius stepped to the edge of the path and sniffed the air.

"What is it?" Hans asked.

Cornelius opened his mouth to speak but no explanation was necessary, for at that moment not one, not two, but three enormous boars came barreling out of the trees. They were squealing and snorting and roaring in the most terrifying manner. Cornelius leaped to one side, shouting at the others to get behind the nearest tree. Gretel did as she was told, though was distressed to find herself considerably wider than the trunk of her chosen pine. Hans lost his nerve and bolted.

"Don't run!" Cornelius cried after him.

But it was too late. Hans's panic had granted him the temporary gift of speed, but he was no match for the wild hogs. Soon they had caught up to him, and by then it was hard to tell whether it was they or he who was squealing the loudest. And then he tripped. The fall took some yards, such was his speed and his weight, and he came to rest up against the trunk of a larch, his face having plowed a deep furrow through the wet earth. In an instant the pigs were upon him, drawing back their tusks as if to gouge at this thing that lay helpless at their trotters.

"Hell's teeth!" shouted Gretel as she charged from her hiding place, screaming at the animals, desperately trying to distract them so that they would leave Hans alone. "Get away, you brutes!" She yelled, waving her arms and attempting to make herself look as fierce as possible. One of the boars hesitated, looking up at her. The other two appeared to be about to bite Hans, but then decided to quarrel with each other instead.

At that moment, a loop of rope whipped through the air as Cornelius lassoed one of the angry hogs. He expertly tightened the rope as it landed around the pig's middle, and in a flash the bewildered animal was upside down and he was trussing its feet. Hans had dug himself out of the mud sufficiently to flap at the nearest boar with his hat. Gretel ran at the third. It was doubtful that such a wild animal had ever in its wild life seen such a wild woman charging at it with murder in her eyes. Certainly the element of surprise won Gretel all the advantage she needed, for as she came within arm's reach of the thing—and realized she had no idea of what she was going to do to it—the pig jinked sideways and tore away through the trees.

The third boar was less easily deterred and by now had Hans pinned against the tree trunk as it ran at him repeatedly. Only Hans's unusually quick reflexes meant that its tusks did not find their target but instead ripped into and splintered the rough bark of the tree. Gretel lost her footing in the slippery, storm-sodden mud and fell flat, so that she could only flounder and watch as Hans whipped his rucksack from his back and used it to beat away the animal. She felt every blow as if it had been struck upon her own body, knowing as she did that her poor wig was most likely being pulverized in the process.

Cornelius ran at the final boar, hollering boldly. He lunged at the bristly creature and wrestled with it. Once or twice it seemed the animal would win the fight, and its tusks flashed dangerously close to the soft flesh of Cornelius's cheek, but in the end he subdued it, and tied its feet with short lengths of cord.

The two boars lay panting, flanks heaving, eyes wide. The three humans did pretty much the same. Cornelius was the first to find his voice.

"I saw someone back there," he said. "Some distance behind the boar."

"Can you describe them?" Gretel asked.

He shook his head. "They were too far away, but it was a woman, I'm certain of that."

"A woman?" Gretel's mind started whirring.

Hans was brushing mud off his pajamas. "I say," he gasped at last. "That was a close thing."

"Why did you have to run, Hans?" Gretel puffed to her feet. "For pity's sake why must you always do the idiotic thing? Can you not just once do as you are told, or must I always be rescuing you from your own cowardice and stupidity?"

She regretted her outburst the instant she had uttered it, knowing her words to be harsh and unfair, but she could not unsay them. Hans's face gave away how wounded he was, which only served to make Gretel feel guiltier and therefore crosser, so that, instead of apologizing while there was time to undo the damage, she blundered on, appealing to Cornelius for support. "You can see how it is, Herr Staunch, surely? Every time I bring my brother with me hoping that for once he will be of some use, and every time I end up having to save his hide, one way or another. Well, I mean to say, it is enough to make anyone cross. It is not unreasonable for me to want things to be other than they are, wouldn't you agree?"

Cornelius's voice was calm and level and not a bit cross. "Hans acted instinctively," he explained.

"And are we animals that can only react? Surely we are reasoning beings and should therefore employ our ability to reason?"

"In the town or city, maybe," Cornelius went on, "but out here, man in the wilderness, gotta trust your instincts."

Gretel wanted to argue further, to point out that those very instincts had almost got him gored and chewed by three very wild boar, but something in Cornelius's expression stopped her. What was it? Hans's hurt was easily identified, but it took her a little while longer to put a name to Cornelius's disappointment. It cut deep. It was like earning the disapproval of a favorite teacher. She had been judged and found wanting, not because of her actions, but because of her cruel words. She might have helped save Hans's skin, but she had inflicted a wound that would leave a scar just the same.

Hans slung his pack over his shoulder once more and jammed his battered hat onto his head.

"Let me know when you consider we have gone far enough to set up camp," he said levelly, though there was an unmistakable tremor in his voice. With that he turned and set off along the path.

Gretel looked at the roped boar, wondering briefly if a bit of crackling and pig's knuckle would go some way to earning her brother's forgiveness.

Cornelius dropped to his knees beside the nearest hog and took out an alarmingly large, sharp knife. Gretel gasped, uncertain that she had the stomach for watching butchery at that moment. But Cornelius merely cut the rope, set the animal back on its feet, and gave it a push into the trees.

"Won't they come after us again?" Gretel asked.

"No," Cornelius freed the remaining boar and sheathed his knife. "They weren't really attacking. They are calmer now, and running in the other direction. They won't bother us again."

"But they seemed so intent on fighting, on biting, on generally goring and gouging—how is that not an attack?"

"They were behaving oddly. It's not normal for them to charge like that, not if they are not cornered and threatened themselves."

"Truly?"

"And they are not given to hunting in packs. The males are very territorial, that's why they started fighting each other." He shook his head. "I've never seen three adult boar running together before. I can't even imagine they all came from this part of the woods."

"You mean, someone brought them here? Brought them and then deliberately set them upon us?"

"That would be one explanation." He held her gaze, clearly expecting her to expand on this idea.

"Our mystery attacker," she said thoughtfully. "Another attempt to scare us off." She felt anger forming a hard lump in her stomach. "Right, I think I have had quite enough of being frightened and battered and bruised. Herr Staunch, if you would be so good as to lead on. We will not stop for luncheon today but forge ahead so that we might reach our destination before dark and put an end to this nonsense once and for all!"

FOURTEEN

G retel walked the following miles carrying the prickly burden of a guilty conscience. She had spoken harshly to Hans and she should not have. That was the long and the short of it. She noticed Cornelius conversing with Hans. She could not make out the words of their exchanges, but she could tell by the subtle alterations in Hans's posture, by his increasingly purposeful gait, by the way he repositioned his hat to its more customary jaunty angle, that Herr Staunch was offering reassurance and encouragement. And that this gentle coaxing was effective in restoring her brother's mood. She was forced to reevaluate her opinion of their cheerful guide.

She had hitherto considered him to be a man of action rather than thought, a man who dined exclusively on handy homilies and snacks of conveniently digestible bon mots. She saw now that this was not a fair appraisal. He was a man sensitive to the needs of others. A person able to comprehend the flaws another person might carry with them, and the damage those flaws could do to others. His current kindness toward Hans suggested that he understood better than most the nature of human frailty, and he was capable of quieting himself to offer kindness rather than bluster when it was needed. Gretel had to admit to herself that this was something she often found difficult to do. Particularly where Hans was concerned.

Their route became ever more twisty and tangled, so that soon they were forced to beat back the undergrowth in order to pass. Brambles and vines snatched at them as they pushed on, and they made frequent and increasingly uncertain checks of the map. Their destination might have been clearly marked on the tattered and crumpled chart, but it was evidently not a place easily found, even with instructions.

Suddenly Cornelius, walking past, held up a hand. Everyone stopped. He crouched low and inspected the forest floor.

"What is it?" Gretel asked.

"Are there more animal tracks?" Hans wanted to know. "More boar, perhaps? Or wolflike things? Or bears this time. There might be bears, might there not?"

Cornelius said nothing for a moment, but stooped to press his ear to the ground. He looked puzzled. He got to his feet and minutely examined the area around the faint path they were following.

"Strange," he said at last. "There are signs of many people having passed this way, albeit carefully, treading so as to leave as faint a trace as possible. And I can detect vibrations some way up ahead that feel like the hooves of heavy animals."

"Horses?" Gretel suggested. "Hunters riding in this area?"

"No, they are moving too slowly and not getting nearer or farther. Almost as if they were walking in small circles. And, well, I know it makes no sense but I am certain there are wheels moving over the ground."

"Cart wheels? But surely, there is no space in which to move a cart, wagon, or carriage of any kind?"

"Not here, at least," he agreed.

They proceeded with a new manner of caution. Dusk was descending, so that their progress through the tangled woods was of necessity ponderous, but now they were also taking greater care to be quiet, to listen, to squint into the caliginosity for an explanation for Cornelius's theories. After a further half hour's walking they found it. Keeping themselves hidden behind a briar bush, the trio stood and stared in amazement at the truth of what lay behind the workaday X on Herr Arnold's map.

The gathering gloom was abruptly punctuated with lights, some bright and steady, others flickering. These lights shone through windows of many shapes and sizes, and were clearly illuminating the rooms of houses, shops, and hostelries. As if it were not sufficiently astonishing to find an entire village hidden at the heart of the forest; as if discovering a whole settlement where only a single dwelling had been anticipated was not adequately dumbfounding; as if coming upon a veritable community living their lives in this remote and secret part of the woods was not astounding enough for anyone on an unremarkable late summer's evening, there was another feature of these houses that made them indisputably extraordinary. Something other. Something else. Something uncommon in the extreme. They were all at least thirty feet above the ground. Each and every one of them was built into—and out of—the trees. They were, indeed, tree houses. There were small homes with quaint shuttered windows. There were taller buildings, outside which swung painted signs advertising accommodation. There was a general store, and a tailor's, and a barbershop, and an inn, and a little farther down more signs offered the services of a smithy, an undertaker, and a physician.

"Great heavens!" Hans exclaimed.

Cornelius was speechless.

Gretel's mind was spinning with new questions and possibilities, not the least of which was that she might at last get a bath and some new clothes. Less urgent, but more important, was the thought that this was a place a person who did not wish to be found could very well live something approaching a life. While what she knew of the sorcerer had led her to resist the idea of him hiding alone in a shack indefinitely, she could imagine him passing his days here tolerably well. And that thought gave her hope that he was indeed still living. It was only then that she realized it did matter to her. She would, after all, be far happier to take her payment from the insurance company for proving him to be alive, rather from Widow Arnold for proving him to be dead.

"Look!" Hans interrupted her thoughts before she could follow them any further. "An inn! And looks like quite a good one too. I for one could do with a stein or two of ale. What say you, Gretel?"

"I say we have earned a little rest and recuperation, but I also say that we know no one here, and that if we were to enter the inn in our current state of dress and unkemptness we might not be welcome. I suggest the following. Herr Staunch, you are still sensibly clothed and reasonably tidy; would you be so good as to venture into that guest house up there, secure rooms for us, and ask if the tailor might be sent over with a selection of serviceable garments? I urge discretion, for if our sorcerer is here somewhere we do not wish to spook him. If he were to learn a detective has strolled into town he might well flee, and I for one have had my fill of chasing through the forest."

"Who should I say we are?" Cornelius asked.

"You should be yourself, and say that you have two would-be wilderness adventurers who engaged your services to learn camping and such like, but who are now weary and in need of such comforts as hot water and beds. Be vague but pleasant, and I doubt anyone will quiz you further."

Hans, for once, sounded a practical note. "But what shall we do for money? I can't imagine you brought sufficient with you for hotel tariffs and bar bills."

"I did not. And what little I brought went up in smoke with the rest of my things at the witch's cottage. Herr Staunch, I must ask that you cover our expenses and add them to your bill. You will be reimbursed as soon as we return to Gesternstadt, you have my word."

"Happy to help," Cornelius said, "though of course we could just set up camp a little way off. I saw a perfect spot for a fire and hammocks back up the trail . . ." The expressions on the faces of his companions gave him his answer. "As you wish," he said, "but if it's all the same to you, once I have done as you ask, I shall sleep out again. I will go to that place and wait for you to send word that my services are required for the return journey." He hurried away to do Gretel's bidding.

The ground beneath the aerial village was inhabited by tethered grazing animals—goats and milk cows in the main—which explained the patterns of hoofbeats Cornelius had correctly identified. He moved swiftly through them, passing the broad sign welcoming visitors to Baumhausdorf, and jogged over to the nearest rope ladder, upon which he made a speedy ascent, untroubled by the way it swung and twisted, his strong arms and fleet feet powering him upward with ease.

"Look at him go!" Hans said in awe. Then, after a pause in which Gretel was sure she could hear the cogs of his mind turning, he asked, "How are we to gain entry to the village and all its delights? I can't see either of us managing that ladder."

When Hans managed to point out an obvious but inconvenient truth, it was Gretel's habit to offer a cutting repost. On this occasion, however, the memory of his wounded face when she had spoke harshly was too fresh in her mind.

"You make a good point, brother mine. The ladders are not for us. Let us assume that not everyone in Baumhausdorf is as nimble and able as our young friend. They must have some other means of ingress. We shall look for it."

They stepped forward beneath the cloak of darkness, moving as quietly as they were able between the pungent goats and masticating cattle. An overly friendly calf took a liking to Hans's hat, which slowed them down somewhat, and Gretel more than once felt her boot squish into a warm pat, but otherwise they encountered no difficulties. At length they came to a wooden contraption manned by a large youth who had not words but was able to indicate the service he offered, which was to work the pulley that lifted a cage that would bear them up into the trees. Having no coin with which to pay him, Hans instead performed a card trick, which the fellow found inordinately amusing. Minutes later, they were installed in the wicker and wood cage and were cranked aloft.

"I say!" breathed Hans as they stepped onto the wooden street.

The tree house village was indeed something to marvel at. It was in all respects the same as if it had been constructed on terra firma, but its being high in the trees gave it two immediately noticeable characteristics. The first was movement, for as the trees gently sighed and swayed or stretched their boughs, so the wooden planks moved. The sensation was unsettling, but also curiously pleasant, reminding Gretel of being aboard a cruise ship. The second thing that was remarkable even in the dark was the new perspective upon the world that the village gave its inhabitants. Although night had properly fallen by now, a moon bright as a newly minted silver coin bathed the landscape with its gentle light. Gretel stepped forward to lean upon the balustrade that ran all along the street.

"Well!" she declared. Before her lay many leagues of forest, stretching in all directions. She was able to look down upon the canopy of leaves and branches as if she were a giantess. The forest was no longer an impenetrable, frightening mass of trees, but a soft, shadowy carpet over which she could cast her gaze to the distant horizon of high pastures and mountains. "Well!" she said again.

"Fraulein Gretel!" Cornelius called softly from a nearby doorway. He gestured for them to join him. "This is both inn and guesthouse, and I have obtained rooms for us."

"Was your story believed?"

"It was. In fact, the proprietor, Herr Uberts, showed little interest in who we are. The tariff is not unreasonable, and there is a door from the lobby that goes into the bar of the inn."

"Excellent," Hans declared, clapping his hands together with glee at the thought.

They followed Cornelius inside and up the stairs. The interior gave no clue to the fact that they were so high up, but seemed in every respect an ordinary guesthouse with something of a rustic feel. There was plenty of wood left unpainted and a preponderance of bare wooden furniture, perhaps, but still there were enough soft furnishings for comfort, if not style. Gretel's room was small but clean, with a simple wooden bed, chair, and washstand. The quilt was patchwork and colorful and Gretel had to resist the urge to flop upon it and succumb to fatigue.

"No," she told herself. "First a bath, fresh clothes, and then a bite to eat in the inn." A course of action that would revive her, but also allow her to begin the questioning of locals that might lead her to the sorcerer, for there was nowhere better to loosen tongues than a bar.

Before drawing the curtains, Gretel looked out through the window, the better to fix her bearings. The inn was situated roughly at the midpoint of the main street of the village. This main thoroughfare, if such it could be called, looped in a freely drawn circle, the center of which was an empty drop to the ground, railed off with the sturdy balustrade. To the immediate left was the barbershop, to the right the tailor's. Other stores and dwellings ran either around the main loop or off down side streets. Gretel noticed a sign above one of the smaller establishments offering the services of a "Physician of Great Talent and Expertise," if not modesty. As she pondered this bit of confident self-promotion, the good doctor himself stepped out to take a breath of the balmy night air.

"Great heavens!" exclaimed Gretel, for there, resplendent in purple—though minus a pointy hat—stood none other than Herr Arnold Ernst himself. She watched him, her mouth open in disbelief. Despite the lack of his appendix, he seemed to be in good health. She had not expected him to be so easy to find. Indeed he seemed to be making no effort to hide himself, and as he was advertising his services, he must be, locally, quite well known. He must surely be using an alias. Would he admit to his true identity, she wondered? Would he run if he realized that he was being tracked, and was about to be ensnared? And what, precisely, was she going to do with him now that she had found him? Gretel faced the prospect of trussing him up and paying someone strong and capable to help her drag him back to Gesternstadt, and it did not appeal. No, she would have to get to the bottom of the mystery of his disappearance. Of what exactly had taken place in his magicarium. Was there anyone else involved? Had he been coerced? He must be missing his beloved wife, and that, she decided, was key to getting him to cooperate. She would stick to her plan and ask questions before confronting him. As long as he did not get wind of who she was and what purpose had brought her there, there was no reason for the sorcerer to go anywhere.

As she watched, he turned to go in, but then hesitated, looking to the sky. A small burr of darkness darted toward him. He held up a hand and Jynx alighted upon it. Ernst smiled and cooed and tickled the tiny creature beneath its chin before taking it indoors. If she had been doubt at all about the physician's true identity, the tiny bat expunged it.

A knock at the door heralded the arrival of a middle-aged woman who introduced herself as the wife of the tailor. She came with a selection of clothes draped over her arm, which she laid out upon the bed as if they were from the latest collection of the finest Parisian designers.

"Take your pick, Fraulein," she said, standing back, hands on hips, confident in the quality of her wares. Or more likely, Gretel thought, the fact that hers was the only establishment selling clothes within three days' march in any direction.

Gretel rifled through the garments on offer. They were all second-, or third-, or fourth-hand. Some showed more evidence of wear than others. The one fashioned from a good quality cotton had a disturbing patch over the heart, as if a jagged cut had been repaired. The dark red muslin was not dark enough to hide the stain down its front that Gretel knew in her bones to be blood. The next was a wedding dress, which was wholly unsuited to anything other than the occasion for which it had been designed. There was, or course, the dreaded dirndl, which Gretel quickly passed over. This left two outfits. One was an ensemble of skirts and bodice of passable quality, of a serviceable green hue. Alas, it had been made for a woman of a considerably less substantial frame than Gretel's, and there was no time for alterations. The last, and therefore only choice, was a dress of royal blue silk. It was the right size and bore no discernible history of violence, which was in its favor. Its cut, however, was less helpful. It had no sleeves, but thin straps instead, and the front was cut so low and so wide as to display acres of flesh to the point, Gretel felt, where it would be hard to persuade any man to maintain eye contact with her, whatever the nature of their conversation. Still, there was nothing else. Gretel paid the tailor's wife too much to part with her own cream cotton shawl and handed over some of the coins Cornelius had lent her for both garments. There were no shoes, so she would have to continue in her boots. The departure of the tailor's wife coincided with the arrival of a maid bearing jugs of steaming water for Gretel's bath.

Half an hour later, she lay submerged, fragrant soap lathering up nicely as she scrubbed her battered feet, her aching muscles and bruised body beginning to feel restored at last. She closed her eyes.

"A little longer," she promised herself, "and then to work!"

FIFTEEN

Two hours later she knocked on the door to Hans's room. The evening was warm, but she had elected to tie the shawl around her shoulders for the sake of decorum. Even so, she was showing rather more cleavage than she was comfortable with. She consoled herself with the fact that it might distract people sufficiently to get them to talk with her. She had washed her hair and piled it high on her head, and the maid had even given her a little powder and rouge, so that the worst of the ravages of her woodland camping were concealed. The soap, while pleasant enough, had a rather powerful scent to it which clung to her still. All in all, the glimpse she had of herself in the long mirror on the landing had revealed her to look worryingly come-hither, but there was nothing to be done about it.

Hans opened the door.

Gretel started. "Why on earth are you dressed like that?" she asked.

"It was this or a butcher's apron. They had nothing else in my size."

"But a clergyman . . . ?"

"What would you have me do, Gretel? I can hardly go out in what's left of those pajamas."

Hans's attire was head to toe that of a country vicar. It did at least look clean, and nothing could have been more respectable, though Gretel was still left with the sense that they were kitted out to attend a costume ball.

"What a pair we make," she muttered as they made their way downstairs.

There was a spring in Hans's step as he took her arm and steered her toward the inn. Gretel thought he was unlikely to be the first clergyman to be so openly eager to get to a bar, but he might have been one of the few to do so while apparently escorting a woman of easy virtue. As they approached the door that connected the inn to the guest house, music could be heard, of the lively and unchallenging kind, and above it chatter and laughter, loud and boisterous. They opened the door and stepped inside.

The hostelry consisted of a single, large room. Despite its size, it was so filled with revelers it appeared cramped. From the entrance, Gretel could just make out a fireplace at the far end, a long bar running the length of the room, and stools, small tables, and chairs in every available space, most currently occupied. And what occupants they were! As her eyes adjusted to the smoke that made them smart and the low light of the wall lamps obscured by so many drinkers, she took stock of the clientele. Most were men, which was not in itself unusual. What immediately struck her was that so many of them were faintly familiar to her. As she turned from one face to the next she was certain she recognized several of them, though she knew she had not actually met any of them. And then it dawned on her: she knew them from their likenesses rendered in ink upon notices. Notices declaring them Wanted Men. The more she looked, the more certain she became. There was Scurvy Sam, a pirate who had not set foot on a ship for decades but instead robbed stagecoaches. And there the Coffin Dodger Dandy, a man of flamboyant dress and advanced years, and one of the most successful jewel thieves in Bavaria. And playing cards with him it could be no other than the Lily Twins, known for leaving a lily at the scene of their crimes, which were mostly, if Gretel's memory served, murders in the course of burglary.

"Gretel . . . !" Hans hissed at her from the corner of his mouth. "Am I mistaken, or . . . ?"

"You are not, brother mine."

"You are seeing what I am seeing?"

"I fear that I am."

"What have we come to?" he whispered urgently.

"A place of safety for outlaws and outcasts, it would seem. Come, there is a vacant table in the corner."

They made their way across the room and took their seats. A serving wench, a tray at her hip, swayed through the throng and dragged a wet rag over their table.

"What can I get you?" she asked.

"A jug of your best ale," Gretel replied, "two glasses, and whatever you have by way of food."

"We've pigs knuckle and potatoes. And some weisswurst."

"With mustard?" Hans asked.

"Of course, Reverend."

"Excellent," said Gretel, letting the confusion over Hans's identity pass. She took from her pocket the last of the money Cornelius had lent her and pressed coins into the woman's hand, and as she did so she asked, "I wonder, does Herr Arnold frequent your establishment?"

"The physician? On occasion, though he's not a big drinker. Needs to keep a steady hand for his work, I suppose." She left them with this thought.

"Look!" Hans leaned close to his sister and nodded toward the far wall. "Isn't that the fellow who robbed the Gesternstadt bank last summer?"

"I believe it is, though it might be prudent not to let on that you've recognized him."

"But, Gretel, I recognize nearly all of them. They are all infamous. Can you imagine if we'd brought Kapitan Strudel with us? Ha! He wouldn't have room for them all in his little jail."

Gretel doubted very much that should the Kingsman ever find his way to this particular inn, he would ever be allowed to leave. All of a sudden, icy fingers seemed to creep around the back of her neck. If everyone here was a nefarious criminal, and all lived openly as such, then the secrecy of the location was of paramount importance. Which meant that only people who could be trusted to keep that secret would be permitted the freedom to come and go. It appeared the sorcerer—or the physician as she must now think of him—enjoyed that freedom. She was more than a little worried that she and Hans might not be granted the same privilege. If anyone recognized her and mentioned the word *detective* it might well be all up for Gretel (yes, *that* Gretel) of Gesternstadt. And her brother. And Cornelius Staunch, were his connection to them apparent.

"Hans," she whispered into his ear, "whatever you do, do not give away our names."

"Not?"

"No. My profession is not a good fit here. If we plan on returning home, with or without Herr Arnold, but with our skins intact, we must maintain the pretense Cornelius started for us. We are would-be wilderness adventurers, remember? We hired him to take us into the woods to teach us the ways of the expert hiker and camper, but we overreached ourselves and wish to remain here only as long as it takes us to recover our strength. Then we will leave. It is also crucial that we do not admit to recognizing anyone. Do you understand, Hans? Hans!"

But her brother was no longer listening to her. His mouth opened and shut but he uttered no sound. His eyes were wide with fear, and he was staring at the bar. Gretel followed the direction of his gaze and was too slow to stop a small cry escaping her own mouth. For there, seated on a bar stool, hairy chin resting on a hairy paw, was a large, ragged, brown bear. As they stared the barman refilled his tankard, and the bear drank lustily from it before wiping his mouth with the back of his paw. He belched and slammed his vessel down, nodding for another. On either side of him sat men completely at ease with their ursine drinking companion.

Before Gretel and Hans had the chance to react further, the main door opened and in from the street came a brawny man with an axe slung over his shoulder, followed by three men of short stature who entered in the midst of an argument and continued it even as the woodsman hoisted them onto barstools and ordered them drinks.

The waitress returned with the ale and set down wooden platters in front of them.

"Tell me," Gretel asked in as steady a voice as she could muster, "that . . . bear . . . ?" She found she could not form a sensible question.

"Him?" the waitress asked, glancing up, as if there might be more than one. "You'd best steer clear of him. He's got a bit of a temper on him. Doesn't help that everyone still calls him Baby Bear, even though he must be thirty if he's a day."

Hans snorted. "He certainly doesn't look like a baby!"

"Names stick though, don't they?" The waitress put knives on the table. "He grew up and left home but everyone knew about the whole Goldilocks business. He never could shake the story off. Started drinking young, got in with a bad crowd." She gave a shrug, "What can you do?"

Gretel took a swig of her ale and nodded at the new arrivals. "And those?"

"Huh, that's posh girls for you. All very handy having seven dwarves when you've no one else, but the minute that Snow White married her prince and got a castle full of servants she dropped them like so many hot potatoes."

"What happened to the other four?" Hans asked.

"Don't know. They never came here. This bunch work with the woodsman now. He'd be on his own otherwise. Never got over Red Riding Hood dumping him to marry a wine merchant. Will you be wanting bread?"

"What?" Gretel's mind was in a spin. "Yes. Bread, thank you."

As the waitress went off to fetch their food Gretel and Hans sat for a moment while the hubbub and raucous laughter bounced around them. Gretel considered their situation. Not only were they in the company of career criminals, but every bit of human—or animal—flotsam and jetsam seemed to have washed up at Baumhausdorf. This was a place for those who could have no other place. All were welcome here. And all could be themselves, for none would ever tell. What better place to hide than somewhere where no one questioned your past, your deeds, or your shortcomings? All were equal, as was their need for their whereabouts to remain secret.

"I say," Hans pointed toward a table by the window. "A card game. Stud poker, if I'm not very much mistaken. Which I don't think I am. Or I ought not to be, at least, after all these years of playing."

"You cannot take part, Hans. Don't even think of it."

"What? But Gretel, such an opportunity. I could win enough to pay for our meal, and lodgings, more than likely."

"Dressed as a vicar?"

"Don't vicars play cards?"

"They are not known for their gambling prowess, Hans. You start winning hands, taking money off the locals dressed as you are, and people will start to smell a rat."

"But . . ."

"We cannot afford to draw attention to ourselves. I don't think you realize the precarious nature of our situation in this place. Ah, here comes our food. Now, eat up, try not to stare, particularly at that bear, and with luck we can have our feed and return to our rooms without talking to anyone."

The meal was passably good—hot, fresh, and plentiful. The ale was sweet and strong. After days of privations, it was a seductive combination, so that Gretel found herself tarrying, staying for another jug of ale and some steamed suet apple pudding with custard. Hans put up no objection. Gradually, the mood at the inn began to shift to something a little more robust and quarrelsome. The piano player appeared to be drinking at the same rate as everyone else, so that his playing was growing in tempo and volume as the evening progressed. The strange patrons became more rowdy, the noise in the room ever louder and more uncouth, so that soon anything near normal conversation was soon impossible.

"We should leave soon, Hans."

"What's that?" He cupped a hand over his ear.

Gretel got to her feet. "We should go!" she yelled, pointing at the door.

Hans nodded and got up to follow her. The room was so full by now, however, that it was not a simple matter to move through the throng, and progress could only be made with a good deal of mouthed *entschuldigen*s and forgive-mes. Hans's new persona went some way toward smoothing their passage. More than once a trodden-on toe that might have resulted in fists being swung was saved by the sight of the clergyman's clothing. Gretel's shawl was dragged from her shoulders as she pushed forward and her low-cut neckline garnered some lascivious glances. She ignored them, even smiling sweetly when she thought it might help. It seemed to take an age to get anywhere, and Hans's attention was snagged by another game of cards. He stopped, gazing long-ingly at the pot in the center of the table as a winning hand was laid down.

Gretel tugged at his sleeve. "Come along, Reverend brother," she shouted into his ear.

"But Gretel, no one would really notice me playing amid all this din. Just one little game? There'd be no need for me to tell them who you are or why you are here," he pleaded.

"I can't hear you!"

"I said . . ."

Hans took a deep breath to put the full force of his not inconsiderable lungs behind his words. Unfortunately, the piano player chose that very instant to pause in his playing, so that Hans bellowed into the sudden quiet.

". . . they don't have to know that you are a detective here to find someone hiding from the law!!"

The quiet deepened into a dark, bottomless silence, as every single pair of eyes turned to stare anew at the vicar and his voluptuous escort, and every single one of those pairs burned bright and hard with the potential for a murderous course of action.

SIXTEEN

There are times when circumstances and events conspire to bring about the downfall of a person who could reasonably protest that their fate was not deserved. When such a confluence of happenings occurs there is little the hapless person in the eye of the storm can do to change the outcome one way or another, nor can they regret what has brought them low, as they were no more in control of their destiny than a leaf caught in a whirlpool. There are also times when quite the reverse can be said: there are people who pull the wrath of all the gods down upon their heads, only to be saved from the consequences of their actions by some simple incident that fortuitously arrives without the smallest effort on their own part. Gretel later admitted to herself that what took place in the inn that night fell into this second category of adventure.

As she and Hans stood hemmed in on all sides by frowning and snarling men—and one bear—for all of whom the very idea of "the law" triggered the urge for a violent response, she searched her mind for something to say that would rescue the situation. She even opened her mouth in preparation for such clever words of explanation as might come. None did. She tried a smile, but it cut no ice at all. Beside her, Hans emitted a little giggle, the result of too much ale and too little sense, added to by an understandable fear for his own, dog-collared neck.

One of the nearest men, whose whiskery, rugged looks were not improved by the many scars that hatched his face, voiced the question all present were, in all probability, thinking.

"Who are you, and what business have you here that concerns *the law?*" These last two words were so distasteful to him he was forced to spit elaborately after uttering them. Several of his fellows evidently felt the same way.

"My brother is confused . . . ," Gretel began, keeping her voice carefree and cheery, which was a fair feat of acting on her part. ". . . He is unaccustomed to ale so powerful as the one you enjoy here."

"Confused or not his name remains the same," Scarface pointed out. "Who is he and who are you?"

There was a chorus of *ayes* and *speak up*s and *let's have it*s!

Hans felt duty bound to do something. It might have been that that something was a thing of some merit, of some cunning, of some guile such as he had never shown in his life before. Or it might have been that that something was something less, something somewhat unhelpful, something somehow more Hans. No one would ever find out, for as he drew himself up to speak, tucking his thumbs in his highly respectable lapels and puffing out his stomach, he took a step back and to the side the better to address the company. Alas, there was no back and very little side to be had, so that instead he trod squarely and weightily on the unshod back paw of Baby Bear.

The great bear roared. Hans sprang forward, barreling into Scurvy Sam, who shoved him into the arms of A.N. Other Outlaw. This burly specimen of the criminal classes drew back his arm and threw a meaty fist at Hans's head, but Hans, still off balance from all the barreling and shoving, teetered sideways and downward at that moment, landing heavily on the sawdusted floor. The punch found its mark instead in the eye of the woodsman, whereupon both dwarves leaped from their barstools to defend their friend.

The entire room fell to brawling. There being insufficient space for a private fight, the hitting spread like a contagion the length of the bar, so that soon everyone was punching or biting or throttling someone else. The pianist struck up a suitably lively tune. The barman took out a cudgel with which to defend his wares. The previous chatter was now replaced with oaths, curses, and shouts.

Gretel dropped to the floor beside her brother.

"Hans! Keep low and follow me," she instructed, turning to scuttle on hands and knees through the lurching and stamping feet. At one point the bear picked up a hefty man and threw him out of the window. His trajectory, and the arc and length of his scream, suggested he had cleared the balustrade completely and made a speedy descent to the ground below.

"Keep going, Hans, for pity's sake!" Gretel called to him.

They forced their way to the side door and hauled it open, standing only to slam it on the chaos behind them. But not before Gretel had glimpsed a familiar figure slipping out through the main door of the inn. A woman. Nondescript and a little plain, but unmistakably a woman known to Gretel. A woman, indeed, whom she had interviewed not more than six days back. For that woman was none other than the wife of the baker whom Ernst Arnold's magic had condemned to a life of tormented, endless laughter.

※

In the sanctuary of her blissfully comfortable bed in her wonderfully empty room behind her reassuringly locked and barred-by-a-chair door, Gretel took stock. At least she and Hans had escaped the bar brawl unscathed. In fact, the fight had provided a vital diversion. Although many of the minds present at the time would have been the worse for alcohol, there were plenty sharp enough to see Gretel as a threat to their continued safety, and indeed the continued secrecy surrounding Baumhausdorf. While hangovers, indolence, and better things to do might buy her a little time, her cover was blown. She was not safe in the village, and would have to conduct her business and leave as quickly as possible. The inn did not appear to have a closing time, so that for hours after leaving she could hear fights and riotous behavior continuing. Outside her window, on the treetop street, and even down upon the forest floor itself, commotion, noise, and drunken revelry continued into the small hours. This disruption and human activity was in sharp contrast to the quiet—if uncomfortable—nights she had spent in the woods up to this point. She thought briefly of Cornelius, and imagined him sleeping peacefully in his hammock some way off.

The facts as she saw them were few but important.

First, the sorcerer was alive and looked to be in good health, despite his missing part. He had evidently set up shop as the village physician and been accepted as such into the singular community of Baumhausdorf.

Second, on their journey through the forest, she and Hans had been attacked three times, with only two sightings of possible attackers. Hans had spotted a figure he described as being a werewolf.

Third, the Gesternstadt baker's wife was staying in the village.

Gretel examined these facts, holding them up to the light and turning them this way and that. She searched for common elements and possible corollaries. She looked for patterns and matches. She thought until her head tightened around her brow as if she were wearing in the snuggest of new wigs.

And then it came to her.

"Aha!" she cried out, sitting up and shaking her head in the gloaming of her bedchamber. "Three attacks: three sorcerer's clients interviewed! The first remained hidden, the second covered in hair—from a distance resembling a wolf-man—and the third . . . the baker's wife!"

The connection made, it stood up to close scrutiny. But why, she wondered? Why had the three victims of Ernst Arnold's failed magic gone to such great lengths to try to stop her finding the sorcerer? Why, she asked herself, over and over, until the repeated word turned into a lilting lullaby and sent her off to sleep.

※

The next morning dawned freshened and bright, sunbeams shining upon a woodland refreshed by the recent rain. There was everywhere the smell of wet timber, trees, and flowers, and birds sang in a such a cheerful manner as was difficult to resist.

Gretel rose early and left Hans sleeping in his room. She wanted to conduct her interview with the sorcerer before word reached him of her presence in the village. She need not have worried that any of the drinkers of the previous night would be abroad before lunch. The wooden walkways were devoid of people, and the swineherds who tended the beasts below lay among the livestock in snoring heaps.

Gretel tied the wool shawl a little tighter around her shoulders. She had dressed her hair as modestly as she could and eschewed powder and rouge in an effort to appear more businesslike and less alluring. Though if she had judged Herr Arnold aright, he would have eyes for no other woman than his beloved wife.

She stood at his door beneath the sign declaring him to be a physician and knocked firmly. Footsteps could be heard, and the door was quickly opened.

"Herr Arnold?" Form dictated that she ask even though she knew the answer.

"Detective Gretel! Did Voigt send you?" the sorcerer paled beneath her gaze. She noticed that he had not shaken his love of lurid colors and flamboyant clothing, so he still looked very much the magician. She wondered if it were a fondness for things past, or the simple fact that a decent tailor was nowhere near, and new clothes, as she had discovered, were limited.

"He did not, and I wonder at your suggesting that he did. It was your good wife who engaged my services."

"Evalina!" The speaking of his beloved's name proved too much for Ernst, and he lost his composure, crumpling into copious tears.

"Perhaps we might have this conversation away from prying eyes?" Gretel asked.

He nodded, his face obscured by a large—purple—handkerchief, and indicated with a sweep of his elaborately sleeved arm that she should step inside. His office, which was evidently his home as well as his place of work, although more spartan, was decorated with the same poor taste and love of junk that had been employed for his house and magicarium back in Gesternstadt. There were differences that were entirely due to the position he held in the treetop village, to wit in place of crystal balls and wands and curious incense and jars of ingredients for magic, there were the instruments of a surgeon and bonesetter, none of which looked pleasant. A fluttering transpired to be little Jynx, disturbed from his rest, come to perform a dance of greeting about Gretel's head before returning to a favorite beam.

"Please be seated, Fraulein," he said, clearing a stack of books and papers from a low chair. He waited until she was sitting and then took a seat opposite on an uncomfortable looking stool. Gretel could not help thinking that Evalina would have set about adding frilly soft furnishings in a thrice. "Tell me, Fraulein, I beg you, how fares my dear wife?"

"As any widow might." This set him to weeping again, so she went on, "She misses you terribly and is left in torment not knowing your fate, Herr Arnold. You could surely not expect anything other, given how she loves you."

"Does she love me still, do you think?" He looked up, searching her face for honesty. "Could she? Would she, if she knew . . . ?"

"That rather depends what it is she does not know, doesn't it?"

"Oh, my poor darling." He blew his nose loudly.

"Herr Arnold, let us begin again. I am pleased to find you living, as Evalina will be."

"Will she? Can she forgive me?"

"She would rather you alive and sinful yet repentant than dead and blameless, I am certain of it."

"But the deception . . ."

"You were clearly a man driven to desperate measures. And on that matter, please do tell me why, and how, you came to remove your own appendix?"

"Ah, that."

"It was not sorcery, this much I know."

He gave a small, dry chuckle. "Alas, I would not be here to talk to you now had I relied on my skill with magic to remove it. Although, there was one aspect of the operation where only magic would assist me. As fortune would have it, this was the one piece of sorcery with which I have always had some measure of success."

"Which is?"

"To be able to render a person—or indeed a part of that person—temporarily senseless of pain."

"Good heavens!"

"Surprising, is it not? It certainly made my task easier. In fact, I doubt I would have attempted it otherwise. A pity I could not have had such reliable results with my other spells."

"But why do it? Such risky surgery, and unaided, all simply to evade your debts?"

"You know of those? Of course you do. Your reputation tells me you would not have come this far without knowing as many facts as were there to be found." He gave a sigh and sat back a bit on his seat, letting his hands fall to rest upon his knees, his eyes at last dry. It was the posture of a man ready to tell all. Gretel had seen it before. "I had not enjoyed good health for some weeks. I had a suspicion that it was my appendix that was making me unwell. I knew, deep down, that it would have to come out. It was then that the idea came to me. You see, had I simply vanished people would have assumed I had deserted my dear Evalina. I needed to leave something that indicated my demise."

"Even your murder?"

"Yes, even that. When I became ill I seized upon the idea. I could cure myself—I was confident of that—disappear, and leave some clue as to my probably fate."

"A cryptic one, if I may say so."

"But not too cryptic for Gretel of Gesternstadt?"

"You imagined I would find you? You hoped to be discovered, even?"

Herr Arnold sighed again. "In truth, it may be that I did. When a man acts out of despair and follows a drastic course, is there not often a part of him that wishes to be found out? To be stopped?"

Gretel knew this to be the case oftentimes, for she had observed it before in some cases she had solved. "A perverse part of human nature," she agreed. "But Herr Arnold, could you not have simply shared your troubles with your devoted wife? Surely together you could have found some other way out of your difficulties?"

"Oh, Fraulein, she is so precious to me: I did not wish to worry her."

Gretel clucked. "Those words are written on the tombstones of so many men," she warned him. She noticed then his appointment book on the table beside her. In it were many names written against dates and times, and many accounts checked and settled, by the look of it.

"I see you do brisk business here as a physician," she said.

"I have the inhabitants of Baumhausdorf to thank for that," he told her. "The nature of their . . . *work* . . . means that they often return home sporting injuries of one kind or another. Then there are the frequent quarrels and brawls here where they sustain further hurts and wounds. And of course, there is the drop," here he paused to nod to the window and the view of the balustrade outside. "I spend a good deal of my time setting broken bones."

"Ah, yes," Gretel recalled the pixie with the broken arm. "I have in fact seen and admired some of your work. Alas, you do not, it seems, have a similar facility for magic. Given which, I do not understand why, when you are such a skilled and accomplished surgeon and bonesetter, you would not choose to follow this career in Gesternstadt? Why did you instead doggedly pursue the profession of sorcerer, despite all evidence pointing to the fact that you had no talent for it?"

Gretel would have to wait for her answer, for at that moment there came an urgent hammering upon the door. The sorcerer-physician was clearly accustomed to such a frantic summons, and moved swiftly but without panic to open the door. A young woman, flushed and anxious, all but fell into the office. Gretel recognized her as the maid from their guest house who had filled her bath for her and helped her with her toiletries. She was a little alarmed when the girl ignored Herr Arnold and addressed her words to Gretel herself.

"Oh Fraulein, you must come quick!" she panted.

"Whatever has happened?"

"Your brother, he found a game of cards and was invited to play."

Gretel rolled her eyes. "Yes, that sounds like Hans. I expressly tell him to do one thing and he does another. Thank you for your concern, young Fraulein, but he is a fair player. I don't suppose he will lose all of our money."

"I'm sure he is a very good player, Fraulein. That is the problem. I think some of those he was playing with were not nearly so good as him and employed methods of which he did not approve, so that now he has accused them of cheating!"

SEVENTEEN

"H err Arnold, kindly accompany me, I may have need of your services," said Gretel. Although there might have been truth in this—and indeed she hoped there was not—she was more concerned that the sorcerer might flee when her back was turned. Fortunately, by appealing to him in his capacity as a physician she had secured his cooperation, and he followed her out of the office.

As Gretel hitched up her skirts and hurried over to the inn she kept telling herself that things were probably not as bad as they sounded, and that with a few careful words and a few rounds of ale, things could be smoothed over and the matter brought to a safe and happy conclusion. However, when she entered the barroom and saw the tableau awaiting her, she had to admit to herself that the situation was indeed ticklish. There were five men seated at the table. Three kept to their seats, their cards laid flat in front of them. The fourth, Hans, still held his hand. He was keeping particularly still, due to the fact that the fifth man—all sinew and bristly chin—had reached across to hold the tip of a very sharp blade to his throat.

"A little soon in the day for a game of cards, is it not, brother?" Gretel asked.

Hans replied without even moving his eyes in her direction. "Ah, but this game was begun last evening, so is in fact a very late game, rather than a very early one," he explained. "After a bite of breakfast I happened upon these gentlemen . . ."

The man holding the knife growled. "Gentlemen, ha! But a moment ago I was a barefaced liar and a cheat. Ain't it strange how a person's opinion can change. Well, you'll not sweet talk your way out of this."

"I'm sure my brother spoke in haste."

"Not *really*," said Hans carefully.

"I'm certain he was mistaken," she said pointedly stressing the final word.

"No," Hans insisted. "I wasn't," he added, his voice rising to a squeak as the point of the blade was pressed a little harder to his throat.

"No one calls me a cheat!" the card player growled.

"But . . ." Hans could not help himself, "there is no other explanation. The cards cannot be as you claim. Our fellow players have theirs upon the table and I count three aces among them. As I have held the fourth since they were first dealt, you cannot also have another. D'you see?"

His adversary shook his head. "Who's to say it ain't you's the cheat? Could be that yours is the fifth ace, eh? What say you to that?"

Hans's voice, though strained, was still impressively determined. "I say my ace gains me nothing, whereas yours gives you the winning hand. See?" He placed his cards upon the table. Even Gretel could see it was a poor collection of unrelated cards and of no value whatsoever, despite its ace.

The knifeman grunted. "If that's all you was holding, why were you raising the bid?"

"I was exercising my right to bluff, rather hoping that you had insufficient funds to see me for long, so that you would be forced to fold, and I would win the pot. A not unreasonable expectation, if I might say so, given that you have only one coin and a broken bottle stopper in front of you and do not, if you'll forgive me, have the appearance of a man carrying a large amount of money on his person."

This remark drew upon the bristly man unwelcome scrutiny from all present. He shifted uncomfortably in his ale-stained shirt and homespun jerkin. "You play an unfair advantage in that respect," he pointed out. "For while you wear the clothes of your office, how are we to know what manner of wealth you might possess, eh?"

This statement put Hans into the sort of mental dilemma Gretel knew he was ill equipped to deal with. On the one hand he had accused someone of playing false, of cheating. On the other, he himself was dressed as a clergyman, no doubt enjoying the small but important quarter that office afforded him, while he was not, never had been, nor was ever likely to be, an ordained priest.

Gretel hastened to steer the discourse back on to safer ground. "It would appear that the case is far from proven, and that there is no satisfactory way to find that proof."

The knifeman glared at her. "Has always been my experience that a sharp edge on a blade can prove a lot of things."

"But would you dull that edge upon a man of the church? That is not something I would wish on any man's conscience. Then again, you have your reputation to protect, I understand that."

"But . . ." Hans tried to protest but Gretel shut him up. He might be about to spill the beans about how he came by his attire, or wail on about the business of cheating. Either way could not bring about a happy resolution.

"It seems to me," she said calmly, "that you are both, despite your differing backgrounds, men who share a passion for the game. Men who enjoy the thrill and the challenge of the cards. Am I right?"

There came an assenting grunt from the knifeman and a squeak from Hans as a result of his trying to nod and piercing his own skin on the knife in doing so.

"As I thought. In which case, you both no doubt hold a grudging respect for the other's skills. There is, I venture to suggest, much you could learn from each other." She waited for this idea to permeate the dense skulls of those listening before continuing. "Hans, I feel certain you have already learned a lesson regarding the hazards of bandying about accusations of an inflammatory nature while among people of brief acquaintance. And you, sir, I suspect, are in fact curious as to how my brother has amassed such a large pile of money in front of him through his brief stint at your table, while you appear to have lost all of yours." There was another pause while the two considered what she had said. After a suitable hiatus she went on. "I recommend a course of action that could please all concerned. I suggest that the current pot on the table be divided equally between all five players," here she was forced to hold up a hand to quell oaths and curses, "so that the game may continue. And during that game, and for subsequent hands, that shared money be used so that Hans can impart his highly particular and effective knowledge to his fellow sharps, so that they too might, in future, enjoy similar success at the table."

"But, Gretel, what of professional secrets . . . ?" Hans started.

"Hans! Consider your current position! Very carefully."

In the end his reluctance was overcome and Hans set to tutoring the other card players. So beloved was the subject to him that he soon forgot what had brought him to this point, and was taken up with enthusiasm to impart all his wisdom and clever tactics. His unlikely students listened attentively.

Gretel and Ernst sat at a table a little way off and the chambermaid was persuaded to fetch them coffee and cakes. Once settled, Gretel was able to resume her questioning of the sorcerer, all the while keeping half an eye on her brother in case of another situation developing from which he would have to be extricated.

"Herr Arnold, it still will not sit right in my mind: why did you insist on plying the trade of magic when your true and notable gift was for bone setting and surgery? Surely there cannot be many physicians able to successfully remove their own appendix? Such skills would be in high demand, and would have earned you a good living."

Ernst dabbed at his lips with a napkin, carefully removing lebkuchen crumbs. His droopy sleeve dipped briefly into his coffee cup as he did so. "I had hoped to improve my work with magic, so that I could support my wife and I as easily that way."

"But why try?"

"There is more to the way a man earns a crust than the work involved, Fraulein. Surely you, as a professional of some standing, will acknowledge that?"

"I do."

"With every title, with each position within a society, come certain associations, certain expectations."

"I grant you that is the case, but I would not have considered sorcery to be a particularly, shall we say, estimable profession? Certainly not over and above that of a uniquely talented surgeon?"

"Ah, but in whose eyes?"

"Anyone's, I should imagine."

"But I am not concerned with anyone. I am concerned only with a certain one."

Gretel drained her coffee cup and frowned while she processed this statement. The only "one" that Ernst could possibly be referring to was his wife.

"Forgive me, Herr Arnold, but I suspect your wife's adoration for you would remain unchanged were you to take to collecting night waste to make your living."

"Darling Evalina would love me still, of course. But . . . there would always be that tiny speck of disappointment. And such irritations can, over time, grow to become intolerable."

"Surely a disappointment can only arise from a thwarted expectation. Only if Evalina had always anticipated marrying a sorcerer would she feel the lack thereof . . ." Gretel stopped. She experienced a joyful moment of things falling into place, of puzzle pieces slotting in where they should go, of reasons for and why fitting into their rightful positions in the case. "Of course! Evalina *had* always envisaged life as the spouse of a sorcerer. To begin with, that sorcerer would have been Otto Voigt."

At the mention of the Head Sorcerer's name Ernst's face darkened and his grip on his coffee cup tightened. "The post of leader of the Sorcerer's Circle carries such cachet."

"It does?"

"Certainly! It is the very pinnacle of our profession. The status, the title, the office itself . . . With it comes a standing in the community of practitioners of magic like no other. As the wife of such a man, all that went with it would have been Evalina's. By giving him up for me, she gave up much else besides."

"Full house!" came the knifeman's gleeful cry from the card table. The others made astonished and congratulatory noises.

Ernst frowned, pushing his plate away, his appetite quashed by thoughts of his rival.

Gretel said, "But give it up she did. And willingly, for she loves you then as she does now. She is not a merry widow, Herr Arnold. She is nursing a broken heart."

"And that thought wounds me as a knife to my own! But what choice did I have? I had so badly managed our money. However hard I studied and practiced I could not perform magic well, not reliably."

"And covering for all those mistakes was a costly business."

"It brought about my ruin. I had taken so much from my dearest wife, at least by appearing to be the victim of a murder she could claim on the insurance policy I had taken out. She will not want for money in the future."

"I fear you may be mistaken on that count. I am not here on her behalf alone, but also under the instructions of the insurers. They wished me to find proof of your death, or proof of your life."

He nodded sadly. "And Evalina? What did she wish for?"

"Your safe return, nothing more."

Tears brimmed in his eyes. "Alas, that is something more I cannot give to her, for if I were to return I would be arrested for fraud and made bankrupt and there would be no payment from the policy. She would face a lonely future, socially outcast, and destitute to boot. My poor darling!"

And with that he fell to quiet sobbing. Gretel signaled to the barman who had come to restock the bar, and he brought over a bottle of schnapps. Gretel poured a generous glug into Ernst's cup.

"All may not be as bleak as you imagine. Come, drink up. Let us remove Hans from his position as instructor as soon as possible and then return to your office. I shall need paper and ink. Can a trustworthy messenger be found?"

"He can. Do you have a plan, Fraulein?" Ernst asked, a tiny glimmer of hope appearing in his expression.

"Naturally, Herr Arnold. I am never without a plan."

It took a further hour for Hans to divest the greater part of his card playing knowledge to his pupils. As soon as he had finished, he and Gretel went back to the surgery with Ernst. Hans had sustained a flesh wound to his throat, so he sat and allowed the physician-sorcerer to tend to it for him.

Gretel took up a sheet of paper and set a quill to it, writing in her customarily haphazard hand. "This letter," she explained, "will go ahead of us, by way of introduction and to set in train what I hope will be a solution to the greater part of your problems, Herr Arnold. Indeed, it should secure a satisfactory outcome to the case for all concerned."

"To whom are you writing?" he asked.

"Allow me to keep that information to myself, for now," she said. She helped herself to sealing wax and used the handle of her lorgnettes to imprint upon the seal a mark that was unique to herself, and she trusted would be recognized as such. Next, she selected a smaller piece of paper and dashed off a note.

"This is for Cornelius," she explained. "I require him to meet us here an hour after darkness falls."

"Are we on the move again?" Hans asked. "Ouch! I say, that does smart a bit," he declared as Ernst applied something stringent and pungent to his injury.

"Don't make such a fuss, Hans," Gretel told him. "And yes, we will be departing very soon. Our presence in Baumhausdorf has become far too visible for our safety. Word of the detective and her card shark clergyman brother will have spread by now. We have remained unchallenged only, I suspect, because the residents are recovering from the excesses of last night. It is likely they will return to the bar tonight, and after a few jars of ale or schnapps they will be sufficiently stirred up to seek us out and demand answers. And whatever answers we were to give would not, I fear, satisfy them that we would keep the secret of their hideout. In which case . . ."

"Oh no, sister mine. Please do not finish that thought!"

"Calm yourself, Hans. We shall be long gone before that time comes. Herr Arnold, I recommend stout walking shoes and non-chafing breeches."

"Am I to come with you?"

"You are."

"But, Fraulein . . ."

Gretel stopped him with a raised hand and a commanding look. "Come you must, sir. It will profit none of us for you to resist what must be."

"You don't understand . . ."

"I understand perfectly. More than you do, in point of fact. Take the matter of the attacks upon myself and my brother."

"The attacks?"

"We came under assault on three occasions during our journey here, and I have reason to believe those attackers were your clients back in Gesternstadt. Why, one of them is even in this village. Frau Webber."

"The baker's wife? Here?"

"Yes and yes."

"I know nothing of any attacks or assaults, you have my word."

"I have more than that. I have logic and facts, and they point clearly in a direction that does not have you at its end."

Hans gave a little chuckle. "She does that, you know. Takes facts and whatnot and deduces things. Quite clever really."

"Thank you so much, Hans. The facts are these: the hapless victims of your blundering magic owe you no allegiance."

The sorcerer sighed. "I cannot disagree with that."

"What they all have in common—aside from a grievance against you—is the state of penury to which they have been reduced. Therefore, I concluded they acted for money. I thought at first you yourself might have paid them to prevent my finding you. The flaw in this postulation is that the want of money is at the very core of all that has driven you to your current situation. I quickly dismissed the theory that Evalina might have engaged them to search. First, she has no money, and second, she has engaged me, and rightly considers me to be the only person whose assistance she requires. There is only one other interested party in this case."

Ernst stared at her. "Otto!" he breathed.

"Precisely. He is, I'd wager a fair sum, pleased to be rid of you. I believe that he believes you to be living still, in which case he most definitely does not want me finding you." She paused as another thought occurred to her. "Tell me, did Herr Voigt know about your ability to numb pain?"

"Oh yes, he knew. He was quite jealous of it, in fact. I should have thought seeing me humiliated, prosecuted, and thrown in jail might have found favor with Otto."

"To some degree, yes, but he would rather you were dead than jailed. Oh, I don't think he would go as far as murdering you himself. It suits him very well that you have arranged for your own 'death.' If you were to be jailed your loyal wife would no doubt stand by you, visiting you frequently, and waiting stoically and faithfully for the day of your release. If you were dead, however, after a very necessary and sincere period of mourning . . ." Gretel tactfully left the sentence unfinished, wishing to spare the sorcerer's feelings, so that he might draw the obvious conclusion silently and privately.

Hans, alas, suffered no such inhibition.

"Evalina could marry another!" he declared, delighted at having been able to follow what was going on, for once.

Ernst sprang to his feet. "No! Otto will make his move! He will woo her while she is grieving and lonely!" He began to pace the room urgently. At last he stopped in front of Gretel.

"I must go to her," he said. "I cannot stay away, whatever the consequences."

"I had hoped you would see it that way."

"Take me with you this night, I beg you."

"You see? Cooperation and good sense and everything will go much more pleasantly for all concerned." She stood up and pressed the letter and the note into Hans's hand. "Take these. Ernst tells me the messenger is to be found at the end of main street. They are addressed and directions given upon them. Give him this," here she handed him a somewhat crumpled note of money, "tell him he will receive the same again after they are both delivered successfully. His trustworthiness and speed will earn him double if no one discovers our plans."

"Consider it done," Hans said, turning to leave.

"Come back here directly you have run that errand, Hans. I will send to the guest house for our things. Herr Arnold, pack a bag if you must."

"We are to return to Gesternstadt?" he asked.

"Ultimately, yes. But in the first instance no. In order for things to work out in your favor you will have to place your trust in me, Herr Arnold, for we must first make all haste and get ourselves without delay to the Summer Schloss!"

EIGHTEEN

They formed a curious and unhelpfully noticeable trio when later Gretel, Hans, and Ernst made their way along the wooden main street under cover of darkness. Even in the gloom, with the feeble glow of the few lamps that were hung up to illuminate the walkway, they still looked out of place, somehow: a large woman in a flamboyant gown and heavy boots; an even larger vicar with a backpack and sporting a small cut to his throat and the remnants of a black eye; and a physician-dressed-as-a-sorcerer, a diminutive bat flying at his shoulder. Nevertheless, Gretel had been right about the likely habits of the residents of Baumhausdorf, and they were able to make their way to the wooden lift unseen. They climbed aboard and Gretel called down to the brawny youth below.

"Lower away, if you please."

He did so, his sizeable muscles powering arms that had no difficulty turning the handle that worked the winch. The cage came to a thudding stop at ground level, but he did not immediately move to open the door.

"Thank you, young man. If you would be so kind as to let us out . . . ?" Gretel asked.

He shook his head.

Herr Arnold fidgeted. "It's rather cramped in here. What is the delay?"

Hans tried to shift over to give the sorcerer a little room, but there was really nowhere to shift to.

"Come along," Gretel spoke in what she hoped was a firm but friendly way. She dare not raise her voice for fear of being discovered by somebody up top, but the longer they stayed in the village, the greater their chances of never being allowed to leave it. "Open up, there's a good fellow."

Again the silent youth shook his head and made a cryptic gesture.

"He wants something," Hans observed.

"What would I do without you?" Gretel asked her brother with a chilly smile.

At that moment Cornelius arrived on silent footfalls. "Is there a problem?" he asked.

"He wants something," Hans repeated.

Cornelius entered into an exchange of gestures and signals with the lift attendant that ended with both of them smiling.

"He wants to see another card trick!" Cornelius explained. "He enjoyed the first one so much, that's his fee for working the lift."

Hans grabbed the opportunity to look smug, for such chances rarely came his way. "Oh, see, Gretel? He wants something!"

She bundled her brother to the fore of the cage and he took his cards from his rucksack. "Choose a short one," she urged him. "We are not yet out of harm's way."

Hans tutted at her, as if she were asking him to rush the painting of a masterpiece, but his fear of being caught was greater than his pride, so he heeded her words. With a sleight of hand that impressed even the sorcerer, he performed a neat little trick that had the desired effect of the young man, who promptly unlatched the cage door and waved them a smiling farewell.

Cornelius was all fresh-faced energy and sensible clothing. He did not question what might have occurred to necessitate a moonlit flit, nor did he comment upon their choice of outfits, and Gretel found she liked him all the more for these small but helpful things. The man was built entirely of the practical, his every bone and muscle existing only to work and work well, but he had at his core a soul with a greater love for mankind, and therefore a tolerance of it, than Gretel could ever hope to possess.

They walked on in silence, save for curses and exclamations uttered sotto voce when one or other of them stumbled into something painful in the dark. The path was reasonably clear beneath a helpful moon, and Cornelius furnished them each with a slow-burning stick for a torch. Despite these assistances, the way seemed strewn with things intent of delivering scratches and bruises at every turn. After two hours, Gretel called a halt. Cornelius led them off the track and found a secluded glade suitable for stringing the hammocks. They could not risk a fire in case a search party came after them. They ate cold sausage and black bread, drank a little ale, and then hauled themselves into their respective sleeping slings. Gretel did not sleep well. Whatever she recalled of the silence of the forest from their inward journey, it now seemed a place jammed full of alarming noises and disturbing sounds. Was that a fox or a wolf calling a way off? Does an owl really sound like that? How many and how large are the creatures that scuttle and scamper about in the dark? She shut her eyes, her ears, and her mind as best she could and chased sleep until a shiny dawn heralded another day.

Breakfasting as they walked, the party struck out again. With both the map and Ernst to guide them, there was less chance of getting lost, and the continuing warm weather devoid of thunderstorms now made the going reasonable. Hans was just starting to mutter about it being time for a proper meal of some sort, and surely they were far enough from the village to risk a fire, when Cornelius held up a hand to stop them.

"That's strange," he said. "I'm certain those weren't there a few days ago."

The others crowded forward to see what it was that perplexed him. In front of them, in a neat line along the side of the path, were four wooden boards, each nailed to a tree. They were similar in shape and size, with small variations, and appeared to be of polished wood, rather than something roughly hewn from the forest.

"Quite quaint," said Hans, stepping forward to run his hand down one of them. "They've no carvings or inscriptions I can see, but they are nicely made."

"What are they for?" Ernst wondered aloud, moving to see for himself.

Cornelius dropped to the ground, investigating the forest floor, searching for footprints and clues as to who had put these peculiar wooden items in this remote spot. He ran his fingers over the damp soil and trampled twigs and leaves.

"Very recent," he nodded before raising his head to peer down the path ahead. "Whoever put these here has only just done so."

"I know what they are," Gretel said levelly. "I have never seen one before, but I have read about them." She too stepped up to take a closer look. "Yes, the right length, neatly lathed wood, polished." She sniffed. "Beeswax."

Hans scratched his hat, which he had reclaimed and insisted on wearing despite it not entirely going with his clerical ensemble. "But why on earth would anyone be polishing bits of wood in a wood? I mean to say, once you start that sort of caper, where would you stop?" He took in the entire forest with a sweep of his arm.

"They have a highly specific use," Gretel explained, "and are always, to my knowledge, made with a fair amount of care. Out of respect for the dead."

"Dead?" chorused Hans and Ernst, striking a querulous note.

"They are *Totenbretter*. Death boards. The tradition predates the use of coffins or caskets," she told them. "The deceased would be placed upon these boards and kept at home for a few days so that all with an inclination to do so could pay their final respects. Sometimes the boards were buried with the corpses, sometimes they were used again, other times they would be taken back to a place the dead person used to frequent. As this region has always been full of woods and those who made their livings from the forests, the boards were often nailed to trees, or set beside a pathway, or both, as in this case. The idea was that they took something of that person back to that place, and that as they disintegrated, just as the body decomposed, they returned to their natural state."

There was an uncomfortable silence while everyone contemplated decomposing.

At last Ernst spoke up. "I've certainly never seen them here before, and I have made this journey many times."

"Oh look!" said Hans, bending down to peer more closely at the Totenbretter nearest to him. "This one *has* got something carved on it. Well, more scratched than carved really. A bit hard to read . . . let me see . . . *d* . . . is it? Yes . . . *d* something . . . *t* . . . hmm, hard to read this bit . . . ah, *v*, yes, definitely a *v* . . . then there's a bit of a gap, so second word—I say, isn't this like charades?—begins with . . . *G* . . . a capital letter. After that, an *r*, I believe, then something, something . . . finishes *el*." He straightened up, his face scrunched with the effort of trying to work out what was written. Suddenly he beamed. "I have it! *Definitively Gruel*!" He announced, tremendously pleased with himself. "Fancy that, *Definitively Gruel*. Curious, but there it is." He turned to find three pale faces regarding him, his sister's the palest of them all.

"I rather think it is not," she said, "a food-based inscription."

"Not?" Hans queried.

Ernst swallowed hard. "I fear it is a name. Yes, I can see it now . . . *Detective Gretel*."

Hans's mouth opened and shut as if his jaw were being worked by an unseen puppeteer. He made no sound, save a thin wail when Ernst went on to point out that there were three more boards, and three more of them. A nervous search showed up no more inscriptions, but nonetheless the idea had taken hold. These were boards for conveying the dead, and someone had thoughtfully provided one for each of them.

"Come along," Gretel struck off down the path again. "There is nothing to be gained by dallying here."

"But, Gretel . . ." Hans trotted after her. "Cornelius said the person who put them here must be quite near. Should we not proceed with extreme caution? Or perhaps, not proceed at all?"

"That is presumably what somebody wants, Hans. I am not about to give in to threats, however creative. We go on! Cornelius, if you would be so good as to take point duty?"

"Of course," said Cornelius, bounding fearlessly ahead.

And so they continued on their way. The forest seemed to have taken on a darker, more sinister aspect now, so that shadows were jagged and the sounds sharp. The little party did not chatter, nor did they graze upon snacks, but instead kept watchful eyes, squinting into the gloomy corners and sunless patches beneath the trees, turning toward unfamiliar noises, alert now for an unknown danger. They paused only briefly halfway through the day in order to feed, and then moved on again, the mood of the group, with the exception of the indomitable Cornelius, somber. Gretel found herself more peeved than scared. She was tiring of being on the receiving end of assaults and tricks and jibes. Having one's nerves jangled for days at a time brought on the manner of exhaustion that took all the color out of life. The sooner they reached the Summer Schloss and she could put her plan into the next stage of action, the happier she would be.

That night it was decided they were far enough from the village to risk a fire. Gretel deemed it a necessity to keep them safe, provide some hot food, and raise morale. When she said as much Cornelius patted her arm, delighted.

An hour later, the fire burning brightly, a meal eaten, and a little more ale imbibed, it was decided a watch should be set, and Gretel elected to take the first shift. While the others slumbered in their hammocks, she sat on a log, poking the embers and low flames of the campfire with a long stick, letting her eyes lose their focus as she stared at the flaring tongues of fire. There was something so very hypnotic about the tiny, flickering orange heart to each one, with its flashes of scarlet and gold leaping to sparks that jumped upward to burn for an instant before melting into the night sky. Gretel shifted her position slightly, leaning back against Hans's rucksack. It had been a testing few days. She was deeply relieved to think that the end of the case was in sight. All she had to do was reach the royal castle, see through her plan to bring about the restoration of Ernst's finances and reputation, take her large and well-earned fee from the insurance company, and return to the relative comforts of her own little home. Not far now, she told herself, not many miles to go, nor many days to tolerate the privations of forest life or the annoyances of people attempting to undo what she was attempting to do. She dropped her stick into the fire and watched the flames consume it. She allowed her eyes to close and her head to loll forward just for a moment, just for an instant, for the watch was hers, and she must not, on any account, allow herself to fall asleep.

※

The first thing Gretel became aware of as she woke up two hours later was the unusual timbre of Hans's snore. Over the years she had become accustomed to the rattling in-breath, the wheezing tremor while it was held, and the puffing, flappy-lipped outpouring of the used-up air. While it was irritating, there was comfort to be had in its familiarity, like the creaking sign of the inn across the street when the wind blew from the southwest, or the *squeak-squerk* of the milkmaid's barrow wheels as she made her early morning deliveries. So it was with a vague sense of something being not quite as it should be that Gretel came to, for the familiar note of the snore had changed and the pitch altered, replaced with a deep, sustained rumble.

The second thing that struck her was that her eyelids were no longer working. Or at least, that seemed to be the case, as, though she thought she had lifted them, she could discern not the faintest chink of light. She rubbed her eyes, sitting up stiffly, and came to realize that they were indeed open, but clouds were obscuring the moon, and there was no light at all from the fire because it had gone out.

"Oh, dung heaps!" she whispered crossly to herself, annoyed at her own stupidity at letting the vital campfire die, as well as falling asleep when she should not have. In fact, judging by the complete out-ness of the fire, she had been asleep some time, and indeed someone else should have taken over the watch, so she was annoyed with them too. She groped inside the rucksack, searching for Hans's lighter, for she was in no mood to attempt using a flint and bits of dry moss to restart the fire. She emptied the entire contents of the bag, but there was no lighter to be found. Deciding that Hans must have it in his pocket she crawled over to where she knew his hammock was strung. She noticed that this seemed to be in the opposite direction from the sound of his snore, which made little sense. But there was the trunk of one of the sturdy trees holding up his hammock, and there was the actual hammock with his actual self in it. Gretel fumbled in what pockets she could find. Hans snorted and gave a small shout of query, but otherwise remained undisturbed by having his person searched.

"Got it!" Gretel declared to the night. She stepped away from Hans and tried to get the thing to light. This required her to flick open the lid and then smartly strike the small wheel at the top with her thumb to produce a spark that in turn would light the oil inside. After a couple of false starts, a spark did appear, though it did not catch the fuel. She tried again, spinning the little wheel more rapidly. Several sparks were produced. As she was busy working the uncooperative device, Gretel became aware that Hans's snore, which was not after all coming from Hans but from a few strides off to her left, was moving a little closer. She did not have time to become unsettled by this fact, because it was only as she noticed it that the fleeting light of the sparks appeared to illuminate an object, large and heavy, that must, in fact, be responsible for the snore. Before she had the chance to react to this revelation, her thumb at last struck a successful blow to the lighter, and the fuel caught. She stood clutching the device, her thumb holding down the lever that fed the flame, finding herself immobilized by the sight that was now shown to her. In the uneven glow, there, not more than a stride from her, stood a large, gray, shaggy wolf, emitting a steady, sonorous, guttural growl.

❈

The combination of shock and terror can bring about a variety of responses. The person who is shocked and terrified might turn and run, screaming all the while, heedless of the wisdom of their actions. Another might take their courage in both hands and fling themselves with a battle cry at the cause of their alarm. Yet another might freeze, as if spellbound, standing unable to so much as utter a cry or raise a hand to defend herself. If anyone had ever asked Gretel what her reaction might have been to finding herself face to face with a hungry-looking wolf in the middle of the forest in the middle of the night, she might have chosen the first of these options as her most likely response. But nobody had ever asked her, and she had never given any proper thought to the situation arising. Whether such a dinner table discussion would have helped prepare her for the event, she would never know. All she could do was allow her instinct for survival—which was large and well-developed—to spring to the fore.

"Wolf!!" she bellowed at the top of her not-inconsiderable voice. "Wolf! Wolf! Wolf!"

Her fellow campers, so abruptly roused from their sleep in their hammocks, leaped into action.

That is to say, Cornelius leapt, Ernst fell, and Hans did his best to sit up.

Gretel had to keep flicking the lighter to create a flame, so that the wolf was glimpsed in a series of terrifying, frozen, split-second images. This staccato illumination made Gretel feel as if she were witnessing some sort of traveling sideshow where all movements are jerky and sudden. As she continued her frantic flicking, she saw Cornelius caught mid-leap in the light; the wolf caught mid-snarl; Ernst caught mid-stumble; Cornelius again, arms low and wide, crouching; the wolf opening its terrible jaws; Ernst scrambling toward the nearest tree; Hans still trying to sit up; Cornelius circling the wolf; the wolf crouching and circling also.

"Ouch!" Gretel yelped as the lighter grew so hot it burned her fingers and she dropped it, removing the only light Cornelius had to help him battle the snarling beast. She dropped to her knees, searching frantically through the leaves and vines on the ground. Dreadful sounds came from the wolf as its growling grew ever more threatening.

"I have it!" Gretel cried as her hand found the lighter. Still on her knees she flicked it again and again. During her search she had moved close to Hans's hammock, and in her haste to work the lighter she managed to set the flame to the fabric, which caught fire with startling ease.

Hans gave a yelp and pitched out, landing heavily, winded, and unable to run. The blazing hammock lit up the campsite. To her horror, Gretel saw that the wolf had Cornelius backed up to a tree and was advancing upon him. She looked around for a branch to set ablaze from the flaming hammock so that she could run at the wolf, but none came to hand.

"Herr Arnold!" she yelled, "for pity's sake do something!"

From his perch on a low branch of a chestnut tree Ernst gave a wavering reply and then started muttering and stirring the air with one hand. Too late Gretel realized he was about to resort to using some of his magic to intervene. She opened her mouth to stop him, but even as she did so a flash of green light bounced past her and enveloped the wolf. The creature did at least pause in its pursuit of Cornelius, which gave him the chance to spring past it, back to the relative safety of the hammock fire. The wolf appeared to pulsate and wobble, and as they watched, both appalled and in awe, it began to shrink. It reduced from a large predator to a medium-sized hound and then a pocket-sized pooch before their very eyes. Alas, whatever magic Ernst had conjured was, true to his previous form, catastrophically flawed. For no sooner had the wolf shrunk to harmless dimensions than it pulsed some more and began to grow again. It grew, back past hound, beyond wolf, and into something nearer the weight and scale of a well-fed cart horse. Its teeth now doubled in size, its body all muscle and violent intentions, it turned to face the group and began to advance once more upon what it clearly regarded as supper.

"Whoops," said the sorcerer quietly from the safety of his tree.

"Don't run," Cornelius warned them.

In truth, there was little danger of this happening. Ernst was in a tree, Hans was still nose-down on the forest floor, and Gretel was on her knees.

"Hold your ground," Cornelius instructed.

This seemed a more realistic proposition.

"We need something to scare him off," Cornelius went on. "Something to get the fire closer to him!"

"There aren't any sticks," Gretel said. "I've searched, there's nothing."

The wolf dropped its shoulders lower and continued to creep closer. It was then that Jynx reappeared. The doughty little bat dispensed with swooping and directly dive-bombed instead, scratching at the wolf's nose. The wolf raised its head to snap at its assailant. Gretel seized the moment. She snatched Hans's hat from his head, wiped it through the flames of the hammock so that it too caught fire, and then ran at the wolf with it, screaming like a banshee.

The wolf had evidently never been attacked by a fierce Bavarian detective with a flaming Bavarian hat and had not a notion of how to defend itself. Instinct kicked in, and the bewildered animal spun around on its great back paws and bounded away through the forest. Gretel was forced to drop the hat and set about stamping upon it in an effort to extinguish the flames. Cornelius dashed away and fetched an armful of kindling so that the fire could be relit with the remnants of the hammock. Ernst slowly descended from the tree.

"Herr Arnold," Gretel spoke with a calmness she did not feel, as her heart, currently performing some version of a tarantella, was a long way from settling to its more usual waltzing rhythm, "should there be another occasion in which we come under attack, kindly refrain from employing your magic as a means of defense."

"I was only trying to help," he said.

"Well, don't."

Hans had at last rolled over and regained his breath and his voice.

"I say! What happened to my hat?" He asked, picking up the charred remains and forlornly turning them over in his hands.

⁂

They sat up until dawn, keeping close to the fire, none of them able to contemplate sleep. When day broke Cornelius kicked earth over the embers and the group packed up and moved on, Hans mumbling sadly all the while about the loss of his hat.

"That was very unusual," Cornelius said to Gretel as they walked.

198

She shot him a glance to see if he was trying to be funny but his face seemed serious enough.

"I don't mean the wolf . . . changing like that," he explained upon seeing her expression. "I mean that it was on its own. It's just not how wolves behave. Where was the rest of the pack? Why did it try to attack such a large group? And why was the fire so completely out?"

"Ah, yes, that . . . ." Gretel began.

"It didn't just burn up all the wood and go out," Cornelius went on. "Somebody put it out. And I suspect somebody put that wolf onto us too."

"Like the three boars, you mean?" Gretel asked.

He nodded.

Ernst piped up. "I believe someone is practicing magic close by. I know you think I don't know anything about being a sorcerer . . ." Here he paused in the expectation that someone might protest against this being the case. No one did, so he continued, ". . . but someone near us is casting spells. I'm certain of it."

"All the more reason for us to keep moving," Gretel said. "Another few hours of this and we should be free of this wretched forest and in sight of the Summer Schloss. A moment that cannot come soon enough for me."

They rounded the next bend and came to a sudden stop.

"Oof!" said Hans, bumping into the back of Gretel. "What now?"

When he stepped to one side and looked up ahead he saw only too well what. The path they had been following, the one clearly marked on Ernst's map, was no longer the simple, single, slightly twisting track it always had been. Now it split into six versions of itself. Each path looked equally firm, equally possible, equally sensible, but only one could be real.

"None of this matches the map," Gretel said.

Cornelius shook his head slowly. "Something's not right here. Those trees shouldn't grow like that, all leaning up against each other and not reaching the daylight properly. It's almost as if they've been reordered, somehow. Repositioned."

"Huh!" said Hans. "You'd have to know how to do magic to shift that bunch around."

Ernst puffed himself up a little and gave a knowing look. Gretel parried it with a glance of her own that warned him against any I-told-you-sos.

"There is deception afoot here, Herr Arnold," she grudgingly admitted. "Your sorcerer's antennae might not have been mistaken after all. Someone is playing tricks on us."

"But who?" Hans asked.

"I suspect Otto Voigt," said Gretel.

"But why?" Hans asked.

"He has not yet given up hope of preventing his rival's return to Gesternstadt."

"But how?" Hans asked.

"First the wolf, now this, who knows what he will try next."

Ernst said, "He is trying to scare us."

"He's succeeding," Hans said.

Cornelius added, "And now he's trying to get us hopelessly lost."

"Not doing badly with that either," Hans said.

Gretel scowled at her brother. "If you have nothing helpful to add, for pity's sake be quiet." She took out the dog-eared map and consulted it once more.

Cornelius read it over her shoulder and put a reassuring hand on her arm. "When a map and a route fail to match up, it's time to stop relying on it. We have to use something more dependable."

"Such as?" Gretel wanted to know.

"That," he said, pointing up at the sun. "It is very simple."

There followed ten minutes where Cornelius talked a lot and the others listened. He hopped about collecting this twig and that stick, clearing a space on the ground, positioning stick 1 at a certain angle from stick 2, stepping out the optimum distance between the two, jabbering on about the trajectory of the sun from east to west, its point at midday, the shadows thereafter, along with the position of their destination, and how a reading of the line of shade, and its angle between the two special sticks would indicate the direction in which they should proceed.

By the time he had finished explaining his theory he was a little breathless, Ernst was shaking his head in astonishment, Gretel had a headache, and Hans had fallen asleep standing up.

"We need to go this way," Cornelius said at last, and the weary group moved off once again.

They walked on and on, Gretel forbidding anyone to rest, ignoring Hans's plaintive words, turning her mind from her own blisters and aching limbs. She refused to let anyone or anything stop them.

"We will continue until we are free of these woods once and for all," she declared, marching forward. She led the way, though they had to stop for Cornelius's specialist navigational skills more than once, and though her feet were screaming for respite. At last, just when she thought she could go no farther, the trees began to thin out. The path widened. Where before there had been ivy and brambles, now grass and wildflowers grew. Larch and spruce disappeared, replaced by oak and birch, and even these became fewer and farther between. Finally, stumbling and sore, Gretel led them from the forest and out into the gentle dusk as it fell upon the high meadows. And there, across the valley, set grandly upon its rocky outcrop, stood the undeniably splendid but faintly ridiculous Summer Schloss.

NINETEEN

When they came within a mile of the castle, Cornelius turned to Gretel. "Well, this is as far as I go with you. It's been a pleasure to share your time in the forest . . ."

"Herr Staunch, your help has been invaluable."

Hans looked almost tearful. "Are you leaving us? Not coming to the Schloss, then?"

"Not this time, Hans. I've promised to take a family gorge walking and whitewater rafting. They're counting on me; can't let them down."

Hands were warmly shaken all around.

Gretel assured him the moment she received payment for the case she would send him his fee.

"We could not have managed without your assistance," she told him.

Cornelius shrugged. "Once you learn the skills you need to survive, it's simple really."

"Your contribution went well beyond the practical," she insisted, thinking again of his patience with Hans and his touching care for the welfare of the whole party.

Cornelius smiled, a bright-eyed, youthful smile full of the love of life and zest for adventure. "If you ever want to climb an Alp, or experience the wonders of the desert . . ."

"I promise you will be the first to know."

They watched him stride away, all waving when he turned to raise his hand in farewell before the path twisted and he was lost from sight. Gretel heard a heavy sigh escape Hans.

"Come along," she said. "There is much to be done to bring this case to a satisfactory conclusion."

"I was rather afraid of that," said Ernst.

"Me too," said Hans.

"Do not be daunted," Gretel said, trying for a bit of Cornelius's morale-boosting, "we go to a place with comfortable chairs, hot water, excellent wine, and fine food. Let that draw us on."

It was good to be free of the woods at last. Only Jynx found the daylight too strong, so that he sought refuge in the sorcerer's capacious sleeve for the remainder of the journey. Everyone else, however, felt their spirits lift. The sun beating on their heads was a novelty rather than an irritation, and the brightness and blueness of the sky was cheerful. The white castle gleamed beneath the summer sun, its myriad turrets and spires, its numerous balconies, its countless windows, all sparkling and beautiful as the day itself. However much the Summer Schloss might stand as a monument to man's vanity and foolishness, it could not help but impress and delight any who looked upon it, whether for the first time or the hundredth.

As they walked, Gretel allowed herself to entertain optimistic notions about how their time at the Summer Schloss might go. She had sent word to Ferdinand telling him of their imminent arrival and taking him in some small part into her confidence, though leaving much for them to discuss. She was confident she would be well received by him, but knew she had a task ahead of her if she was to convince King Julian—or more accurately, Queen Beatrice—of her idea.

She glanced sideways at Herr Arnold. He was still dressed in the robes and droopy-sleeved purple garments of a sorcerer, and he looked like a man worn down by the woes of the world. He had not bathed nor shaved for three nights now, and it showed. It was worrying, therefore, to think that so much of the success of Gretel's plan rested on his fatigued shoulders. Looking at herself and Hans she was further depressed to realize how ragtag they all looked. Her indecorous garment was hardly suitable for an audience with royalty, and Hans was still dressed as a clergyman. There was little to be done about it, however. She would simply have to rise above these disadvantages and trust to her own ability to put forward a convincing argument. That and Ferdinand's affection for her. On that matter, she was less confident than she might have been but a few weeks earlier. He was now affianced. Perhaps he might not wish to be reminded that there existed a frisson between the two of them. Certainly, one would think, his fiancée might not wish to learn of it.

It was as Gretel was mulling over all the obstacles between her and success that a detachment of the King's Guard appeared at the top of the path, galloping out to meet them. Either they had been sent as an escort by Ferdinand, or . . .

"In the name of King Julian, halt!" screamed the sergeant at arms.

Gretel sighed. This was not her first encounter with the shouty, bumptious officer. He was not, she recalled, an easy man to deal with.

"Good morning to you, sergeant," she called to him, raising her voice to make herself heard above the hoofbeats of the prancing horses as they circled around them, the jangling of the bits and bridles, and the clanging of the somewhat excessive amounts of weaponry the soldiers were equipped with.

"Who approaches the castle of King Julian the Mighty unannounced and without invitation?!" the sergeant demanded. Loudly.

"You are correct in as much as we do lack an official invitation. However, our arrival is not unannounced, as I have written to Uber General Ferdinand von Ferdinand to inform him of our visit. My name is Fraulein Gretel—Detective Gretel—of Gesternstadt, and I am expected."

This gave the officer pause. He could never be seen to contradict his commanding officer. However, he had evidently not been apprised of the fact that these visitors were expected. To admit this fact might make him seem less than vital in the Uber General's life. But should he be so easily convinced by the word of a civilian? Particularly one with whom his previous dealings had been difficult? To be made a fool of by someone so apparently unimportant and downright shabby would be to make himself the laughingstock of the regiment. Then again, if he did not treat a guest of the Uber General's with the proper respect, all prospect of advancement in his career would vanish.

"You will all come with us!" he bellowed. He gestured at his men, who formed a ring of iron and rattling steel around the hapless trio. In this way they proceeded toward the castle, the horses fidgeting against the painfully slow pace at which they were forced to travel.

Gretel was relieved that she'd been able to win the albeit reluctant cooperation of the sergeant. However, her relief was short lived, as when they reached the castle they were not taken to a grand reception room, nor even to Ferdinand's quarters. Instead they were bundled through a lowly rear entrance, marched down a series of corridors and stone stairs, and ultimately shown into a bare room. Indeed, it was made entirely of bareness. The stones of the walls were exposed and unadorned; the flagstones upon the floor were bare of rug, carpet, or even straw; the bars that latticed the small window were bare, being free of drapes or shutters; the wooden bench held not a single cushion to relieve its own bareness. When their escort left the room, slamming the heavy, featureless door, and the sound of the key turning in the lock echoed around their drab room, Gretel could barely contain her fury.

"For heaven's sake!" she hissed beneath her breath.

"Never mind," Ernst sought to pour oil on troubled waters, "we have reached our destination, have we not? I'm sure we will be more cordially received once it is understood why we are here, Fraulein Gretel. In the meantime, we can take our ease."

Hans let loose a *Ha!* before dramatically pressing his arms against his sides as if squeezing into a tight space. "Alas, I cannot take my ease, so overwhelmed am I by all the *comfortable chairs, hot water, excellent wine, and fine food!*" He added another bark of mirthless laughter before pointedly turning his back on his sister, choosing to stare at the wall rather than look at her.

Gretel was forced to rein in her own ire. Hans was rarely pushed to the limits of his temper, but when he was a concrete stubbornness set in. Gretel recognized the signs. It would take a deal of gentle cajoling to bring him out of this state, and if there was any hope of their situation improving she needed him to at least do nothing to make things worse.

"Come, come, let us not fall into despair. The sergeant is merely being thorough. It is his job to protect the castle and the royal family . . ."

"Oh, well," Hans retorted without troubling himself to turn around, "it is entirely reasonable then that he should throw three unarmed, travel-weary local people into a cell, as we do present such a threat!"

Gretel told him as patiently as she could that this was not, in fact, a cell, and that she was only too well acquainted with the accommodation true villains and ne'er-do-wells were thrown into at the Schloss, and that therefore they clearly were not considered properly criminal. She then turned her attention to the sorcerer.

"Herr Arnold, soon it will be down to you to act; you will only get one chance. Are you ready?"

"I hope so, that is, I'm sure I will be. Can you tell me again exactly what it is you want me to do?" he asked, his face paling a little.

"If the king is still suffering from his injury, which I am confident he will be, given the quacks he keeps around him who call themselves physicians, you are well placed to earn yourself a pardon for your crimes. Without that, you can forget returning to Evalina and picking up the threads of your life, so for pity's sake, do pull yourself together."

"Of course," he nodded, straightening up a little and mustering a determined expression.

"Better," Gretel told him. "Now, the idea is this. I will put your case before the king, painting the whole sorry business of your failed magic, covering up your ineptitude, and attempting to defraud the insurance company of a large sum of money, in as flattering a light as I am able. After that, I shall extol your skills as a surgeon and physician, and advise the king that he could find no one better to mend his painful foot."

"Will he listen? Will he allow me to treat him, d'you think?"

"The king himself is not difficult to persuade of anything, providing you can make yourself heard." Gretel experienced an uncomfortable memory of a recent encounter with the king's deafness coupled with the overreacting tendencies of his aides and guards. "No, he will be the least of our challenges. Our greatest task will be to convince Queen Beatrice that you are a suitable and safe person to let loose on her husband. You will need to appear as sensible and serious as you have ever done in your life, Herr Arnold, make no mistake."

"I understand."

"I will bring the discussion around to the pain the king is experiencing, and this will be your cue. We do not know the precise circumstances in which we will be speaking, nor who will be present. It may be that I have to take . . . extreme measures to steer the discourse in the direction that suits our purposes. You must attend to my every word."

"I shall!"

"Watch me closely, and wait for my signal. Let us say there will be a special word." She thought for a moment, searching for something that would trigger a response in Ernst. "I have it! Jynx."

"My little friend!" exclaimed the sorcerer, peering up his sleeve to smile at the sleeping bat.

"Quite so. When you hear that word, step forward and apply your spell for quelling pain."

"As soon as I hear that word, yes."

"What is more, you are to use only—and I stress, ONLY—the spell you work for the benumbing of pain. Nothing more."

"Of course, yes."

"This is of the utmost importance. No other magic *at all.* Do I make myself clear on that point?"

"Perfectly."

"Good. Once you have removed the pain from the royal foot, it is my belief that all present will be impressed, and the king himself will be so relieved, that you will be allowed to proceed with your treatment as a physician and set the bones. I will bargain your skills against a pardon for you."

"Fraulein," the sorcerer began to look a little tearful and took hold of Gretel's hand. "I cannot thank you enough for helping me like this. To think that all might yet be put right, and that I might be permitted to return to my darling Evalina . . . well, I shall be forever in your debt!"

"On the subject of which, we must also extract something of a fee from the royal purse, so that you might set your finances straight once and for all. There are those who will demand recompense yet for your calamitous magic."

"You think of everything!" he exclaimed. "But tell me, if Evalina is unable to claim on the insurance policy because I am living still, how will we be able to also pay the fee you have so diligently earned and so greatly deserve? It is a matter that preys on my mind, Fraulein, for I cannot see such devotion to duty, such hard work, such care go unrewarded, and yet I am at a loss to see how I might pay you your due."

Gretel hesitated. She wanted to tell the sorcerer not to concern himself with this problem, but to explain why she was not concerned would mean revealing to him that, aside from taking his wife's instructions, she had taken on the case on behalf of the insurance company too. She knew they would pay her when she provided proof of Herr Arnold's existence, and given how things had turned out, it was as well she had had the foresight and perspicacity to hedge her bets in the way that she had. However, she could not rid herself of the sense that she had backed both boxers in the same ring. There was something a little unseemly, or perhaps lacking honesty, in working on a case where she would be paid if the missing man were alive, and paid by someone else if he were dead. Put so plainly, her position smacked of overriding self-interest. She preferred to think of it as astute business acumen, but even so . . .

"Do not concern yourself with my fee, Herr Arnold," she said at last. "It is enough for you to know that I will be paid, but that I will not press yourself for that payment."

Ernst did not have the chance to question her further as brisk footsteps interrupted their conversation. A key was turned in the lock once more. The hefty door was pushed open. And there stood Ferdinand. He looked every bit as attractive and manly and handsomely turned out as ever, which stirred within Gretel a complicated mixture of feelings. She did her best not to let any of them show.

Ferdinand stepped into the room and bowed low, his manner formal yet cordial.

"Fraulein Gretel, I beg your forgiveness. My sergeant is known for his zeal, which is sometimes misplaced."

Gretel allowed him to kiss her hand, then wished she hadn't when she noticed how grimy her fingernails were. Ever the perfect gentleman, if Ferdinand noticed he gave no indication of having done so.

"Your man is to be congratulated for carrying out his duties so conscientiously," she said. "We have suffered no ill treatment."

From Hans there came a small noise of dissent that everyone was able to ignore.

Ferdinand offered Gretel his arm. "Please allow me to escort you to more suitable rooms. I imagine you are all fatigued from your journey . . ."

"Indeed we are!" Hans put in.

". . . and would welcome the opportunity to take some refreshment and perhaps bathe," he said, tactfully not sniffing or looking at their clothes while he spoke.

"If I might trouble you for a change of clothing, Herr Uber General?" Gretel asked, taking care to address him in a businesslike manner. "As I indicated in my letter, I require an audience with His Majesty, and we are none of us currently in a fit state . . ."

"I will have the housekeeper find something more suitable," he assured her. "Now, perhaps you would give me a little more detail regarding your plan?"

Gretel took his arm. "Of course," she replied as she let him lead her out of the horrid room and up toward the more pleasant areas of the castle. "But first, tell me, how fares the king? The injury he sustained while out hunting, has it healed? Is he recovered completely?"

"Sadly, it has not, and King Julian still suffers greatly."

"Ah!" Gretel exclaimed, failing to keep the triumphant note out of her voice. Two of the attendant guards and Ferdinand himself looked at her incredulously. "I mean to say, *ahh*, such a pity. It breaks my heart to think of our noble ruler suffering at all. Is it very bad?"

"Our physicians have made him comfortable while he is abed. However, the moment His Majesty tries to move," here Ferdinand shook his head with genuine sadness, "well, then I am sorry to say the king experiences terrible pain that no one has yet successfully rid him of. And the broken bones in his foot are reluctant to heal."

"Fear not, for I bring with me one who can effect a swift and painless cure."

Ferdinand looked from Hans to Ernst and back again, evidently unconvinced by the possible candidates for this important task.

"Fraulein, as ever I trust your judgment, but . . ."

"I ask for that trust to continue, Herr Uber General. It is not misplaced. I know well that your loyalty to the king is beyond question and that nothing would please you more than to see him cured. I promise you, all will be well."

They walked on through numerous grand rooms and halls, each with more marble, more gilt, more of everything that gleamed and glittered.

"There are rooms close by the main entrance that you may use. It is but a short walk then to His Majesty's bedchamber. It is where he is currently receiving all visitors, as it is more comfortable for him to do so." Here he indicated a grandly columned doorway to their right. "While you prepare yourselves I will inform the King and Queen of your arrival and your offer of assistance."

"Do you think he will see us?" Gretel asked, briefly allowing her confidence to wobble.

Ferdinand did not have time to answer, for it was then a furious commotion erupted outside the main door. Raised voices and angry warnings echoed through the hallway, a passionate visitor having succeeded in having the door opened to allow him to enter the castle.

"What's this now?" Ferdinand muttered, slipping away from Gretel to stand squarely in the center of the hall, his hand on the hilt of his sword.

It was a surprise to everyone present to see that the fuss was all caused by a single, unarmed man. A man soberly dressed, exceptionally neat in his appearance, but his face showing the rage that he brought with him, his stride telling of the urgency of his business at the Schloss.

"I will see the king!" he insisted loudly. "I must see him! It is imperative for His Majesty's continued good health, nay his very life, that I be permitted to speak with him!"

There were gasps all around, followed by a *good-heavens*, from Hans, a *you!* from Herr Arnold, and a *give-me-strength!* from Gretel.

Ferdinand held up a hand. "State your name and your business here, sir."

"I am Otto Voigt, Head Sorcerer of the Gesternstadt Sorcerer's Circle," he announced loftily, "and *that man*," here he paused to wag a finger at Ernst, "is a charlatan and a fraud and should not be allowed anywhere near the king!"

Ernst stepped forward as if to speak but Gretel got there first, determined not to let him snatch defeat from the jaws of victory. They had come a long way and were now, literally, within strides of an audience with the king. She must not let this moment be taken from her.

"*This* man," she declared, pointing at Otto, "has been responsible for three assaults on myself and my brother, and has himself on one occasion put our very lives in peril. His word is not to be trusted, for he has long wished to be rid of Herr Arnold and will, it seems, stop at nothing to bring about his downfall, no matter who else is harmed in the process."

"You are certain of this?" asked Ferdinand.

"I am."

Herr Voigt fairly spat with fury. "Foundless and groundless accusations! Where is your proof?" he yelled.

The door to the king's chamber opened and a pale-faced aide hurried out.

"Uber General Ferdinand, what on earth is going on? Queen Beatrice has sent me to demand this racket be stopped immediately."

"My apologies to Her Majesty," Ferdinand said quickly. "There is no cause for concern."

"There is indeed cause for grave concern!" Herr Voigt shouted. "This man . . . I will not call him *sorcerer* for that would be to denigrate the title . . . this man is dangerous, I tell you! To have him in the same building as our beloved sovereign is to invite calamity!"

At this point the assembled company fell to arguing, shouting over one another, bellowing, remonstrating, accusing, and denying all at once and with such force and volume that not one of them could be properly heard nor understood. Ferdinand did his utmost to quell this riot of slander and vitriol, but stopped short of having them all dragged away by the guards. Such a course of action might have been the only one left him, had not the door to the bedchamber been thrown wide and the queen herself appeared upon the threshold.

"What is the meaning of this hideously disrespectful and injurious noise?" she demanded. She was a plump, short woman, with unremarkable features and a thin voice, but her position, her royal blood, her terrifying power of life and death over just about anyone, lent a serious force to any words she uttered.

Silence descended.

Gretel seized the moment.

"Your Majesty," she said, bowing low, trying to put from her mind the fact that she looked like a trollop and had been sleeping in a forest, "I bring good news—a physician capable of healing His Majesty this very day!"

Whereupon Otto Voigt began shouting again, Ernst joining in to defend himself, and the late-to-the-party sergeant-at-arms generally shrieking at everyone.

Queen Beatrice drew herself up and snapped. "Enough! Uber General, you may speak, and no one else. Is it true, what this . . . person says?"

Gretel would like to have reminded the queen who she was and shaken off the title of "person" then and there, but this was not the moment. She had to trust Ferdinand to make her case.

He too gave a low bow. "Yes, Your Majesty, I believe it may be."

"May be? Am I to admit this curious rabble to the king's bedchamber on the slender assurance of a may be?"

"I believe Fraulein Gretel is sincere in what she says, Your Majesty."

Another silence took hold, filled with tension and unspoken thoughts. The queen considered the possibilities. In the end they came down to an ill husband or a healed husband. It had to be worth a try.

"Have them enter," she said. She turned back into the bedchamber, but not before she had warned Ferdinand. "On your head be it, Uber General."

Gretel and Ferdinand exchanged glances. His was manfully oblique. Gretel hoped that hers was reassuring. She took hold of Ernst and bundled him through the door ahead of her. There was something of a scuffle as Otto Voigt insisted on being present too. Ferdinand, evidently wishing to avoid another scene, allowed him to stand at the back of the room between two guards. The sergeant took up his position beside his king.

The room was, or course, stupendously grand. The ceiling floated somewhere up above Gretel's sharpest range of vision, but even so she could make out murals of cherubs and angels amid clouds and flowers, all in vivid colors and picked out with gilding. The room itself was all white walls bearing scrolling cornices and intricate plasterwork. Chandeliers dangled, as chandeliers are wont to do. The tall windows were swagged and swathed in Chinese silk. Gretel couldn't help being struck by the singularly lovely shade of blue employed for the braiding, and decided it would look perfectly charming on an evening gown. There was no furniture at all save for the gargantuan four-poster bed at the center of the room. While the monarch reclined, everyone else was expected to stand.

Propped up against satin bolsters, a brocade coverlet covering most of him, lay King Julian the Mighty. In his youth he had been strong and straight backed, if never large. At least that youthful vigor had made sense of his name. Now, shriveled by years of ruling and managing his own squabbling family, the king was a small scrap of a man, dwarfed by his bed, his surroundings, even his little consort, who stood on his right. Next to her was the king's aide, then his physician—a willowy man in black—and two servants, just in case. On the other side of the bed stood Princess Charlotte and the sergeant. Guards were posted at each post. While Gretel got as near as she could, Ferdinand placed himself between his monarch and Ernst. Trust was one thing; gambling with the king's life was another.

"Your Majesty," he began, and then clearly remembered the king's deafness and raised his voice. "Allow me to present Detective Gretel of Gesternstadt. She has brought with her a physician."

"What's that?" King Julian squinted through wire-rimmed spectacles. "Defective metal, you say?"

"Gretel, Your Majesty!" Ferdinand beckoned to her to step a little closer.

Gretel did so, bowed again, and affected a sorrowful expression. "King Julian, I am distressed to see you suffering so," she said. Loudly. "But be of good cheer, for I bring with me the answer to your woes!"

"What's she saying?" the king asked.

His aide leaned low to the monarch's ear and then yelled, "She is sorry for your suffering!"

"She is?"

"She has something to make you feel better!" he explained.

"Oh yes?" He nodded, looking hard at Gretel now, taking in the frothy nature of her gown, the low-cut neckline, the creamy expanse of bosom on display. A small smile tugged at the corners of the royal mouth. "Well, that would be nice," he said.

Gretel thought it best to press on. "I understand your foot still pains you greatly," she yelled.

"My what?" he asked, cupping a hand to his ear.

"Your foot!" she repeated, pointing.

"Oh don't worry about that," he continued to smile. "It only hurts if I move it."

Gretel took a step closer to the bed. The sergeant reflexively leaped forward.

"Stand back!" he commanded, barring her way with his sword.

"Well, *really*!" Gretel muttered.

"It's all right, Klaus," the king assured him. "Let the pretty lady come here. She's going to cheer me up, you know!" he chuckled. The queen huffed and puffed.

Gretel had a nasty feeling that the conversation was getting away from her. She distinctly heard Hans snigger. "I have with me a man with a talent like no other, Your Majesty. He will be able to take away your pain and mend your broken foot." Here she indicated Ernst, who was standing a little way behind her.

The king flapped a hand at his aide and a servant. "Help me sit up," he insisted. They did so with great care, but still the king winced and squawked. Once a little more upright he asked. "Who is it she wants me to see?"

"The man she has brought with her!" yelled the aide.

"What, the clergyman?" The king gave another chuckle. "No, no, my dear. I cannot marry you. Ha-ha, how quaint. She wants to marry me!"

As the king was laughing everyone present was required to join in. Gretel felt the glare of the queen upon her and noticed that she was definitely not laughing. Hans realized that he was somehow the cause of some merriment and so laughed all the louder.

"Not him, Your Majesty," Gretel went on, stepping back to reveal Ernst. "This man! He is a physician like no other!"

"Him? The sorcerer?" The king thought this was funnier still.

"Do not be confused by his attire, I promise you his talent is for removing pain and mending broken bones. You will not find a finer fellow for fixing feet anywhere, I'll wager."

But the king's mind had wandered. "Beatrice, why is there a conjurer here? Is he going to do some magic tricks?"

The king's own physician now piped up. "Sire, you cannot even consider letting this sorcerer put his hands upon your royal personage!"

It was too much for Otto. "He is no sorcerer!" he screamed. "Ernst Arnold is a fraud. His spells are disastrous, I tell you! I have witnesses. Let me bring them forward!"

Queen Beatrice held up a hand for quiet. "Witnesses?"

"Yes, Your Majesty. Their testimony will rid you of any doubt upon the matter of this rogue's fraudulent nature."

The king's aide and the queen conferred for a moment. At last she nodded to Herr Voigt.

"Let the witnesses be brought in," she said.

There was a great deal of confusion within and without, but at last two figures were bundled through the door. Gretel immediately recognized them as the baker himself, weak from laughter and still gripped by merciless chortles and guffaws, and the hirsute Herr Winkler. "Here!" Otto shouted, waving his arms in such an agitated manner that he was quickly surrounded by more guards. "These poor people will tell the truth of what it is like to bear the brunt of Ernst Arnold's failed attempts at magic!"

Gretel groaned. Her chance to convince the royal couple to let Ernst do his stuff was slipping fast away from her.

"Psst, Ernst," she hissed beneath her breath, though she need not have worried about the king hearing her. "Be ready!" she told him. He was worryingly distracted by the sight of his erstwhile clients, but Gretel felt she had no choice but to go on with their plan. She took a breath, aware that what she was about to do was both risky and more than a little brutal. But there was no choice. If there was no pain, there was no pain for Ernst to remove. The king must be made to move so that he was reminded of his own suffering, and then Herr Arnold could swoop, remove the agony, convince everyone of his gift, and go on to reset the bones of the royal appendage.

"Oh heavens!" she cried, turning and raising a hand to her brow. "So long without food and proper rest. How faint I feel! How unsteady on my feet! How very much as if I might swoon! There must be a Jynx upon me!" She half closed her eyes as she teetered forward, nearer and nearer the bed, twirling and dodging all the while to evade the outstretched arms that attempted to catch her as she swooned. She must fall upon that bed, even upon that very king. Nothing less would do. "I tell you I am Jynxed!" she cried, hoping that the signal she and Ernst had agreed upon would strike home. He must be ready to cast his spell at once, for if the king's suffering was too great they would all be swept from the bedchamber before he could act and the moment would be lost.

"A Jynx!" she fair bellowed, before throwing herself in the direction of the frail, startled-but-really-quite-pleased-looking recumbent king.

It wasn't a bad plan. There were elements of risk to it, true, but it was carefully thought out, with the minimum of people involved, and few variables to contend with. Unfortunately, one of the people who was not meant to be involved, and who turned out to be a large and significant variable, was Hans. Unaware of his sister's intention of providing the opportunity for Ernst to remove pain from the monarch's freshly provoked extremity, he saw only that his sister was about to faint on top of his king. His large, robust, big-boned, some might say *heavy* sister, on top of his tiny, fragile, bird-boned king. Even Hans's brain was able to compute the likely outcome with some speed. Without care for his own well-being, or really thinking the thing through at all, truth be told, Hans hurled himself at Gretel. With a warning cry—though intended for whom it was hard to tell—he ran two paces and launched himself through the air, an airborne cleric, arms outstretched.

Through her half-closed eyes Gretel saw him coming but there was no time to take evasive action. She felt him connect with her, felt the weight of him increased threefold by the momentum of his leap, felt herself pushed through the air, away from her intended target, and down, down, down onto the marble floor. Marble has many qualities, but softness is not counted among them. There was a sickening *snap! which* echoed around the bedchamber, audible to all even above the general commotion and alarm that had broken out. Most did not know what it signified. Some had a rough idea. One knew precisely what it meant.

"My leg!" Gretel screamed, struggling to push Hans off her. "Argh! By all that's holy, My. Leg!"

Hans rolled over three times, coming to a halt at the feet of the astonished Princess Charlotte. There were shouts of "The King!" "The King!" Ernst, clearly remembering he had a part to play, rushed forward, but found King Julian in no pain at all. He dithered. The sergeant screamed that the madwoman and her entourage should be dragged from the bedchamber. Ferdinand shouted—quite anxiously, Gretel later recalled—that the Fraulein was injured and was not to be moved. Hans could be heard asking if the king was all right. Gretel was in such torment that she had temporarily been rendered speechless.

However, she soon found she was once again able to scream and did so with such force that all present hushed and turned to look at her. What they saw caused the princess to whimper, several people to gasp, Hans to faint, and Ferdinand to drop to his knees at her side.

"Stay calm, Gretel," he said softly. "Don't move."

Gretel paused in her screaming to look at her own leg. She wished that she had not. Her skirts and petticoats had risen immodestly during her fall so that all below her knees was exposed. One leg looked very much as it should, even if the stockings were laddered and grubby. The other leg, however, was very much not as it should be, with the knee pointing in one direction, the toes pointing in the opposite, and a suspicious lump beneath her hosiery halfway down her shin. The combination of shock and pain all but overwhelmed Gretel. She closed her eyes, summoned all her strength and bellowed, "Ernst, if you value your life, Jynx!"

"Oh!" he cried, at last remembering what was required of him. He stepped forward, raised his hand, and cast a swift, silent and skillful spell in Gretel's direction. It cut her off mid-scream. Everyone watched.

"Has it stopped hurting?" Ferdinand asked.

"Yes!" she said, as amazed as everyone else. "I feel no pain at all."

Queen Beatrice peered down at her. "None at all?"

"Not a twinge," Gretel assured her, sitting up as best she could. Ferdinand took hold of her so that she could lean back against him.

Ernst shook his head. "Try not to move around," he said. "I still have to set those bones."

"Can you do it?" the queen wanted to know.

"Oh yes, if someone could bring me two short wooden planks, some plaster of Paris—or clay if you have none—string, cotton wadding . . ." He reeled off a list of things and a servant was dispatched to find them.

"What's going on?" the king asked, unaccustomed to having the attention focused on someone other than himself. "What's happened to that lovely lady who was going to cheer me up?"

Princess Charlotte leaned over and took his hand. "She's having her leg mended, Papa," she told him.

"By the sorcerer?" he asked.

"Yes, Papa."

"Yes, indeed," said the queen. "And if his bone setting is as good as his pain numbing, then we shall permit him to attend to the royal foot!"

Gretel allowed herself to rest limply in Ferdinand's arms.

"That was quite a fall," he said to her quietly.

"All part of the job," she said. She wanted to enjoy being held by him, even if he was someone else's fiancé. She felt she had earned the right to a little tenderness and affection, if only for a fleeting moment. But the sorcerer's spell was making her feel woozy, and her eyelids had become unhelpfully heavy. And then there was the laughter, for the poor baker had shifted from a short time of tittering to set off again more gustily, helplessly chuckling and then belly laughing, clutching at his sides. Hans, fearing he had missed a joke, joined in. The king followed suit, so that everyone else was obliged to guffaw and chortle also. It was to this cacophony of maniacal laughter that Gretel finally lost consciousness.

TWENTY

The royal carriage that whizzed down the broad drive away from the Summer Schloss was built for both showing off and for comfort. Even so, Gretel struggled to find a tolerable position on the fatly padded seating. The cast Ernst had so expertly applied to her broken leg was cumbersome in the extreme. While at least most of it was concealed beneath her skirts, she was unable to wear a left shoe and sported instead a ridiculous amount of swathing. She could set the foot to the ground, but not take much weight upon it, so that walking involved a cane and a great deal of limping. It was an improvement, she told herself. The first three days after she sustained the injury she had been forced to hobble with two crutches in the most ungainly and unattractive of gaits. Ernst had insisted on her staying put until he was satisfied the repairs were working well enough for her to, as he put it, gad about again. This meant that the three of them had remained at the castle until the morning dawned when her leg was declared fit to travel.

Now, as they sped through the picturesque countryside toward Gesternstadt, Gretel experienced a confusion of feelings. She had barely glimpsed Ferdinand in the last few days, and when they had met it had been in the company of others. She had twice seen—and once acknowledged with courteous greetings—his fiancée, a winsome and elegant reminder of just what might have been keeping Ferdinand from calling in to see how she was faring. In addition, Gretel had not had the opportunity to say a private thank-you and farewell to the Uber General. She told herself that it was for the best. He had made his choice, and there was the end to it. She refused to allow herself to care enough to appear lovelorn. After all, there had been nothing agreed between them. Nothing significant had occurred. No, it was too ridiculous to chase after a man, at her age, and with her standing in the region, and her professional reputation. She would bedeck herself in her finery for Herr Mozart's concert, hold her head high, demonstrate that her pride was intact, and while she was at it remind Ferdinand of what he had let slip through his fingers.

At last the carriage slowed to negotiate the narrow streets, sauntering pedestrians, and cobbles of the little town. On Gretel's instructions, the driver took them directly to Herr Arnold's house. As they approached Ernst looked anxiously out of the window.

"Will she forgive me, do you think?" he asked Gretel. "Can she?"

"She has been informed of your imminent arrival and I would confidently put a large sum of my hard-earned money on the fact that she will be overjoyed to have you home," she told him. "Trust may have to be rebuilt, but you have time and excellent circumstances in which to do just that."

"I confess," he said, brightening, "matters have been resolved so well . . . I could not have hoped for a better outcome."

"Nor a better future to offer your dear wife."

Indeed, Gretel reflected, the couple's fortunes had changed significantly for the better. After observing Ernst's work on her own leg, it was agreed that he should treat the king. After a tense few hours, the monarch was up and about, hopping around on his new cast, free from pain, and very, very grateful. So impressed was he—and his queen—that Herr Arnold was appointed the new (and only) Royal Physician, on the proviso that the only magic he ever employed would be the now-famous numbing spell. Already word of this singular talent was spreading throughout Bavaria and beyond. Soon Ernst would enjoy reputation and status that far exceeded his wildest imaginings. Along with the job—and substantial and generous remuneration—went a grand suite of rooms in the west wing of the Schloss, and plans were in train to equip one of the towers as his very own office. There would be ample money to pay off any remaining debts, and of course a complete royal pardon was issued for any charges of fraud, with immediate effect.

Otto Voigt had been arrested and charged with conspiring to assault, as well as attempted murder by wolf. An unusual law, but one that carried a dire sentence. King Julian always enjoyed a nice, grisly execution, so it had taken some work on Gretel's part to persuade him there was a better course of action. For all his lack of scruples, Herr Voigt was an accomplished sorcerer, and he alone could restore the health of the laughing baker, the hairy Herr Winkler, and all others who had suffered Herr Arnold's blundering magic. The king was reluctant to miss out on a bit of drawing and quartering, but was finally persuaded when Gretel pointed out it would not do for the Royal Physician to have examples of his failures and ineptitude wandering about. How poorly that would reflect on the king's choice of doctor. He grudgingly agreed, throwing in banishment from the realm. This threw up a vacancy for the position of Head Sorcerer, which Gretel quickly forbade Ernst from ever applying for.

The horses were reined in and the carriage came to a halt, jolting Hans from his slumbers on the seating beside Gretel.

"What's that? The king! Oh, where are we?" He came to blearily.

"I bid you both farewell," Ernst said, shaking first the hand of Hans and then Gretel. "Come to the Schloss at the end of the month, Fraulein," he said to her, "so that I can remove your cast. I am confident you will make a full recovery."

"I am thankful for it, Herr Arnold."

"Me too," said Hans. "I'd never hear the end of it otherwise."

Gretel shot him a look that said, healed or not, it would take a long time for her to forgive him for causing her leg to snap like a piece of kindling.

Ernst went on. "And of course, should either of you ever fall ill, you know where to find me."

"A comfort indeed," Gretel told him.

There was a small movement in his sleeve and Jynx appeared. The little bat flitted around the interior of the carriage for a moment before alighting on Gretel's shoulder. She stroked his furry body.

"You are officially now a physician's assistant," she told him. Jynx hooked his tiny claws around her proffered finger and she handed him back to his master.

Ernst climbed out of the carriage and had barely set foot to the ground when Evalina came running out of the house to fling her arms around him.

"Oh, husband! My dearest, you are returned to me!" she cried as she wept tears of joy.

"My darling wife!"

If Ernst had thought he would need sweet words to win back his wife's affection he had not taken into account the strength of her love for him, nor the potency of a sincere kiss. The two stood in a loving embrace, heedless of the stares of passersby, lost in their own happiness.

Gretel felt both satisfaction at a case well handled and a satisfied client, and sour envy at their delight in each other. She rapped upon the ceiling of the carriage with her cane and called up, "Home, driver, if you please."

Home. However humble the little house Gretel shared with her brother, however quaint its window boxes and shutters, however provincial and parochial, there was nothing like it for returning to after a trying case elsewhere. Once Gretel had been helped from the carriage by Hans—who knew his sister would milk her injury and his guilt for as long as possible and could do nothing about it—and as soon as she had overcome the familiar disappointment at finding the place smaller and shabbier than she remembered, the sight of her own daybed in her own living room cheered her enormously. Sunshine fell through the south-facing window, carrying dizzy dust motes in their carefree dance. The room smelled of shut-up air, and gone-out fire, and forgotten schnapps in glasses on the mantelpiece.

"Wonderful!" Gretel declared as she sank into the welcoming embrace of her tapestry daybed and its assortment of silk cushions. "Simply wonderful."

"Another case successfully solved, sister mine," said Hans, setting down their rucksack and the baskets of comestibles he had obtained from the cook at the Schloss. His action of saving the king, even at the cost of his own sister, had marked him out as something of a minor hero at the castle. His back had been slapped thoroughly and often, and he had been given gifts of wines, cheeses, some splendid wurst, preserves, and mustards. The three days he had spent waiting for Gretel to be fit to travel had been both fruitful and enjoyable. "I shall fix us a light meal. You must rest, and soon all will be as it should be again."

"Almost all," she said, tapping her cast with her cane to make the point. "Some things may take a little longer."

"Oh look," said Hans, ignoring the remark. "Some post has been delivered. Let me see." He picked up a small pile of letters and notes. "Coal bill. Milk bill. Butcher's bill . . . ooh, better settle that one quick sharp. Someone selling windows. Huh, can't they see we already have them? What's this? Looks important."

He handed Gretel a letter written on expensive vellum, with an elaborate seal. She opened it.

"Ah-ha. Excellent. 'Diligence Insurers are pleased to enclosed your full fee, as agreed . . . blah, blah, appreciation . . . blah, endeavors, etcetera, etcetera.'" She checked the banker's draft. "Oh yes, that will do very nicely indeed."

"Enough to keep us in wurst and ale for a while, eh?" Hans asked.

"Happily, yes. And more besides."

The more, Gretel had already decided, included the rather sumptuous gown she had required the seamstress to make while she was away. It would be ready by now. She would go for a fitting that very afternoon. There were only three days before the concert, and she would need all of them to expunge the ravages of the forest and make herself glorious for the concert.

"A light meal would be most welcome, brother mine. And then a nap. Later, I must trouble you to fetch the bathtub and light the fire. I shall get myself to the dressmaker as soon as possible, but not before I feel fully restored."

With that thought she lay back upon her wonderfully familiar bolsters and pillows, closed her eyes, and fell into the manner of sleep only ever experienced by those who have recently completed a challenging and exhausting task.

⁂

The evening of the concert was pleasantly warm, the season having begun its downward descent into the cool dip of autumn at last. Gretel was grateful for the change of temperature. She was pleased with her new gown and knew she could look her best in it, particularly without the high color summer heat could bring about. The dressmaker had excelled herself, and the only final alterations necessary were, for the first time Gretel could remember, some taking in. It seemed her time spent marching about in the forest and living on berries and whatnot had robbed her of some of her voluptuousness. Thankfully, enough of it remained to do the new gown justice. Before setting out for the town hall she appraised herself in her full-length looking glass. Running her hands over the melon-green silk, smoothing it over her pleasing curves, she nodded, satisfied.

There was a moment's mourning for her lost wig, which alas there had not been time to replace. And it was hard to ignore the unsightly boot she was forced to wear over her leg cast, but most of it was hidden by her skirts. She would need her cane for a while, but had cheered herself up a little on this front by purchasing an elegant ebony one with a silver and amber top to it. On the whole, she felt she would present the very best version of herself to the great and the good of Gesternstadt. And to Ferdinand. Not that she cared.

"Hans!" she called as she went downstairs. "We shall be late!"

"Fear not, I am ready," he said, emerging from the kitchen chewing on a sandwich. "Just partaking of a small snack. Can't digest music on an empty stomach," he explained.

"On that we are in complete agreement, brother mine," she told him, removing the sandwich from his hand as she passed and biting into it. "Mmm, very good. Although perhaps a little more mustard next time . . . ?"

They walked through the town, slowed a little by her injury. Hans, on Gretel's insistence, was turned out fittingly for the occasion, with not a trace of Bavarian peasant on show. If his tight-fitting hose were less than flattering, the finely tailored velvet cutaway jacket made up for it, and the overall effect was of a well-to-do gentleman. As they neared the town hall, which stood as the theater and concert hall when the need arose, other music lovers began to throng the streets. People had made an effort, much to Gretel's delight. Everywhere was evidence of money having been spent, Sunday best having been spruced up, and a general air of expectation and excitement. If Gretel hadn't felt the painful twist of cobbles beneath her Italian leather shoe she might have imagined herself, just for an instant, in some sophisticated city, where such cultural events were the norm. Everyone who was anyone, and quite a few who weren't, had turned out. Evidently, even the people of Gesternstadt had recognized the importance of having a renowned composer visit their insignificant home. It was an occasion not to be missed.

She was a little surprised, therefore, not to see a royal carriage among those now depositing bejeweled ladies outside the venue. She reasoned that any members of the royal family would prefer to arrive fashionably late and make a grand entrance. No doubt Ferdinand and his fiancée would do the same. Gretel could not afford to be late at all, for she would have to fight for a good seat, not having the privilege of a royal box to ensure she would be able to see, and, more importantly, be seen. She and Hans bustled their way through the foyer and into the auditorium. There were rows of cushioned seats in the stalls, with benches up in the balcony. Gretel, having purchased superior tickets, made straight for the front row of the orchestra, hoping to better enjoy the great composer's presence, and be in the sight line of the royal party from their box.

"I say," said Hans, "this is all rather grand, isn't it? Not your usual Saturday night in Gesternstadt, have to say."

But Gretel wasn't really listening. She was using her lorgnettes, freshly polished and recovered from their woodland trek, to scan the audience. She saw many clients, past and present, neighbors and their guests, even Kapital Kingsman Strudel, but no one betitled. No one royal. And crucially, no one with a burgundy cape with gold silk lining with a skinny fiancée on his arm. Gretel let out an exasperated sigh. She did not want to admit to herself how much she had wanted to see Ferdinand that night. Did not want to face the fact that she did not, in fact, wish to merely show how content, how happy indeed, she was without him, and perhaps make him experience a twinge of regret at having passed her over for another. For the truth was, she now saw, that she had hoped for one last chance to change his mind. One final opportunity for him to sit amid the stirring and beautiful music of Herr Mozart, to gaze down upon Gretel at her very best, to ponder the frisson that had fizzed between them for so long, and to realize that he could not, after all, live without her.

"Stupid woman!" she said at last of herself and to herself.

"What's that?" asked Hans.

"Nothing. But budge up, these seats are rather small."

"Aren't they just," he agreed.

Gretel stopped a second sigh escaping and attempted to pull herself together. She had done all she could. She could do no more. There was nothing left to do except allow herself to be soothed by the balm of the maestro's magnificent music.

The rest of the audience took their places, the rows of seats were quickly filled, the excited buzz of the music lovers hushed, a charged quiet filled the hall, and at last the curtain went up.

There is a line of thought that states that misery loves company. There is another that holds bad things happen in groups of three. Gretel was not aware of the dictum that insists disappointments travel in pairs, but she was beginning to see evidence of it. Only seconds before she had had to accept that Ferdinand would never be hers, and that this mattered to her a great deal. Now, as she held her breath for the majesty and miracle that was the gift of a sublime talent and his orchestra, she was instead presented with Herr Wolfgang Alfred Mozart and his ensemble of Alpine Horns. The sight of them was sufficient to draw a gasp from the crowd that suggested Gretel was not the only one present to have been sold her ticket under false pretenses. As if unaware of the fury building in the building, Herr Mozart—a man of advancing years and retreating hairline—beamed happily as he took center stage, raised his baton, and encouraged his musicians to put their alphorns to use.

Even above this aural onslaught scandalized expostulations could be heard: "Monstrous!"

"Outrageous!"

"Utterly unscrupulous!"

"A full refund, or there will be blood spilled!" one particularly enraged gentleman insisted.

Through it all the band played on, with Herr Mozart But Not That Herr Mozart even turning occasionally to smile broadly at his audience, apparently oblivious to the reception he was getting. Gretel could only surmise that he was genuinely unaware that anyone might mistake him for a composer of operas and requiems. And why would they? She, for one, felt more foolish than furious. She sat still, conscious of the exodus of many of the more disgruntled music lovers behind her. She knew she could not sit through an hour of being blown back in her seat by the lusty blasts from the admittedly impressive horns on stage. She would wait until the initial rush had died down and then make her escape discreetly. She had no desire to enter into a group rant on the pavement with other foolish Gesternstadters. To her left, from Hans there came the sound of humming and a thigh being happily slapped in time to the music, if such it could be called.

Taking a side exit from the hall, Gretel hoped to slip away unnoticed. She had left Hans enjoying the performance. Herr Mozart had at least gained one new follower. Gretel put her head down and hurried along the narrow street away from the square, her cane rapping against the cobbles as she went. So intent was she on fleeing that she did not see the man standing on the edge of the street and barreled straight into him.

"Oh! I beg your pardon," she muttered, attempting to step back from the stranger who now held onto her arm.

"Fraulein, are you hurt?" asked a voice that most definitely did not belong to a stranger.

Gretel looked up. Ferdinand looked down at her.

It took all her self-control not to squawk.

"You are too late to take your seat for the concert," she told him as levelly as she was able.

"I have had a lucky escape, judging by the speed at which you appear to be running away from it. With your leg still healing, is it wise to move so swiftly unaccompanied?"

Gretel gathered what little self-respect she had left in both hands and set her mouth in a determined line. Being spurned by the man was bad enough; she would not tolerate him laughing at her also.

"My experience of alphorn music tells me we were not being given the best," she said.

"Indeed?"

"Quite so. I paid good money for my ticket, and I refuse to sit through second-rate horn playing."

"Is that so?"

"It is."

"I see."

"Good."

"I was not aware of your expertise on the topic of alphorn and Kuhreihen."

"No reason you should be."

"Another of your hidden talents."

"There are many."

"I don't doubt it."

An itchy, irritable pause worked its way into the equally irritating exchange. Ferdinand still had hold of Gretel's arm and seemed in no hurry to relinquish it. After a while he spoke again.

"I should like to discover more of your hidden talents."

Gretel widened her eyes at him. "I'm sure you would!" she said, more than a little crossly. She could not fathom what manner of game this was for a man to be playing when he was about to be married to a woman other than the one with whom he was playing it. Suddenly the complexity of this thought and the memory of the alphorns brought on a sharp headache.

And then Ferdinand leaned forward and kissed her, full on the mouth.

And the headache went away.

And somewhere distant a bird sang.

And Gretel felt as if possibly her feet had lifted a little off the ground.

And then she recalled a skinny countess with engaged-to-the-Uber-General stamped all over her, and the headache came back.

And then Hans appeared.

"I say, sister mine, wasn't that the most splendid music? Don't you think? Oh, good evening, Herr Uber General. You've missed the first half. I just stepped out for a breath of air during the intermission. Splendid stuff, have to say, quite splendid. Don't dally now, or you'll miss the second half."

"Go away, Hans," Gretel told him, but he had already gone, scuttling back to enjoy what was clearly the musical highlight of his year.

"Where were we?" Ferdinand asked, evidently not expecting a reply as he moved in for another kiss.

It took Gretel all her resolve and self-control to pull back. She held up a hand. "I am not in the habit of kissing other people's fiancés," she told him.

"I am very glad to hear it."

"Or being kissed by. Other people's. Fiancés."

"I would never have believed you capable of behaving otherwise."

"Then why do it?"

"To my knowledge I have not."

"But you did, just then. You kissed me."

He raised his eyebrows a fraction. Gretel was annoyed to find this singularly attractive. "Do you have a fiancé?" he asked.

"I do not!"

"Then we do not have a problem."

"But you have."

"A problem?"

"A fiancée!"

"I do?"

"Do you not?"

"I do not!"

"But . . . what about Countess Whatsername? Tall woman, young-ish. Skinny, some might say angular. Sharp hip bones, one might imagine. What about her?"

"Countess Margarita? What about her?"

"You are engaged to her, to be married, for heaven's sake!"

"That, Fraulein, is news to me."

Another pause stepped in. This one was altogether different from the first, for although it was fidgety and uncomfortable, it clutched close to itself a small, bright nugget of hope.

Gretel chose her words with care and spoke them clearly and calmly. "Am I to understand, then, that you are not affianced, not betrothed, not engaged nor promised to anyone? At all?" she asked.

"I am not," he confirmed.

"You have not plighted your troth to the woman of your choice and are about to be married?" she double-checked.

He shook his head. "Not yet," he said, smiling.

And then he kissed her again. And this time lots of birds sang. And sweet gentle music played inside Gretel's head with not a single alphorn involved. And her heart lifted as she returned the kiss with rather less restraint than a woman of good reputation should risk, standing in the street in broad view of any who happened by. Happily, none did. Gretel pulled away, quite breathless, uncertain in a fashion that was wholly unfamiliar to her.

Ferdinand stepped back, bowed, straightened, and then offered her his arm.

"Fraulein Gretel, would you join me for a stroll?" he asked.

She nodded, forcing herself to try to appear nonchalant but feeling pretty certain it wasn't convincing.

"I should be delighted, Herr Uber General," she replied, taking his arm.

"Oh, I think it's high time you started calling me Ferdinand, don't you?" he said as he led her away.

❋

When Gretel skipped through her own front door an hour later she found herself, despite her cast and cane, unable to resist performing a little dance in the hallway. Her feet, tired as they were, moved as if on air. She laughed out loud, and then felt quite mad, and then laughed again at that thought.

"Is that you?" Hans called out from the kitchen.

"It is."

He emerged clutching a bottle and a glass of wine. "The Uber General not with you, then?"

"He walked me to my door and then took his leave. His duties at the Schloss demand his attention," she explained.

"Why are you grinning like that?" Hans wanted to know. "Have you been drinking? Can't imagine Herr Uber General taking you to the Inn."

"He did not. We perambulated," she told him.

"Good for you," said Hans and then, brow furrowing slightly, he asked, "Is that allowed? Perambulating, I mean. When a fellow is engaged to another?"

"Ah, but he is not, Hans."

"Not?"

"No. It seems that was all a misunderstanding."

237

"Oh, but I thought, I mean, I was told, I was informed . . ."

"What have I always warned you about gossip? What have I always said regarding the folly and dangers of listening to tittle-tattle and wagging tongues?"

"Well! So, no wedding for poor old Ferdinand, then?"

"Oh, I don't know about that, Hans," Gretel said with a small, secretive smile. "Perhaps one day. One day."

"Oh well, in that case, he'll need some decent wine. Can't have a wedding without a nice drop of something drinkable."

Gretel sighed. "You are rather missing the point, Hans. As usual."

"He needn't worry. Tell him to come to me," Hans said. "Or indeed, us, because now that I think about it, this delivery did actually have your name on it."

"Delivery?"

"Yes, when I got home I found a case of this on the doorstep. Look."

He handed her the bottle he had been holding. Gretel couldn't help noticing it was already half empty. The label declared it to be from a family-run vineyard in eastern Bavaria. She removed the cork and sniffed.

"It smells rather good."

"It is," he assured her, taking a glass from the mantelpiece, blowing off the dust, and offering it to her.

Gretel poured herself a generous measure of the crystal clear white wine and drank deeply, the events of the evening having left her more than a little unnerved.

"Oh," she said, scrutinizing the label on the bottle again, "that really is very good indeed. Who sent it?"

"There was a note. Haven't read it, thought I'd better not, it being addressed to you . . ." He took the squashed letter from his pocket and passed it over.

"Didn't stop you opening the wine," Gretel reminded him. She broke the elaborate seal on the expensive paper and held the writing up to the lamplight. "It seems," she summarized, "that the youngest daughter of an obscure royal family is in peril. She recently eloped to marry the owner of a vineyard on the banks of the Rhine, and not two weeks later he has been found dead in a wine vat."

"Good heavens! What a way to go," said Hans, sounding rather more impressed than appalled.

"Murder is suspected. The family fear for their daughter's safety, but she is now wedded to the memory of her late husband, and determined to uphold the name of his domain out of love and respect for him. She has taken to the world of winemaking and refuses to leave. She has become expert on grape varieties and all aspects of vintnery, and plans to produce her very own white wine. Her father fears a rival neighboring vineyard wishes her ill and will stop at nothing to prevent her success."

"And I suppose they want you to go and investigate? It's all work for you, sister mine, isn't it? No rest for a detective, eh?"

Gretel took another swig of the superior wine. She was still dizzy from the new turn her relationship with Ferdinand had taken. She could still smell his cologne upon her clothes, still feel the memory of his arms about her and his lingering kiss. But she was a woman of action. She was independent and had her business as a detective to attend to. Not to mention household bills and expenses to cover. The payment from the insurance company would be used up soon enough. She must not allow herself to become distracted by romance. After all, Ferdinand had fallen for a woman who valued her professional reputation and her work greatly; she was not about to let that change. They had exchanged no promises, as yet. She must be sensible. If Ferdinand's feelings for her were genuine, they would stand the test of a little time and separation. She would write and tell him that she would be leaving town again directly, for her talents were required for a new case: that of the Princess and the Pinot Grigio.

"Another bottle, Hans," she said, draining her glass, "and then the maps, if you please."

ACKNOWLEDGMENTS

Many thanks to my tireless agent Kate Hordern, the ever-imaginative Adam Fisher for the cover design, and the team at Pegasus for their continued support and enthusiasm.

Thanks also to Stephanie Carter, a lovely reader who has all the grit and determination of Gretel herself, and who came up with the name Jynx for a very special character in this book.

ABOUT THE AUTHOR

P.J. BRACKSTON is the author of the *New York Times* bestseller *The Witch's Daughter; The Winter Witch; Nutters*; and three previous books in the acclaimed "Brothers Grimm" mystery series: *Gretel and the Case of the Missing Frog Prints; Once Upon A Crime*; and *The Case of the Fickle Mermaid*. She has an MA in Creative Writing from Lancaster University and is a visiting lecturer for the University of Wales, Newport. Brackston lives in Wales with her partner, Simon, and their two children.